A ROYAL PROTECTOR ACADEMY NOVEL

RANDI COOLEY WILSON

Aequus
Copyright © 2017 by Randi Cooley Wilson

Published by SECRET GARDEN PRODUCTIONS, LLC

Content editing by
Kris Kendall at Final-Edits

Copy editing by
Liz Ferry at Per Se Editing

Cover design © Hang Le

Interior Design & Formatting by
Christine Borgford at Type A Formatting

AEQUUS (A Royal Protector Academy Novel, Book Two)
Randi Cooley Wilson
Printed in the United States of America
First Edition March 2017
ISBN-13: 978–1519394224
ISBN-10: 1519394225

ROYAL PROTECTOR
ACADEMY

ALSO BY

RANDI COOLEY WILSON

THE ROYAL PROTECTOR ACADEMY
VERNAL
AEQUUS
NOX

THE REVELATION SERIES
REVELATION
RESTRAINT
REDEMPTION
REVOLUTION
RESTORATION

DARK SOUL SERIES
STOLAS
VASSAGO
LEVIATHAN

For Dave—
Because when the wind rises, you always shield us.

She made herself stronger
by fighting with the wind.

Frances Hodgson Burnette
The Secret Garden

ONE
THERE'S A STORM COMING

SERENA

THE DARK TEMPEST LURKS ON THE horizon, casting an ominous shadow over the cloud-filled sky. Heavy gusts slice through the graying atmosphere in quick, angry bursts. With each surge of air, the ache in my chest recedes, allowing me to breathe. To feel. To exist.

For me, the wind is the epitome of strength and power, and in an odd way, I've always envied the currents because they move freely and can't be captured—or tamed.

As I'm an elemental gargoyle, air nourishes my spirit and strengthens my supernatural gifts; the currents are essential to my well-being, allowing the gargoyle vitality to flow freely within my royal protector blood. It is a strong reminder that there is more to our worlds than what we see.

The dry riverbank beneath my feet is a stark contrast to the lush forest that surrounds me. My gaze roams over the Killarney National Park and slides up Torc Mountain, focusing on the peak of the waterfall. A shudder runs through me at the thought of the entrance to the woodland realm hidden behind the cascading liquid.

Where *he* is.

Mere steps from me, but worlds away.

With a quiet growl, I shove thoughts of *him* away to focus on my surroundings and the task at hand.

I ease back into a comfortable position and calm my breathing while manipulating the wind's speed. I strain to move the currents until I'm exhausted.

I'm hoping the directional changes will bring the Irish mist and end the drought.

The way the air floats between the clouds and trees determines if a storm will appear. And right now, more than anything, I need the rainfall.

The howling wind calms into a soft sigh as I drop my hands from exhaustion and everything around me stills.

My eyes float across the unmoving land. It still amazes me that with a simple flick of my wrist, I hold the power to create calm and peace or chaos and destruction.

I miss the days when the skies naturally became dark and the raindrops fell lazily from the sky in their gentle dance.

Three months. My heart stutters at the thought. It hasn't rained in three months—not since Tristan left.

Tristan Gallagher.

My gargoyle protector.

And prince of the woodland realm.

When Tristan returned to his court, not only did he take my heart, but he also took the rainfall. And in its place, the angry winds arose, both in nature and in my core.

As time stands still, the ache in my chest spreads. I savor the shadow of darkness that has fallen across the land.

It's a dark reminder of the sadness and emptiness I feel.

It was only a few months ago that, like the wind, Tristan blew into my life, bringing the storm with him and taking it when he went away, leaving me with the quiet of the curling air, devoid of the tiny drops of water.

I hate the calm. I used to love it, but now, it's too still.

The lack of chaos provides time to think.

To remember.

To allow the hurt to seep in.

Once it had been second nature to savor moments of peace like this. Once I dreamed of being someone else—until I knew Tristan existed. Then all I dreamed of was a day when it was just me and him.

I release a throaty laugh, because that's not likely to happen any-time soon—or ever—considering he is betrothed to another: Freya, the princess of the water realm.

Even though Tristan is half gargoyle, he was raised by his mother, Queen Ophelia, in her kingdom, the woodland realm. Months ago, Tristan killed a royal protector, an enemy who had infiltrated the woodland army and planned to murder the queen.

Though he acted in the name of protection, he spilt gargoyle blood and almost started a war between our worlds. The violation could not go unpunished by my clan, the London clan of gargoyles. The royal family.

As a favor to his old friend—and Tristan's estranged father—Gage Gallagher, my uncle Asher, king of our race, assigned Tristan to protect me, which he begrudgingly agreed to, avoiding his sentence of stone petrifaction.

While it may seem cruel, Tristan's severe punishment was merited in our world. Instead, he was ordered to protect me against a possi-ble attack by the Diablo Fairies—a legion of ancient warriors who practice black magic.

They're a new breed of supernatural creatures, created by the king of the Nine Hells to end my existence. After the death of his mate, Lady Finella, the demon Asmodeus declared revenge on my family and the entire protector race, making it clear that I'm a primary target. As such, my family felt it vital to add another level of protection to my royal guard.

Enter Tristan Gallagher.

If Asmodeus and the Diablo Fairies succeed, it leaves the protector race open to attack, ending our existence—and the future of the human realm.

The Diablo Fairy army has backed off—for now.

Our victory was short-lived because Tristan is also half satyr and next in line to the throne of the woodland realm.

For centuries, the woodland and water realms have been teetering on the brink of war. It's a power struggle between the two dimensions—one that has escalated over the years.

To solidify their alliance, Tristan was promised in marriage to Freya, daughter of Oren, emperor of the water realm. He doesn't love her, but such is the cruelty of the supernatural world.

Soon after beating Kupuva and her Diablo Fairy army, Tristan left his post as my protector and returned to his realm to fulfill his oath and secure peace for his kingdom.

I look up at the clouds and, with a quick, angry flick of my wrist, attempt to coerce water to fall from the sky.

Manipulating the wind releases the storm that stirs within me, but the rain . . . the rain stabilizes me.

Calms me.

Since Tristan left, it hasn't rained. Not one day.

"If you keep forcing the elements to bend to your will, out of anger, you'll create a nightmare of a shitstorm."

I inhale, not recalling the last time I heard that voice.

"Besides, you will fail. The water realm is the reason for the lack of rainwater," he adds. "It's Oren's way of throwing his power around the supernatural worlds."

As my anxiety picks up, so does the wind. It hisses through the trees as Zander approaches me from behind.

Zander, Tristan's stepbrother and best friend.

I peer at him over my shoulder with a vacant glare.

His strides are measured as he approaches and steps next to me. Nervously, he brushes raven strands of hair away from his sympathetic eyes. When I meet his gaze, it causes me to release my hold on the elements; the chaos I've created around us falls silent and the forest stills.

"Serena," he tips his chin in a gesture of respect.

My lips twitch. "Zander."

The nymph lowers his voice. "The strong winds you keep conjuring have spilt over into the woodland realm. The trees are bending painfully and the leaves are trembling in fear, as if something dark is on the horizon."

My response is a one-shouldered shrug. "Maybe it is."

Zander watches me with his stormy jade eyes and inky rock-star hair. He looks nothing like his brother.

Tristan's hair is a warm caramel color, and it's longer on the top and messily styled. The flecks of gold in his serious, cognac gaze are deep, allowing you to become lost in them.

Tristan looks like the calm before the storm, whereas Zander looks like the darkness that will overtake you.

Appearances can be deceiving though, when personalities come into play. Zander is lively, warm, and inviting. Like a blanket. Tristan is full of darkness, a haunted coolness, and an impassive indifference.

Except with me.

"This upheaval wouldn't have anything to do with my brother's upcoming nuptials to a certain nymph princess?"

At his words, rage consumes me, and the winds lift again, whipping around us.

The reality of my situation hit me full force ten seconds after Tristan walked out of my life. Since then, the gloomy days match my dark mood.

Male protectors should come with a warning label.

They aren't good for the heart.

Period.

The End.

"I guess that would be definite yes," Zander teases.

My attention snaps to his face as thunder rolls in and lightning strikes over the lake multiple times.

Zander's attention shifts to the sky. "You need to get past this, champ. He needs to focus on his duties and oaths."

I scowl.

"You should know, whenever the clouds roll into the realm, he frowns, knowing it's you hurting," he continues.

When he came into my life, I was given a taste of freedom. Something I'd never had before. Yet, that free will wasn't unrestricted; it came at a price—the loss of my heart.

In order for Tristan to safeguard me, his protector mark was infused with my blood. It's the only way a gargoyle can truly protect a charge. Once it's broken or begins to weaken, the blood-bonded gargoyles become short-tempered and sullen.

I've been told that with time, the hostility will fade.

Just like my memories of Tristan.

I shiver, feeling lonely and rejected.

"The bond we share doesn't leave me a choice," I snap.

Zander doesn't get angry at me for my short temper.

Instead, his demeanor becomes softer, understanding.

"You do have a choice," he pacifies.

Elemental chaos reigns around us with my heightened emotional state. "Wrong," I state sharply. "If I had a choice, I would have chosen Tristan and he would have chosen me."

Zander swears under his breath and pinches the bridge of his nose. My gaze homes in on the dark circles that frame his eyes, and I'm suddenly aware of how drawn he appears.

His lips pull into a tight smile. "You think he likes this, Serena? Do you think Tristan isn't hurting in the same way you are? My brother is miserable. If you thought he was dark and broody before his time with you, he's worse now. Each time the lightning strikes our realm, a sharp pain literally rolls through him," he forces a bark-laugh. "It's true. He rubs at his heart—daily—at an ache that has settled there, a longing," he pauses and calms. "For *you*."

My words catch in my throat and my shoulders fall in defeat. I know Tristan feels this too. How can he not?

Maybe I should move on.

At the thought, the small mark behind my ear comes to life, reminding me it's there. I lift my hand and rub at it, trying to soothe the sudden burn.

Zander's ink-clouded focus narrows in on the motion.

"Have you told him yet?" he asks.

"About what?" I feign ignorance.

Rolling his eyes, Zander folds his arms across his muscular chest. "The mark. Behind your ear, Serena."

I look away. "Why would he care about a freckle?"

"A freckle in the shape of his insignia," he counters.

Tristan wears the Sun of Vergina symbol on a necklace.

It marks him within the supernatural world as nymph royalty. Oddly, the same mark is branded on my skin.

Sighing, I shake my head, suddenly losing the ability to argue anymore. Instead, I swallow the dryness in my throat.

"I have no idea why it's there, Zander. Until I do, Tristan doesn't need to know. Not now anyway—with everything else he's dealing with," I whisper.

Zander shakes his head in disagreement. "There is a deeper meaning behind it. It isn't just a coincidence."

He's right. Before Tristan left, he handed me a note, which read: *The Sun of Vergina is our cessation.*

The words contain a hidden meaning that I can't decipher. I've been going over and over them again in my mind, trying to figure out their importance. Exactly, how, or what, the insignia will stop or end, I have no idea.

"Do not tell him, Zander," I demand. "Until I understand it, Tristan doesn't need to be bothered with it."

"He'll be pissed off that you withheld this from him."

"I'm not afraid of Tristan's wrath," I mumble, kicking and staring at the dry gravel under my feet. "I fear nothing."

He releases a heavy sigh. "You're too stubborn for your own good. Fear is not a sign of weakness, but of strength."

Slowly, I raise my head and lock eyes with Zander.

"Why are you even here?" I snap.

"Freya's father has moved up the date again."

I try unsuccessfully to hide my surprise at this news.

"I wanted to let you know in person before you heard about it another way. I thought—well, you should know."

"Why?"

He smiles sheepishly and waves toward the winds twisting the landscape. "Given how you took the news the last time, I thought perhaps I could convince you to harness your anger and fear into a less *elemental* outlet."

I school my features, pretending not to have heard him.

"Serena?" Zander questions at my quiet state.

"I meant, why has Oren moved the ceremony up, *again?*"

He shrugs. "I assume it has to do with Tristan's recent visit to the earth realm. Freya has her father's ear and I'm sure she has mentioned my brother's newfound fondness for you, which most likely made him afraid that Tristan would change his mind. As you are aware, *Your Highness*, this agreement binds the two most powerful lands across all realms. It doesn't take a genius to smell Oren's desperation and desire to solidify that partnership. And quickly."

I glance from the good-looking nymph to the waterfall cascading gently behind him, and then back to him again.

The tightness in my chest constricts, and I'm forced to push out a sharp breath. Something about this seems off.

"I think the real question is why the desperation? Why does Oren seek the backing of the woodland realm with such furiousness that he's willing to force nuptials for land he will never govern?" I ask. "It's as if he's afraid, or knows something is about to happen to threaten the realms."

His face pinches. "Perhaps he plans to rule both."

"That's impossible. The only way Oren could rule both realms is if Queen Ophelia and Tristan—" My brows rise. "You don't think he's planning to kill them?"

Zander shakes his head. "Oren is too smart for that. That said, he won't be able to control my brother once Tristan reigns. No one can," he adds with pride. He pauses, looking around uncomfortably before dropping his voice. "Perhaps Oren is hoping Freya and Tristan will produce an heir right away, one that he eventually *can* control?"

I swallow the bile in my throat at Zander's words.

"Then he'd be out of luck. Tristan would never—I mean . . . he wouldn't let a—*his* child, be controlled by Oren. Or anyone else," I bark out. "As his best friend, you know this."

"Maybe it's truly as simple as Oren fearing Tristan will change his mind, given his feelings for you," he reasons.

"Ophelia and Oren signed the decrees when Tristan and Freya were a day old. Royalty cannot break marriage decrees; their agreement is binding. Not to mention Oren pushed the first date up *before* Tristan was assigned to me."

"True."

"And even if they were to be married tomorrow, the queen has a long reign in front of her. Other than solidifying their alliance, rushing their marriage makes no sense."

"Unless," Zander whispers.

"Unless, what?"

"What if Ophelia and Oren are truly working together, as a united front? Think about it, the two most powerful supernatural realms in existence coming together, seeming to be enemies, yet they're working behind the scenes to secure even more influence? Total realm domination."

I stare at Zander because his theory is plausible.

"It would also explain why the queen is holding Tristan to his promise, knowing he has feelings for you," he adds.

His words seep in, before I speak in a hushed tone.

"Zander, what you are describing is marital coercion, with the purpose of undermining the line of succession."

"Yes. I am speaking of high treason," he confirms.

"Holy shit," I blow out in a sharp exhale.

"Deceitfulness in any form within our world is a clear show of disloyalty—even if committed by the sitting queen and emperor."

I scoff. "If your theory is true, as the future heir to the *protector* throne, I can't intercede in matters of supernatural sovereignty unless directly attacked. Regardless of my feelings for Tristan. If I step in, my own actions could be looked upon as threatening the security of the two largest and most powerful immortal realms. These accusations could very well trigger a war—and get me killed."

His gaze narrows. "As the gargoyle princess, you can arbitrate without your uncle Asher's approval if human souls are in danger, or a protector's existence is threatened."

"What does that mean?"

"It means, if they are plotting realm dominance that will include the earth dimension, which places humans in danger. It is your duty to protect them. Not to mention, Tristan is half gargoyle and therefore your subject. It is within your rights to also safeguard him," he points out.

"Notwithstanding, we have no evidence or facts to support the conclusion that the queen and emperor are conducting high treason," I retort. "It's a theory we *just* came up with ten seconds ago."

Zander's expression turns sheepish as he watches me.

My eyes narrow. "Wait, did you really come here just to share news of the change in date, or was it to convince me he's in danger, hoping that I'd charge in and protect him?"

I stiffen as the satyr prowls toward me, ignoring my accusations. "We'll find the evidence, together."

I stare into his unyielding gaze, trying to decide if his conspiracy theory has merit. Zander has no reason to lie.

"Are you trying to start a war? She's your stepmother."

"And he's my brother. You love him. And he loves you. So stop letting fate and titles decide both of your futures."

Without a word, I continue to hold his fierce stare.

"Isn't he worth starting a war for, Serena?" he asks.

My anger vanishes, as does the storm around us.

Silence settles between us, and over the land.

It's as if the universe is waiting for my answer.

Do I want to start a war to protect Tristan?

I look over Zander's face for a few moments before coming to the realization that if this conclusion is true, Tristan is in danger. I have no choice but to protect him.

"I need a favor," I demand with a firm resolve.

"Do you now, champ?" he counters with amusement.

"Your Highness." I bow as confusion falls across his features. I look around, uncomfortable but committed. "I understand you're in need of an escort to a celebration?"

My eyes plead with him, hoping he plays along.

"What?" he asks, confused.

I press my lips together; he clearly doesn't understand what I'm doing. "My presence in the woodland and water realms has been forbidden. It was declared by a royal order."

Zander frowns. "By whom?"

I bristle. "The future king."

"Tristan banished you?" He sounds surprised.

"He signed the order himself," I say in a soft tone.

"That would explain why you haven't come to him."

"Yes, well—" My arms fold across my chest. "Anyway, you're his brother. I know he wouldn't deny you anything. As second in command of the Woodland Nymph Royal Guard, and a prince of the realm, you are permitted to bring anyone you'd like to the future king's marital ceremony."

"You want to be my date to your true love's wedding?"

I growl. "I'm a princess. You're a prince. I would be permitted back into the realm for political reasons—as your date. Then perhaps *we* could find the evidence you seek."

Zander falls silent as he studies my features. "You do realize we would be insinuating that we are . . . *together*?"

I breathe in through my nose and nod my response.

He falls silent again and looks around at the trees that line the expansive lake as he works through the idea. After a moment, he speaks again. "Your uncle would have to approve my courtship, even if pretend, and send word to Queen Ophelia of our blossoming . . . *relationship*."

"You mean we can't just change our Facebook statuses?"

He tries not to smirk at my joke. "I think this would fall into the *it's complicated* category."

"My uncle Asher will approve of it. Of us."

"And Tristan?"

I avert my gaze. "Once he knows why, he will be fine."

A disbelieving laugh escapes from Zander's throat. "No, champ. He fucking won't. Trust me. He'll kill me. Most likely in my sleep. Shit! And what about Magali?"

"She'll understand too," I lie, hoping my best friend and roommate, who has fallen hard for Zander, will.

Since one of Magali's supernatural powers is the detection of deceit, I know she'll pick up on this fib quickly.

After a moment, he sighs. "Once in, what's the plan?"

I smile brightly. "We find evidence that the queen and emperor are consorting to commit high treason, stop a wedding, start a supernatural war, and dodge death."

"Sounds easy enough," he scoffs.

"You asked," I point out.

"My mistake," he grumbles.

I lift my chin. "Tristan *is* worth fighting for."

His gaze narrows as he takes a step toward me. "So you're saying you feel the crazy, obsessive, *I will die for you* kind of love for him?" he asks, pinning me with a look.

Zander once asked me if I felt that way toward Tristan, and I lied and said no. But I do. Deep in my bones, I know.

"I am crazily, obsessively, and totally in love with him."

Zander falls silent and blows out an exaggerated breath.

"What?" I inquire, unsure of his response.

"You just used like twelve adverbs in a row."

I frown. "It was only three."

He runs his hand through his hair. "I love my brother like that too. So, in the name of protection, we'll do this *pretend* courting thing. But Magali needs to know from the start. After what happened with Ryker and Ireland, I won't lie to her, or lead her to believe anything is going on between us. She doesn't need to go through the heartache again of her friends coupling behind her back."

Relief floods me as I nod my agreement.

Without Zander, I don't have access to the woodland realm. If I am going to protect Tristan, I need his help.

"I have another condition," he says in a serious tone as he takes my hands in his. "I mean, if this is to work," he adds.

I tilt my head back, curious. "What's that?"

"You can't cry. Not even a little. I mean it. My heart—well, I won't be able to handle it," he explains.

A small smile cross my lips. I found out the hard way that tears make him beyond uncomfortable.

"I won't shed a tear," I vow.

"You lie; one look at my brother and you're a goner."

"Care to wager?" I challenge. "The winner gets to pick the reward. Anything of their choosing."

"Anything?" he repeats as his eyes narrow on me.

I try not to bristle at the way the word rolled off his tongue, with an underlying roguish sound.

I dip my chin in confirmation. "Anything."

"I accept," he smirks. "This is going to be fun."

We shake on it. "This is business, Zander. Not fun."

"Lighten up; life is supposed to be fun. On that note," he takes a knee. "Serena St. Michael, would you kindly escort me to this small family function I have coming up soon?"

"I would be honored."

He kisses my hand. "Then let the *fun* begin."

TWO
FADE TO RED

TRISTAN

THE CANDLELIT ROOM IS A BLUR of dancing, shadowed in false pretenses, and draped in elegant silk décor and crystal place settings—all conceived out of a nightmare.

My fucking nightmare.

I close my eyes and behind the lids, all I see is *her*.

Visions of sapphire eyes and waves of auburn hair floating in the wind assault me, cutting me to my soul and stabbing at my heart like daggers. Serena St. Michael.

I snap my gaze open and swallow, trying to remove her ghost from the space it's embedded itself in. Of its own accord, my hand lifts and rubs my protector tattoo; the throbbing is a constant reminder—of *her*.

The gargoyle princess haunts my every waking moment, and in the night's darkness, overtakes my dreams.

Since walking away from her, I've been unable to concentrate on anything. Except how she tasted. The ache in my chest grows and I flex my hand in a fist in frustration.

It's been months. Months since I've been entranced by her flowery spring scent or lulled by her laughter.

Attempting to pull myself together, I focus on the pounding of my heart as the sweat builds along the collar of my designer tuxedo. I tug at the material, trying to alleviate the choke hold it has on me. Christ, I miss my fucking jeans.

An ancient, silver-plated goblet filled with crimson liquid suddenly appears in front of me. I take it from the rough hand covered in brown leather fingerless gloves and swallow the entire contents in one swig, ignoring the burn of alcohol sliding down my throat.

Liquid courage.

It doesn't help.

Sadly, I can't drink my fate away.

"This is supposed to be a happy occasion, son. Perhaps a smile would be appropriate?" my stepfather, Rionach, suggests, while gazing into the sea of supernatural dignitaries and royalty celebrating with us this evening.

Out of the corner of my eye, I see his lips twitch as he fights to hide a smile. He knows I hate every second of this charade, but my uncomfortable manner amuses the commander's kind-hearted spirit.

As usual, the leader of the queen's guard looks like a combination of ancient Greek warrior and Irish guerrilla.

He's wearing his general's uniform, no doubt chosen to match my mother's emerald and gold gown. A long, sleeveless, leather vest sits over his garb, an attempt to hide his military appearance—but the sword on his waist is a stark reminder that he is not to be trifled with.

When I was little, I thought Rionach was a god. I knew he'd protect me from any harm that would come my way, not just because it was his job, but because I was his son. His love for me runs deep. Even if I'm not his by blood.

But even he can't stop this lie playing out in front of us.

"Where the hell is Zander?" I bark out, agitated.

A deep crease forms in Rionach's forehead as he runs a hand through his once-golden hair, now peppered with gray, then over his wide nose, before pinching his large chin between his callous fingers, deep in thought.

"Your brother will be here," he states with pride for his biological son. "You should relax, after all, Your Highness," he waves at the room. "This is all in your honor. Tonight, the realms toast to the happiness of their future king and celebrate the peace you've secured for our borders."

I tense as my heart beats wildly in my chest. Lately, I've been struggling to find any beauty or peace within my realm. For me, the world no longer has light in it—just darkness. I'm simply existing. Inhaling, smiling, nodding, and speaking all when I'm supposed to. Nothing more.

The burden of my title and oaths cast a shadow over everything.

The Renaissance music emanating from the lutes and virginals echoes around the ballroom as the prestigious guests waltz to each song. It's normally a soothing melody.

Sadly, the reality of this moment—this situation—makes tonight's music the most gut-wrenching sound in existence.

With each toast and sip of wine the lords and ladies make in my honor, I forge a smile. It's a bogus act on my part, but not Freya's. The water nymph princess flits around the room along with my mother, the queen, personally greeting each guest, smiling, and dancing with our realms' nobles.

The princess of the water dimension is enthralling and beautiful, her existence meant to lure. Her silver eyes are filled with warmth and kindness as she enchants.

Sensing my stare, Freya's eyes lift and meet mine. My childhood friend smiles before dipping her head toward me, as a show of respect to her fiancé and future king. She's been trained well in matters of court manners. The perfect host.

The candlelight's amber hue shimmers off the flecks of glitter in the white twigs that adorn her crown, and the similar branches that frame her slender face. In the light's warmth, her skin appears less silver—less cold.

After a moment, she drops her gaze, hiding it under her long, thick lashes, before flashing a pretty glance at the lord standing before her, causing him to smile brightly.

I inhale my displeasure at being here—with her.

It's all an illusion. The poetry, the sheer beauty of everything that surrounds nymphs—it's all designed to lure you in, to make you feel happy, loved, and beautiful. The reality is, it's all a sham. A ruse created around desire.

I mutter under my breath as I watch the maddening scene, praying the wine is poisoned—to end my misery.

"You should calm down," Rionach suggests. "You look pale and sickly."

"I'm just tired," I grumble, correcting him.

Maybe it's because every night when I lay my head on the pillow, it's *her* I smell, preventing me from sleeping.

"We all are." He slides me a knowing look. "Every one of us that is witnessing this is exhausted."

A server walks by with champagne glasses. We place our empty cups on the silver tray and Rionach takes two more, shoving one at me.

"Drink. It'll help you get through all this nonsense."

I take it gratefully and raise my glass to him. "*Yamas.*"

After I down the contents, my heart slows back to its normal rhythmic pace. I force myself to breathe in and out, because that's what you do when you're lost. You continue to exist, as a shell of the being you were before.

"Your bastard son looks like he's about to have a panic attack. His pale face makes me think that I should have offered my daughter to the vampires, instead of a half-breed satyr prince." Oren barks.

I growl as the Nordic-looking water emperor approaches us. The crown on his slender head tilts, sliding down his white, shoulder-length, stick-straight hair. He reminds me of a weasel. Both in appearance and manner.

Hard silver eyes focus on me as he gets closer.

Angrily, I take a step toward him, but Rionach slaps me on the back before tightening his hand around my shoulder in a firm grip, holding me still as he steps between us.

"Watch how you speak to my son, Emperor. My wife may need your good favor, but I certainly don't give a fuck."

"Queen Ophelia and I both agree that this betrothal is the perfect occasion to celebrate our rekindled alliance. I suggest the prince appear enthusiastic of my generosity."

"Your generosity?" I repeat.

"The offering of my daughter's hand. You should be honored to be part of such an alliance and match. I suggest you show some gratitude, half-breed, before I turn my unkindness in your realm's direction," Oren threatens.

"There are those that say too many alliances make a ruler look weak," Rionach counters. "I may not have been born with a crown, but this realm relies on my sword and allegiance. I'd be careful, Oren, how you threaten my son."

Oren narrows his eyes. "You may speak like a king, but marrying a queen does not elevate you to the level of one."

"And Freya may have a realm, but Tristan has an army, should he need it. One that I command. Remember that."

The emperor lifts his chin. "And let me remind *you* of something. Both you and Ophelia should be kissing my ass for allowing your son's illegitimate hands anywhere near my daughter," Oren sneers. "For the sake of peace, I'm overlooking who his real father is—knowing that if Freya bears sons they'll carry his tainted mongrel bloodline."

I cringe inwardly at the thought of having children, let alone with someone that I do not love or care to be with.

Rionach leans close to the emperor's face. "*I* am Tristan's father. In every way that counts. I also oversee his protection. Before I cut out your tongue for disrespect, remember whom you are speaking to—the future king."

Oren snaps back as though he's been slapped, before righting himself and presenting me with a cruel smirk.

"Does he fight all your battles for you, young prince?"

"Yes. He's the head of my army," I reply sarcastically.

"Threaten me again, Rionach, and I'll see you beheaded, at my command," the emperor adds before taking his leave.

I exhale. "For the record, there will be no sons, or daughters, produced from this façade of a marriage."

Rionach faces me with a disappointed expression. "Kings have consorts for a reason."

I lift a brow at his statement and he rolls his eyes.

"I'm not suggesting you take one, just that there is a reason in court for them . . . you could do worse than Freya."

"I don't love her," I all but shout. "He's right about one thing, though," I sigh. "Given my mixed bloodline and the stigma it brings with it, I'm lucky to be anyone's ally."

"Alliances shift. And you're more than just a bloodline."

I straighten my shoulders and glare through each visiting royal and dignitary. My jaw tightens with the need to take my aggression out on someone or something.

The reminder that I'm Gage Gallagher's son, half gargoyle, claws itself back into my consciousness.

Gargoyle.

Like *her.*

The sea of guests parts as Freya and my mother make their way to us. Rumors of my mother's beauty don't hold a candle to the truth. Her long golden-blonde hair is tied up off her neck this evening, decorated with multiple braids entwined with her favorite lime leaves.

The queen offers us a warm smile before sliding her matching cognac gaze toward me, then back to her husband. "I noticed Oren was speaking with you both; I trust everything is all right?" Her voice is tight.

"As always, my love," Rionach answers. "Oren was simply wishing Tristan a lifetime of happiness," he charms.

My mother's lips twitch. "There are many things I adore about you, Rionach. Your inability to lie is not one."

She places her delicate hands on his chest and smiles up at him with nothing but love and adoration.

"Come, my queen, let me liquor you up so that I might have my way with you later," he teases, taking her hand and leading her away before she can continue to question me.

Freya's gaze meets mine, and she offers a shy smile. "The ballroom seems larger than I recall. Is that possible?"

"I suppose, given that we haven't been in here since we were small children," I reply. "During your game of chase."

"I hated that when we were younger I was always following you around, never able to catch you," she sighs.

"You still haven't." I state firmly, as a reminder that I am not hers, despite what the royal decree says.

She frowns. "Do you like my dress? It's from Paris."

I study the strapless, forest-green gown. It's short in the front and long in the back, showing off her lengthy legs.

Some sort of red-and-pink flower design outlines the opening that drops in the front, reaching to her stomach.

Her perfect breasts are on show for the room and me.

The same flowers cascade down around the skirt.

Freya looks lovely, but it's not something I'd have picked out for her, or anything that I particularly like.

"It's very pretty," I lie.

"I was hoping it would please you. I had several to choose from. It was difficult deciding which you'd like."

Annoyance floats over me that she's worried what I like.

"Why not just pick one that *you* liked?"

Serena would have. Her stubborn streak wouldn't give a fuck what I thought. She'd just wear her favorite.

"How was your dance with Lord Valka?" I change the subject, because every thought I have comes back to Serena.

Freya sighs. "He smells bad and speaks very quickly."

An honest laugh escapes my lips because it's true.

She smiles, seeing my happiness.

"I'd much rather dance with you," the nymph coos.

My eyes float around the ballroom. I suppose now is as good a time as any to stop sulking and embrace my reality.

I dip my chin and hold my hand out to her. "Shall we, then?"

A shyness falls over her as she takes my hand. I pull her into my arms and begin to twirl her around the ballroom.

When I notice that all eyes are on us, I try to control the urge to run and escape. Instead, I smile politely to the crowd and wish it were Serena in my arms, not Freya.

"You're going to be a great ruler someday," she whispers. "Your mere presence commands respect."

My gaze follows hers at the eyes watching us. "I do believe they're staring at you, not your dance partner."

"I disagree. It's obvious how drawn they are to you."

"They're drawn to power and what I can do for them."

"I'm not," she states, her gaze finding mine. "Impressed by your power or title. Or what you can do for me, that is."

"Frey—"

"I prayed for you. Did you know that? As a child, you were all I wanted. I prayed that you'd find the courage to see me. Love me. Whatever the future holds for us, Tristan, whatever may come, I will forever choose you. Loving you will be the best thing I ever do. I promise."

Her words force me to stop dancing. All I can do is stand here, look in her eyes, and hold onto her hands—speechless.

The truth is, I will break her heart. And believe it or not, the thought pains me, because she doesn't deserve this.

None of us do.

I breathe in deeply and close my eyes. Like a spring breeze before the storm, the scent of fresh flowers assaults me.

My head jerks up and I snap open my lids. Releasing Freya, I spin on my heel and lock gazes with a set of deep blue, uncertain eyes as they flicker from me to Freya.

At the sight of her, my entire body seizes and the world around me ceases to exist. All I see is Serena St. Michael.

I hold her stare, afraid to look away, afraid this feeling of peace she brought will leave me as fast as it appeared.

And it does.

Zander steps to her side, taking her hand in his, kissing it, and my world fades to red. All I see is red. Fucking red!

Rage boils within me and before I know what I'm doing, I take a furious step toward them, ignoring Freya's small hands around my elbow as she tries to stop me.

With a harsh yank, I toss her off my arm and continue to storm toward my brother and Serena, ready to tackle him and hammer my fists into his chest and face.

Zander smirks with amusement and takes a slight step in front of Serena, causing me to stop dead in my tracks, confused.

What the fuck is he doing? Protecting her? From me?

The room falls silent.

All laughter and music has ceased.

A crack echoes in my ears and tugs at my core.

Lightning?

No. It's my heart shattering into a million fucking pieces, along with the last piece of my protector bond to her.

Serena's eyes widen and she presses her hand over her heart, feeling our bond disappear. The fierce protector in front of me suddenly looks weak, terrified, and wrecked.

The emptiness hits me so hard, I'm forced to suck in a deep breath. My chest cracks, just a bit, as I mindlessly stare at her, and she back at me—both of us panicked.

Sensing something is off, Zander presses his lips together in a tight smile, walks over to me, and wraps his arm around my shoulder before announcing aloud, "It's okay, please continue to celebrate. My brother is just taken aback by how good-looking and sharply dressed I am."

A light murmur begins to float around the ballroom as the music picks up and the room comes to life again.

"What is happening?" Freya asks, confused, as she appears in front of me with a worried expression.

I ignore the concern in her eyes.

"I'm afraid Tristan has lost his way," Zander states.

What the hell is he doing?

"You're making it worse," I whisper-growl. "Just stop."

"His way?" Freya repeats. "Are you okay?" she asks me.

Zander takes Freya's hand and squeezes. "Do not fret, princess, he will find it again. Because if he doesn't," he turns to face me, "I imagine the other half of his soul will be disappointed, and the last person our future king needs to disappoint is the one he lives for," he finishes. "Right?"

Freya turns to face Zander, her gaze shifting from my brother to Serena. "What in the water realm are you babbling on about? And what is *she* doing here?"

He clears his throat. "She's with me. We're courting."

I jerk away and mutter, "I have to go."

"Tristan, wait!" Freya yells after me, but I ignore her and stumble out of the ballroom.

With every step, I try to catch my breath. I make a beeline for the front doors, pushing them both open with enough force to bring down the entire castle.

Resentment and anger boil under my skin. I release a painful roar that is so raw, it slices through the realm with a fierce shake, as I fall to my knees and yank on my hair, trying to pull oxygen into my burning lungs again.

After a few moments, I stand and run. Toward the only place in the realm that I know I'll be safe. Secure. Alone.

THREE

FIGHT FOR YOU

TRISTAN

MOMENTS LATER, THE WELL-LIT, MODERN CABIN appears through the forest. Home. I follow the cobblestone pathway, climb the stairs, and open the front door, falling in.

One inside, I slide my back down the door and sink to the hardwood floor with an uncaring thud.

My palms rub away the moisture on my cheeks as the tears fall from my eyes and sheer pain overtakes me.

Zander's right. What little direction I had left just disappeared, along with Serena's and my protector bond.

Serena and I are no longer connected. My heart continues to thud and rumble in my chest as if it has permanently lost its reason for continuing to beat.

Almost instantly, my brother appears out of thin air. I lift my angered gaze and pin him with a menacing look.

His black velvet suit shimmers with each movement as I curb the desire to strangle him with his vernal-colored tie.

"Dude! Are you . . . crying?" he accuses, shocked.

I stand in a fierce pose and sneer at him. "I told you to watch over her and protect her. Not bed or COURT her."

A guilty expression falls across his face. "When you're king, you'll have to be a bit more specific with your orders."

My swing is hard and fast as my fist connects with his jaw. Zander's head snaps to the side with a loud popping sound that ricochets off the walls.

"What the hell, Tristan? Warn me before you try to kill me," he barks, and pushes me so hard I fall on my ass.

I lift an eyebrow, seething. "Fucking warn you?"

"Look, I know you're all heartbroken and shit, but do you have to be violent toward the one being who has always had your back?" He turns to the side and spits out a mouthful of blood. "You have to trust me. You asked me to protect her. I can't do that if I'm dead."

"Valid point," I grind out.

"Now," he holds his hands up in surrender. "No attacking me. I'm going to help you get to your feet, and then we can talk about all this. With words, not fists."

Zander holds his hand out and pulls me upright.

"Such a gentleman," I growl.

He grins. "That's what she said," he teases, and I lift my fist to punch him again, but then she steps out of the shadows.

"Stop!" Her voice wraps around me like the warmth of the sunshine. "Please," she whispers, gutting me.

A long, silent moment passes between us as we just stare at one another and the rest of the world fades away.

"Hi," she says softly, breaking the silence.

My brows rise. "Hi?" I repeat, my voice pitching higher in surprise.

Her shoulders fall. "I'm not sure what else to say. This is way more uncomfortable than I thought it would be."

"Maybe you could tell me what the hell you're doing in a realm that has forbidden your presence. Or perhaps you'd like to explain to me why you're attending my premarital celebrations." I narrow my gaze. "Wait, how about we start off with something simple," I shrug. "Like why the fuck it is my brother is apparently COURTING YOU NOW!" I roar.

"Calm down." Zander says in warning.

My focus snaps to him. "Are you seriously protecting her? Did you not just see how your actions in the ballroom shattered our bond?" I bark, and notice Serena bristle.

She steps forward. "During Zander's unrelenting and insufferable presence at the Academy, we've become friends. He needed an escort to your upcoming celebration, as Magali was unable to attend. My clan, your mother, and I all agreed to allow him to court me so that I might accompany him into the realm because, well," she pauses, then screams, "YOU BANISHED ME!"

"FOR A REASON!" I shout back, and quickly inhale my anger through my nose as not to explode on her again.

This is the first time I've been this close to her since I trampled all over her heart and ruined any future chance I had of being with her. And it hurts. It fucking hurts.

"I did it to protect you, so that you didn't have to watch me marry another. Yet, here you are. Willingly," I state.

My brother clears his throat. "I'm just going to step outside and let you two work this out."

"You do that," I snip.

He stares me down. "Don't hurt her—any more than you already have."

"Is that a threat?" I snarl.

Zander sighs. "I refuse to get into a pissing match with you right now. Believe me, her love for you is unwavering."

Once he leaves, I lift my gaze and stare at her as the bitterness festering inside me keeps getting worse. At any moment, I am just going to go ballistic from it all.

I close my eyes, trying to convince myself that if I can't see her, it won't hurt as badly. Her being here—it cuts deep.

I want her.

But I can't have her.

She isn't mine.

"Tristan," Serena whispers next to me.

I stiffen, refusing to open my eyes, because if I look at her face, or if she touches me, I'm done for. Game over.

"Don't be like this . . ."

"I miss you," I admit in a quiet voice. "So damn much, and I wish . . . I wish I wasn't bound to Freya, but I am. I must respect who I am and what I'm meant to do. And you need to understand that. You should go back to the Academy. Our bond is severed. You're free." I swallow the lump in my throat and open my eyes but still refuse to look at her. "I have to keep my promises to my monarchy. If I don't, realms will fall. I can't have innocent blood on my hands, especially when it could be yours. I have no choice."

Serena is in my face so fast that I jerk back with a curse as she presses me against the wall, pointing a finger in my chest as she pins me with her narrowed gaze.

"There is always a choice. I refuse to allow you to justify your actions by saying your hands are tied. You once told me that you believed we can change the outcome of our destiny. That history proves it to us, over and over again. Don't give up on this—on us—as easily as you are."

I reach for her hand, but she pulls away.

"You should be at the Academy, where you are safe, *princess*." A pregnant pause beats between us.

Anger crosses her face at being called princess. I know she hates it, which is why I used it. For a second, I think she might just take a swing at me. It wouldn't be the first time.

Instead, she exhales slowly and backs away, making her way toward the door . . . and no doubt back to my brother.

With her hand on the knob, she tugs it open, but before walking out she turns and faces me, speaking firmly.

"Until all the air has left my lungs, I will fight for you. I will protect you. I will choose you, because you're my fate."

FOUR

A CHILL IN THE AIR

SERENA

I IGNORE THE SLIGHT CHILL IN the air as I step onto the front deck of Tristan's cabin. Exhaling slowly, I seek out Zander. He's sitting in one of the Adirondack chairs by the fire pit. Full lips are pressed into a hard stare as he silently watches the flames dance in the evening's darkness. His jaw is swollen where Tristan hit him and he's stretching his neck from side to side, probably trying to alleviate the ache.

Quietly, I approach him. "Well, that went well."

He chuckles. "We're both still alive, so I think it did."

Offering a small smile, I sit in the empty chair.

"Sorry that Tristan used your face as a punching bag."

He shrugs. "I expected it. I would be pissed off too if the love of my life were suddenly being courted by my brother."

"You didn't deserve his anger, or moment of insanity."

A flash of something crosses his face. "Don't I, though?"

I press a hand over my heart. Now that the adrenaline has worn off, the emptiness and ache caused by the severing of our protector bond is settling in. It's funny, for the first few months I didn't even realize we shared the bond, but now that it's gone, completely, I don't feel whole.

"You okay?" Zander motions with his chin to my heart.

"It hurt for a second, but—now, it's just a dull ache."

"I'm sorry if my stepping between you two snapped it."

"It was just a matter of time before it disappeared fully."

His lips twitch as a comfortable silence falls between us.

"This is going to be so much harder than I thought it would be. Seeing him—with her—tonight . . ." I trail off.

"Hey," Zander takes my hand and squeezes. "You're not alone here. You've got me; we'll get through it. Together."

"If you were smart, you'd run for the hills."

"I don't run," he holds my gaze. "I stay, and fight."

"Thank you," I whisper.

"And don't think I'm being nice, either." He sits back and folds his hands behind his head. "I have a bet to win."

"What a lovely sentiment."

He grins, and I can't help but laugh at his goofiness.

"It's nice to see the two of you getting along so well."

Zander and I dart to our feet and bow before Queen Ophelia. Freya steps to the queen's side, wearing an ugly scowl on her face as she looks us over with annoyance.

Ophelia smiles gracefully. "Freya, be a dear, would you, and go check on my son. I have no doubt that seeing his betrothed will do him some good after this evening's . . . events," the queen orders, in a bright tone that makes it sound more like a suggestion.

"Of course, Your Majesty. It would be my pleasure."

Freya dips her chin and quickly brushes past us.

Once the water princess has disappeared inside the house, the queen's stance morphs into a less formal one as she steps closer to us, while narrowing her parental gaze.

"You two," she nods between us, "sit."

Zander and I share a side-glance and do as she orders.

She moves toward the fire, placing her hands near it for warmth before speaking regally. "I had no idea Tristan signed a banishment order against you, Serena." The queen's tone is suddenly full of disappointment. She sighs. "Unfortunately, your clan took it as a personal insult. I've extended my deepest apologies because I do not wish to have a strained relationship with the gargoyle race. This is why I've allowed Zander to court you—although given the timing, and his fondness for your protector friend, Magali, I'm not sure why the allowance has been asked of me."

"I appreciate the kindness you've shown," I appease.

Ophelia rolls her eyes as if she were not royalty, but instead, my mother. "It wasn't kindness. I don't know what the two of you are up to, but I will figure it out. And when I do, you can be sure that if it hurts my son in any way, regardless of whether we're family or allies, I will not hesitate to take actions against either one of you." She lifts her chin. "My husband is quite fond of you. As are both our sons. Make no mistake, you're here now because *I* believe it is better to keep you close—given your obvious feelings for Tristan, and his for you." She pins me with a look. "If you interfere with his duties and obligations, my favor with you will become nonexistent. Political allies or not. Are we clear?"

"Crystal, Your Majesty," I reply.

She dips her chin before walking over to Zander and placing a palm over his swollen cheek. "I love you as if you were my own. Tristan is impulsive and prideful. Neither of you should be behaving in this manner at court. Be more mindful of each other's feelings. You are, after all, brothers."

He places his hand over hers. "We will. On my honor."

"Tristan has decided to stay at the castle before his nuptials. Freya is there as well. Therefore, it might be best for you both to stay here at his cabin while in our realm."

"Of course, Your Majesty."

"Good. Go inform him then, please," she directs.

Zander looks between the two of us with uncertainty before standing and making his way back to the house.

Queen Ophelia takes his empty seat; her expression is soft and crestfallen as she stares into the auburn flames.

A welcome silence falls between us as we watch the embers glow before her quiet voice fills the night's air.

"If there is anything I took from my brief moment in time with Tristan's father, Gage, it is that gargoyles protect and fight hard for those they love. Your kind are true warriors. And while it may seem that fate is fighting against you and my son," she twists her focus to me, "it is not."

"I'm sorry, Your Majesty, I'm not following."

"I saw what occurred between you and Tristan earlier. The bond severed in the ballroom," her shoulders sag. "I may have even heard his heart shatter when it dissolved."

My hand automatically finds my heart and presses down, a silly attempt to ease the emptiness it now feels.

"Gage is proof that when love is fated, not even death can break a protector's bond." She lowers her voice so it's barely audible. "Search your heart; Tristan will be there. Regardless of his words or his actions. You must trust in the journey. For true love is everlasting, even in death."

Wordless and confused, I watch as she stands, pats the front of her gown down, and disappears into the trees surrounding the cabin.

Dumbfounded, I study the inky forest in disbelief and dissect her words. Trust in the journey? Even in death—was that a threat against Tristan's existence, or mine?

"So you're staying?" Tristan interrupts my pondering with his calm, cool, detached voice, and approaches me from behind.

My gaze swings from the forest to the fire and back again, as his mother's words float around in my head.

If he's in danger, this would be the time to warn him.

"Tristan."

"What?" He stands in front of me with tense shoulders.

I study him, trying to form a plausible reason why I'd be accusing his mother of plotting murder, but can't.

Not without proof, anyway. Wrong time.

Suddenly, I'm chilled, and rub my arms.

"You're blocking the warmth," I point behind him at the flames. "I forgot how cold—and dark—your realm can be."

Something flashes in his eyes as he takes a step to the left, allowing the last bit of heat from the dying fire to wash over me. I see by his annoyed expression that he took my insult as personally as I meant it. He's so detached in my presence, it's physically choking me.

"Classes at the Academy start soon. You'll be needed."

I snort. "Is that so?"

"I understand you, Magali, Ryker, and Ireland were assigned to the school's protection after you graduated," he points out. "You took oaths and have a duty to see through."

"Once again, your panache for stating the obvious is mind-blowing," I reply drily.

"You need to go." His tone is almost pleading.

I flinch and play with my protector bracelet, a habit of mine when I'm uncomfortable or rattled.

His eyes fall to my wrist.

The reminder of my obligation annoys me. All I've ever wanted was to choose my own life and path. Yet, I'm right back where I started, at the Royal Protector Academy.

After a gargoyle graduates from the Academy, the royal family grants each a prestigious protector assignment.

Some of my friends and I have been assigned to the school, not because of our ability to safeguard it, but because it's where my clan feels that I am the safest.

This summer I went home to London. In the early hours of morning, the Diablo Fairy leader, Kupuva, attacked my family, killing my bodyguard, Rulf, during the harsh battle.

Once the army was defeated, I returned to the prison the Academy has become to me. Hidden away, for safety.

"We both know the reason for my assignment," I snip.

Tristan tilts his head as his eyes slowly inspect me. A glimmer of softness touches his eyes as he speaks. "It's the safest place for you to be. An entire school made up of the elite within the gargoyle race. At your disposal if the Diablo Fairy army attacks again. Ready to give their lives for their future queen if need be," he repeats his words from a previous conversation we've had. "Asmodeus and Kupuva are still a threat to you. Your safety takes priority."

"For who?" I challenge. "You?"

"Yes," he changes his tone from chilly to warm. "Me."

As if realizing what he just said, he stands straighter and his face once again becomes masked with indifference.

I would have expected him to look gentle and kind to match his tone, but instead, I can't read him at all anymore.

Cognac eyes blink at me slowly, causing me to shiver for a second time, but this time, it's not from the cool night air.

"Chancellor Davidson gave me a short reprieve so that I could come here with Zander," I admit softly. "My clan agreed, knowing you and your realm would keep me safe."

His shoulders sink as he looks directly at me. "We can't change the circumstances surrounding our births. Our bloodlines are our fates. We're leaders. Royalty. The future of our respective races. It is a heavy burden to carry," he pauses, "one that comes with outrageous rules and ancient decrees. But regardless of what is hanging between us, you're always safe within my realm's walls. And with me."

"Not all of me is safe with you," I say in a shaky voice.

Recognition flares in his eyes. He knows I'm heartbroken and still harboring feelings for him.

Emotions he's crushed.

"Feelings aren't luxuries those like us are lucky enough to be afforded. Oaths. Duties. They are our fate."

"And love?"

His eyes roam over my face. "Interdimensional balance and power rely on levelheadedness and focus. There is no room for love when you are the future king or queen."

"So—you're admitting that you do love me?"

He hesitates, and his perfect lips press into a firm line.

"Your silence isn't very encouraging, Tristan."

His lips twitch, fighting off the smallest hint of a smile at my tease before his expression turns into one of indifference. "Do you want me to lie to you?"

I swallow the thickness in my throat; he already has.

A haunted sadness falls across him, reminding me there is protector blood running through his veins. It might not be mine anymore, but there is no hiding it. Gage's presence is in the very air he breathes and the way he carries himself.

I stand and lean toward him, needing to feel his warmth.

"You are my fate." I whisper into the night air.

He shoots me a pained expression. "I have to go; I'm wanted at the castle to prepare for tomorrow's celebration," his voice turns harder. "Since you'll be staying in my home, as my *brother's* guest, I expect you to sleep in my room and Zander in the guest room. You are a princess and should be mindful of your reputation."

I burst out laughing. "Is that so?"

"That's so, raindrop." His tone is serious.

A huff of annoyance escapes me and I lower my voice to a more seductive one. "You didn't seem to mind my *reputation* back at the Academy, professor."

"We aren't at the Academy anymore. In my realm, at my court, you are titled. The heir to the gargoyle throne." He pushes into my personal space. "Which is why you should heed this warning: a princess with a blemished reputation is like a queen with burned lands."

I hold my breath and lean in a sliver more, so our lips are almost touching and I can inhale the breaths he releases.

"In what way?"

"Each may have once been lush and alluring. Yet, the heat of the flames overtook and consumed them, leaving only dark, scarred blemishes on something once beautiful."

My eyes fall to his lips as I listen to the double meaning.

"Remember that, when my brother puts his hands on you tonight," he adds in a cruel whisper before jerking away.

I avert my gaze, needing a moment to gather my composure, but when I swing it back to scathe him with my snarky response, he's gone.

Vanished into thin air.

No doubt teleporting himself back his fiancée.

Trying to catch my breath, I watch as the last flicker of the glowing ash dies out. The sting of tears threatens, but I hold them back, turning and heading toward the house, hating myself for letting Tristan affect me the way he does.

I storm in and slam the glass doors shut behind me with a frustrated growl before stomping toward Zander, who is waiting for me by the pool table, amused at my state.

"Your brother is a moody, arrogant ass."

Zander stands taller and twirls the pool stick like a sword. "Your Highness, is your honor in need of saving?"

I narrow my gaze. "Nope. Just my pride."

"Pride is for the foolish of heart, champ."

"Then my heart is officially the queen of foolishness."

He puts the stick on the table and walks toward me until he's standing right in front of me. Sighing, he reaches out and touches my cheek. His lips break out into a tense smile.

"Serena, we're born to be real, not perfect. My brother bleeds just like everyone else." He frowns as if the thought upsets him. "There is a heavy weight on his shoulders. He is to be the future king. He is engaged to someone he doesn't love, or even like very much for that matter. His realm is on the brink of war. And the one he's allowed himself to fall in love with just showed up to his unwanted wedding on the arm of his brother, who happens to be a devilishly good-looking, smart, sexy warrior. He has reason to be a moody ass. Wouldn't you agree?"

I frown. "You might have overexaggerated a tiny bit."

He pinches his brows. "How so?"

"Well," I exhale. "For one, you aren't that good-looking," I tease. "Even if Mags gets all weak in the knees whenever you walk into a room and her eyes go all dopey."

A bright grin forms on his lips. "Goddamn, she's beautiful. Speaking of hot and sexy gargoyles from South Africa, Magali checked in. The Academy is silent and all is well. There have been no signs of the Diablo Fairies."

My body sags with relief. "That's good news."

"It is, which means we can focus on the task at hand."

I eye him curiously and slowly pull my cheek away from his warm palm, unsure of his intentions. "Which would be?"

He intertwines our fingers and drags me over to the couch, pulling me down dramatically.

"Finding evidence of treason against Oren and Ophelia."

"You're still stuck on that?"

He pins me with an unamused look.

I feign innocence. "Just confirming. What's the plan?"

"Tomorrow morning, Queen Ophelia and Empress Consort Lily, Freya's mother, are hosting a brunch on the castle grounds. You remember the gardens, right?" he asks.

"How could I forget?" My tone is dry. "You dragged me through the labyrinth when Ophelia announced it was Tristan who was to marry Freya, not you, during my last visit to the realm. I'm pretty sure I threw up on her roses."

"You totally did; it was pretty gross—yet awesome at the same time." He makes a pinched face and clears his throat. "On the other side of the coin, the gardens are where you and I became friends," he ends on a light note, patiently waiting for me to respond and agree with him.

I lighten my tone. "Yes, of course. Good times."

"And fond memories and all," he adds, nodding.

"Please focus," I plead.

"The plan: I figure, while everyone is toasting my brother and his future bride over bagels and schmear, you and I will take a little stroll through the castle, maybe raid the queen's chambers, and see what we can find out."

"Bagels and schmear?"

"It's brunch."

"Yes, I know—just, schmear?"

"Don't judge; nymphs love cream cheese."

I exhale loudly. "I see now why my dad agreed to our courtship. It's weird how alike the two of you are."

"They say most girls fall in love with guys who remind them of their dad," he nods fondly. "And Callan is the best."

I throw him a pointed glare. "We are not in love."

"Because you picked the tortured, brooding, bad boy. Why do girls do this to themselves?" He pouts. "The good news for you is there is still time to change teams. Pick the handsome, funny, good guy," he grins widely.

"No."

"Oh!" he exclaims. "We could totally love triangle the shit out of this . . . ," he trails off, deep in thought.

"Zander," I snarl.

"Focusing. As I was saying, I've paid off some of the servants, asking that they keep their eyes and ears open. Hopefully someone has overheard or seen something."

I glare at him. "Talk about invading your family's privacy. Employees are not meant to be used as pawns."

"I can't help it that the staff gossips."

I bite down on my lower lip. "What about Tristan?"

Zander seems confused. "I'm not sure it would help to pay him off; he has no idea about any of this. For a gargoyle who protects, you're very bad at this espionage stuff."

I roll my eyes. "I mean, don't you think it will be weird if he sees us just get up and leave in the middle of brunch?"

"Oh," he laughs. "No. Whenever I bring someone that I am sleeping with, it's common for us to dart out of meals."

I eye him. "I'm pretty sure I should slap you on behalf of women everywhere for that comment."

"I'm a nymph. Bedding the opposite sex is what I do. Anywhere. Anytime. Even over quiche," he counters.

"But we aren't sleeping together," I remind him.

"Yes, but Tristan doesn't know that." He winks. "Nor does anyone else attending these events. In this realm, it wouldn't seem odd for a male nymph to take the girl he's courting out of sight for a bit. In fact, it's expected."

"On that note, *you'll* be sleeping in the guestroom tonight. I'll be in Tristan's room," I announce. "Clear?"

Zander frowns. "You don't want to cuddle?"

"No offense, but no. Not with you."

"Afraid that you'll like it?"

I press my lips in a firm line. "I'm afraid *you'll* like it."

He pushes some hair out of his now-serious gaze. "All teasing aside, Serena, what I like is the way you love my brother. It's honest and raw. Fierce and unwavering. True."

I squeeze my eyes closed. "None of that matters."

He takes my chin between his fingers. "He loves you."

I open one eye. "You're still sleeping in the guest room."

"I should remind you that this charade was your idea. When we're out, it should appear as if we're a couple who are courting and dare I say, perhaps even like one another."

"Understood."

"Then stop flinching whenever I touch you."

"I don't flinch," I argue.

"It's like you can't get away fast enough."

"Sorry. It's just weird."

"Weird or not, I'm a nymph prince and general, which means at court, I have a reputation to uphold," he states.

Tristan's earlier warning floats around my head.

"As do I." I remind him with a pointed look.

He considers my words before nodding his agreement.

"We'll keep it to hand holding and cheek kisses."

"I'll agree to that, but not in front of Tristan."

"If it can be avoided."

"Fair enough."

"Just so you know, as a creature who loves wine, women, and physical pleasure, I've never had to practice restraint," he mumbles. "I'm warning you, I'm not sure how good I will be at it."

"Restraint builds character."

Zander presses his lips together and leaps off the couch, motioning for me to follow him toward the stairs. "We should get some rest, because tomorrow we seek answers."

We climb up the staircase, my heart jumping with each step closer to Tristan's master suite. It's silly, but I'm feeling weird and anxious to enter the room again. The last time I was here, it's where we stayed—together.

Once we reach the doors, I freeze, unsure if I want to enter. Seeing my hesitation, Zander reaches around me, twists the knobs and pushes them open.

Silently, my eyes take in the expansive room, lined on one side with open french doors that lead out to the stone balcony, overlooking the realm's large lake.

I inhale as a memory—of Tristan and I standing on the terrace, in the rain, kissing—assaults me.

Quietly, Zander slips away and I step into the room.

Immediately, I'm hit with Tristan's scent—citrus and spice. It's calming. Safe. Frightening. Just like him.

I walk farther into the room, toward the two chairs facing the lake, and my heart squeezes a little when I see that the blanket I love to curl up in is still in my preferred chair. I pick it up and inhale his smell, letting it wrap around me. It's then I realize the gas fireplace is lit.

My brows pinch in confusion, because I remember Tristan saying he never uses it. Placing the blanket back on the chair, I walk over to the switch on the wall to turn it off, but at the last minute, change my mind, deciding I like the warmth, and leave it on.

Wanting to get comfortable, I turn toward the bed and see my bags placed by the closet. Rifling through them, I pull out what I need to get ready for sleep. When I stand to head toward the bathroom, I notice a T-shirt lying across Tristan's comforter. Walking toward it, I stop in my tracks when I realize it's the one I wore when I stayed here before.

I look around the room and it dawns on me. Tristan's scent is fresh, as if he were just here. Not dull and lingering.

Tristan—he put the fire on, knowing I like it. He left the blanket and this T-shirt. I smile, knowing he did all this—for me. I walk toward the bed and run my hand over the soft cotton before picking it up and bringing it with me into the bathroom. Once I slip it on, I feel safe and happier than I have in months. Surrounded by him.

Tired, I slip under the soft, warm blanket, settling deeper into the oversized chair. My gaze roams over the lake blanketed in darkness before I shut my eyes tight, desperately recalling memories of him.

His touch. His taste. His sounds.

The way he looks at me.

Tristan cups my chin firmly between his fingers.

"Look at me," he demands, using an arrogant voice.

My eyes blaze with fury at his tone. "I am."

He smiles. "There you are. There's the spark of life."

His fingers on my face relax my core, bringing me back to myself. I try to pull away, but he wraps his free arm around my waist and wrenches my body against his, locking me to him.

Tristan's lips graze my ear as he speaks through the thunder.

"Trust me. To protect you. To protect us."

I stiffen and try to push away, but he holds me tighter.

His lips brush across my neck in the barest of touches before he pulls back and cups my face with shaky hands.

Only a sliver of air exists between our lips as his hooded gaze meets mine. He brushes a thumb over the pulse at the base of my neck, as if he's trying to push life into it to keep my heart beating.

I tremble beneath his touch.

"I've got you. You. Are. Safe." He doesn't release me. He simply waits until

I get myself under control and give in.

"I believe you," I concede breathlessly.

My lids flutter open reluctantly, not wanting to let go of the vision. Movement outside has my focus shifting, and that's when I see him. Like a dark angel covered in shadows and bathed in moonlight, Tristan is standing near the lake's edge, staring up at me through the open doors.

Holding his stare, I stand and walk out onto the patio, adjusting the blanket around my shoulders as the cool air caresses my bare legs.

When he sees me, his expression turns wounded at the same time his eyes slide down my body. Over his shirt, slipping down, taking in my bare legs before gliding back up and landing back on my unwavering stare.

Then he's gone.

Just when I'm ready to turn and head to bed, he reappears on the balcony in front of me, breathing hard, as if he sprinted up here instead of teleporting.

Within seconds, his large, warm hand is at the base of my throat and he walks me backwards until my back hits the side of the house. I still, understanding what he's doing.

As an empath, he's reading my feelings. His hand slides up even farther, until his fingers and palm are flush against my neck. His eyes close as he scans my emotions.

I let him, unmoving, because the feel of his skin against mine is an overwhelmingly welcome sensation. I shiver.

"Are you cold?" he whispers, his breath fanning my lips.

"No," I breathe.

"You're shivering," he observes.

"It's not because of the chill in the air," I barely manage.

He steps closer, and when his chest meets mine, our gazes lock. Tristan runs his fingers over my jaw, slipping his hands behind my neck. His palms conform perfectly to me as he drops his forehead gently to mine.

"You're wearing my shirt," he speaks hoarsely.

My hands white-knuckle the blanket and my lips part slightly when his breath falls in waves across my mouth.

I'm afraid to move.

Afraid if I do, he'll scare and run away.

"What if I said I just want you? What if I just want that one thing?" He croaks as if in pain. "What would happen?"

"You have me. I'm yours. But you have to fight for us."

I tremble as the coolness from his rings soothes my neck. Stepping closer, I wrap my hands around his wrists and cling to the leather of his protector bands, searching his eyes. "I'm yours," I whisper again, firmly this time.

FIVE

CHOSEN

TRISTAN

ONE HUNDRED SEVENTY-THREE DAYS. THAT'S HOW fucking long it's been since my last cigarette. I swallow the last sip of my fifth cup of coffee, wishing it were laced with nicotine to soothe the edgy twitching that's overtaken me.

I shouldn't have gone back to the cabin last night. But I had to be sure that Serena slept in my room and Zander in his. The moment I saw her, wearing the shirt I'd laid out for her, *my* shirt, I lost it. All self-control—gone. Right out the fucking window, which is why I banished her in the first place. I can't focus on anything else when she's around.

Then I left.

She declared herself mine and my response was to run.

I literally disappeared from her arms without so much as an explanation or warning. Just like Gage does.

"Goddamnit!" I growl aloud.

A silvery hand slides over mine. "Are you all right?"

Blinking several times, I come back to reality and see several faces watching me with concern, including Freya's.

"Sorry. I just wanted pancakes and I don't see any," I lie.

The nymph's eyes dart around wildly, as if on a mission, and after a moment, she places her napkin politely on the table and pushes herself into a standing position, squeezing my hand. "It's nothing to fret over, I'll fetch you some."

I clench my jaw, feeling like a jerk. "You don't have to."

"Nonsense. You're to be my husband and the king someday. If it is pancakes that you desire, then you shall have them." She flutters away as Zander enters with Serena.

My gaze narrows at their intertwined hands. Zander leans toward her ear and murmurs something that causes her to laugh. My blood boils. I can handle a lot of things, but my brother whispering sweet nothings in her ear? No.

I play with my brow piercing as I watch them, trying to shake the feeling that this is my fault in the first place.

I knew better. If I had just stayed away from her in the first place, we wouldn't be here right now. Instead, the pull she had on me was so magnetic, I found myself falling for her. Hard. And now, here I sit, watching her grace my brother's arm, contemplating throwing it all away and starting an all-out war just so that I can have her.

Am I really that selfish? To put love in front of duty?

Zander runs a hand through his dark hair and I can't help but wonder. I know why Serena agreed to Zander's courtship, for no other reason than entrance into the realm. Because after last night, one thing is for damn sure: regardless of what's happening outwardly, she's still mine.

The real question is why my brother agreed. Last I knew, he had strong feelings for Serena's best friend Magali.

Something about this feels off. What are they up to?

I observe as he makes her a plate of breakfast items. A smile crosses my lips because he adds pineapple, which she loathes, passionately. That alone confirms this is a hoax.

He hands it to her with a small kiss on the cheek, and I curb my desire to teleport over there and break off his face.

Like a stalker, I stare as they take seats next to Rionach and my mother, smiling and engaging in polite conversation.

Serena pushes the pineapple with her fork to the side of the plate while fixing it with a dirty look, and I laugh.

My moment of triumph vanishes when Zander notices her distaste for the fruit. He picks it up off her plate and tosses it with great dramatics over his shoulder into the woods. Serena tilts her head and smiles at him like he's her fucking hero. I try not to appear as irritated as I feel.

I'm two seconds away from losing my shit.

Her auburn locks fall over her slender shoulder and my chest tightens. I can't decide if it's from her sheer beauty or the fact that Zander gets to be her knight in shining armor.

Hell, maybe I did this. Maybe I pushed her into someone else's arms, knowing mine are the worst ones for her to be in. I'm not the good guy. Zander is. He's everything good and safe. He's someone she deserves.

I, on the other hand, can barely look at myself in the mirror anymore. With the way that I've treated both Freya and Serena over the past few months, fucked up doesn't even begin to describe my situation.

A steaming plate of pancakes is waved under my nose.

"Pancakes." Freya chirps and places the plate down in front of me. "I apologize for the delay. The chef had to make them special. For some reason our mothers did not want them present or offered during brunch," she explains.

I force myself to look at Freya and fake a smile.

She frowns at the gesture and looks at Zander and Serena before returning her uneasy attention back to me.

"Thank you." I try to appear nonchalant as she retakes her seat. "I appreciate you doing that on my behalf."

"No thanks are necessary," her voice is small.

"Still, I appreciate the effort," I add sincerely.

"We're to be married. Pleasing and taking care of you are part of my duties. Your happiness brings me great joy."

"Frey—"

Her eyes glide back to Zander. "Does it bother you?"

"What?"

"That your brother is romancing the gargoyle princess?" she asks. "I mean, if they marry, she will be around all the time, here at court. As your brother's wife."

I flinch. "I'm sure their courtship will end as fast as it began. Zander prefers—variety over commitment."

"A cruel trait that appears to run in your family. No?"

"It's not something to agonize about. We don't know what the future holds. Worrying helps no one," I state.

Her expression becomes crestfallen. "Do you not worry how it will affect me, having her here, all the time?"

I place my fork down and lower my tone, trying not to take this out on her. "Our engagement is strictly business."

Freya fidgets with her napkin. "Do you have any idea how it feels to watch him parade your lover around court?"

I grunt in frustration and stand, trying to escape.

Freya grabs my hand. "Where are you going?"

"Somewhere other than here." I answer in a calm tone, removing my hand, because gods help us all if I truly lose my shit in front of everyone at our engagement brunch.

"You are not the only one with a realm to consider. I'm sure my father will disapprove of Serena's continued presence here at court and within the realm," she threatens.

In the blink of an eye, I grab her elbow and use my protector gifts of speed and teleportation. We disappear so fast that no one has time to see us even leave. Seconds later, I reappear on the top of the castle, overlooking the ocean.

I release her with enough force that she stumbles to catch her footing. "If you are ever going to become queen someday, you should understand something. Kings don't tolerate threats made by their wives. Especially me."

Angrily, the nymph stomps closer to the castle's wall. She falls silent, her eyes fixating on the castle grounds, her hands resting on the stone railing.

I release a long exhale, calming myself. I need to stop taking my anger out on her. "I shouldn't have said that."

Silence.

"There were other ways of handling it," I continue in a gentle manner, "than how I did. I'm sorry, for my temper."

"Handling me, you mean?" she replies, with an edge in her voice, and faces me. "It's what you truly meant, is it not?"

When I don't respond, the Nordic beauty presses her lips, displeased with my silence. "You do realize we're to be married. It is not a maybe, or perhaps, but it is indeed fact."

My eyes roam across her face, admiring the white branches that frame her slender appearance. She's stunning, smart, and kindhearted. Freya is everything any king could want or be lucky enough to have in a queen and partner.

Except she's nothing I want.

She isn't my heart's choice.

She peers at me angrily from under her overly long, thick lashes. "I'm to be your wife. Your realm's queen."

"Believe me, I'm aware." My tone is bored.

Her silver eyes narrow. "We've been engaged since childhood. Do you not think we owe it to ourselves, our families, and our realms to give us a fighting chance?"

"It's not that simple."

She rears back. "What is not simple about this, Tristan? It's already all arranged. All you have to do is accept it and open your heart to me. Learn to love me, as I do you."

"STOP!" I roar. "My realm comes first. Nothing else matters beyond that. Right now, a war with your father could destroy not only the supernatural dimensions, but every realm that relies on the woodland and water lands to maintain their survival. This marriage is nothing more than a business agreement. Please, accept that. My heart has never been, is not now, nor will it ever be open to your love."

Freya regards me, considering my words before lifting her chin in defiance and speaking again. "Well, it's not your decision. It's Queen Ophelia's, and her decree has been made. You and I will be wed. We will exchange vows that will not, and cannot ever be broken. You will be mine and I yours. You will learn to love me, as I do you. And nothing will stop that," she bites out, attempting to sound unkind, but in truth, she simply sounds frightened, fragile, and weak.

I cock my head to the side and offer her a cruel smile.

"You don't see my mother rushing us to the altar anytime soon. As a matter of fact, I'm beginning to think these extensive celebrations and closed-door meetings are her way of stalling. Your father, however, certainly is in a hurry, which can only mean the water realm isn't as strong as you think. I'd be careful if I were you, nymph. You want to threaten me? Declare war on me? Go ahead. I'm waiting."

Silence falls over us before her gentle voice cuts through it, "I have loved you since I was a small child. Even then, your interests lay elsewhere. I knew this when I agreed to my father's terms." She takes a small step toward me and interlaces her fingers with mine. "In time, if you allow it to be, our marriage could be more than just an alliance. Our love could be great. It doesn't have to be this way."

I study her face and recall the carefree girl who used to chase me through the woods for hours on end. "I know it's not what you want to hear, Freya, but our marriage is meant to hold an alliance. That is all it will ever be to me."

Her expression becomes crestfallen as I pull myself free of her tight grip. "It's because you love her, isn't it?"

I look her straight in the eyes so there is no misunderstanding. "With every breath that I take."

"It matters not," she whispers. "You've made it clear that love is irrelevant here," she motions between us. "All I am asking you to do is wait and see how things develop between us. To be sure. To keep the peace and prevent war."

"There is no us," I state firmly. "There is only her."

Her shoulders sag and her expression turns defeated. "You're a fool whose heart will get us all killed," she argues.

I stiffen. "Are we throwing insults now, nymph?"

"Do you really think it's love for her you feel? It is not. It is the bond only," she claims, her voice void of emotion.

I curl my hands into fists. "Our connection is severed."

Her gaze grows intense. "Not the protector bond."

"What?"

"The emotional link is what tethers you."

I stare at her. Simply stare, without expression or words, because I need to know what she knows, or thinks she knows.

After a few moments, she speaks. "Do you really not know what your mother has done?" she asks, her voice grave. "What she did all those years ago?"

I cut her off by taking a threatening step toward her, forcing her back to hit the wall. Once she's trapped, I lean over her and cage her between my arms. "Enlighten me."

Confused eyes search mine. "By the gods, you don't."

"My patience with you is thinning, nymph."

Freya solemnly nods. "Do you ever wonder why my mother was promised to my father? A simple woodland nymph without a drop of royal blood in her body, promised to the emperor of the water fairies, the ruler of the second most powerful realm in existence?"

"As I understand it, Lily was my mother's best friend, her favorite lady. Our realms then, like now, were on the brink of war, and their union, like ours, was negotiated to secure alliances and peace," I reply in a cool tone.

"That is the tale they tell in the light of day. My mother has another version. One that she would recount to me as a small child in the dark hours of the night. For years, I thought it nothing more than a bedtime story. A fairy tale."

"Go on," I bite out, humoring her.

"Do you wish me to share it with you?"

I crack my neck. "Isn't that what we're doing? Sharing?"

"Years ago, on a warm summer's eve, the archangel Michael visited Queen Ophelia. The meeting was a secretive affair, held in Her Majesty's private chambers, with only her most trusted lady present as witness."

"Continue." My interest is piqued at the mention of Michael's name.

"He spoke of a daughter he'd given life to, a human, who was in grave danger because the dark forces hunted her."

"Are you speaking of Serena's aunt, Eve?"

"Yes."

"Keep going," I demand, now engaged.

"Years prior, the Angelic Council and the dark army signed a peace treaty, but the time had expired on it, and a new accord was needed. The archangel had placed his daughter's life under the protection of the gargoyles, but the royal clan was facing treachery and deceit within their own race. Fearing his daughter's protection would be short lived, he went directly to Asmodeus and negotiated a second treaty."

"An archangel negotiating with a demon lord? Why?"

"As I recall, Asmodeus blamed the gargoyles for the death of his mate, Lady Finella, and for that, Michael promised to grant him revenge. An eye for an eye. He told Asmodeus of the baby that Serena's mother, Abby, was carrying—the next heir to the protector throne. In exchange for promising to no longer hunt Eve, Michael vowed that the Angelic Council would step out of the way if Asmodeus chose to go after, and end, the future heir."

"Serena?" I push away from her and ponder her words.

"The gargoyle princess," she confirms.

"What does this have to do with my mother, or me?"

"After the second treaty was agreed to by both sides, Michael searched for a way to protect the unborn child. I'm unsure how, but he became aware that Queen Ophelia had a son who was half gargoyle. He was desperate to safeguard the unborn child, knowing the fate he'd brought upon it."

My eyes roam over the grounds surrounding the castle as realization dawns on me. "Michael couldn't go to Asher, the future king, or anyone else within the gargoyle race to ask for their protection of the child, because they would have learned of his deceitfulness against them." I pause and tighten my jaw as I put the pieces together. "He could, however, go to the one protector hidden within the woodland realm. The one that no one knew existed."

"Except Her Majesty," she adds.

I slide my glance back to Freya. "Tell me more."

"At first the queen refused, but then—" she stops.

"Then what?" I ask, irritated, and step next to her.

"Michael threatened to tell the child's father of his existence if she did not agree. Therefore, the queen had no choice but to acquiesce," she sighs. "Or so the story goes."

"The child being me. And the father is Gage," I surmise, and she dips her chin in affirmation.

"My mother went on to tell me that Michael introduced Abby to Queen Ophelia under the pretenses that Her Majesty would assist with décor for Asher and Eve's mating ceremony and Asher's coronation gala," she continues.

"That's why she allowed me to go with her that night."

"Michael had his brother, Uriel, distract Gage and Callan, Serena's father, under the guise of last-minute security preparations and discussions. He feared they would see what was happening and prevent the bond," she finishes.

"The bond?" I repeat. "A blood link would have been needed to tether us," I think aloud. "I didn't blood bond with Serena that day, I simply placed my hand on Abby's stomach," I mutter aloud. "How did we bond so quickly?"

"You're half satyr. An empath. Even you are aware you can emotionally connect with an unborn child in the same manner that a protector can bond through blood," she points out. "My guess would be that once your blood mixed with hers all those months ago, it heightened your pre-established attachment to her, strengthening the link."

I shake my head, trying to figure this out. "If my mother knows this, why the hell would she agree to our marriage?"

Freya's watery eyes meet mine. "Queen Ophelia wanted you to have a cessation. Me. I am your way out, Tristan."

"What?"

"A powerful seer once told my mother in Her Majesty's presence that her only child would be a daughter."

"You," I assume.

She nods. "Queen Ophelia struggled for weeks after you bonded with Serena. She never wanted you to be part of the protector world, or linked to someone without free will."

"So my mother devised a backup plan?"

"As her best friend, my mother knew she had to help ease Her Majesty's burdens," Freya whispers.

I look away. "So, Lily agreed to marry Oren. Then our mothers, knowing Lily would have a daughter, promised their children in marriage. Peace for our realms was simply a byproduct of their secret. Does Oren know all of this?"

"No."

I reach under my shirt and pull out my insignia, which hangs off a leather rope. "How does the Sun of Vergina play into all of this?"

The nymph princess opens her mouth and then falls silent, as irritation creases her brows before speaking.

"Freya," I warn.

"Her Majesty arranged for the god of the sun to enchant it before you bonded with Serena," she admits.

"Why?"

"Queen Ophelia feared that if you linked to the unborn child, you would unknowingly choose her as your bonded mate. You were young; she did it to protect your heart."

"Or control me." I stare across the gardens toward the brunch where everyone is gathered. "What does the magic do?" I ask, already knowing but needing to hear it aloud.

"It's a prophetic charm. The Sun of Vergina prophecy states that of your own free will, you shall choose your love and she will bear your mark for all to see that she is yours, and yours alone." Her hand wraps around my arm. "It is your decision, Tristan. Not even a link can force it. Once you choose, the gods and goddesses will bless your fate."

And there it is.

"It marks your fated love's body with your insignia." I repeat to myself, working through the conversation.

"You see," she slides in front of me and holds my face in her palms, forcing my attention. "The Sun of Vergina is your cessation. Once we are married, and you choose to love me, I will bear your mark and you will be free of your emotional link to her, forever. You don't love her; you're merely tied by a bond. And in the process, we will prevent war and secure peace for our realms. There is no downside."

I stare at her with a blank expression.

She has it wrong.

The Sun of Vergina prophecy has already been fulfilled.

I've already chosen.

And the gods and goddesses have blessed it.

It is to be war, not peace for our realms.

SIX

WAR NOT PEACE

SERENA

HEAVY BOOTS STOMPING ON STONE ECHO through-out the silent halls. They stop abruptly as they near us, and Zander looks at me over his shoulder, bringing his index finger to his lips, silently telling me to remain quiet as the castle guards finish their rounds. Seconds later, the sound picks up again and becomes softer as the guards walk in the opposite direction.

I stare at the back of his shirt, trying not to make a sound. A few moments later he motions for me to follow him and we make our way through a few empty hallways before coming to a large, heavy, wooden door.

Zander pauses for a moment, staring at it with a confused look on his face.

"What's wrong?" I whisper.

"It's unguarded," he matches my quiet tone.

"So?" I look around nervously.

"The queen's chambers are never unguarded. It's odd."

"Odd or not, we don't really have time to ponder it."

Agreeing, he grabs the knob of the door, opening it and ushering me in before closing it, encasing us in darkness.

"Zander?" I call out, unable to see him.

"Hold on," he replies quietly.

In an instant, the tiniest sliver of sunlight beams past a heavy, regal, velvet curtain, offering just enough light for the room to appear shadowed, but still allow us to move without tripping over something. I'll have to rely on my gargoyle supernatural vision for the rest of my sight.

"Okay, if the queen were to keep important paperwork or documents, it would be in this room," he speaks softly. "Be mindful that anything could be of importance."

"Got it."

Slowly, we make our way around the eclipsed chamber and begin open and closing drawers, rummaging through them, looking for anything that would tie Oren or Ophelia to signs of treason, or attempts on Tristan's life.

After what feels like hours, we are still empty-handed.

"I don't see anything," I say.

He groans. "Gross. Did you eat onions at brunch?"

I put my hand out and accidentally smack his face.

"Why are you so close to me?"

"I thought you might want to make out," he replies.

"I don't. And stop fooling around. We're never going to protect Tristan if we don't find anything," I scold.

"Wait, what's that?" he queries. "That's new."

I follow him over to an old chest hidden under a faded tapestry. He fidgets with the lock, and within seconds it pops open. With pride, he looks up and offers me a smirk.

"How did you do that so quickly?" I ask, awestruck.

Zander wiggles his fingers at me. "Practice. I can also take off your bra within five seconds—if you ever want."

I narrow my eyes at him. "I don't, but good to know."

"Save that for later." He smiles and opens the trunk farther.

We rifle through its contents before he pushes air slowly through his lips on a low curious whistle.

"What?"

He pulls out a small piece of paper. It's tea-stained and thin—almost transparent—ancient-looking. On it is a drawing of a golden sun containing sixteen triangular rays.

The name Helios is handwritten on the bottom after lines of Greek. They've faded and are hard to read.

"Isn't that Tristan's insignia?" I study the symbol.

"Don't you mean, isn't that the freckle behind my ear I haven't told Tristan about, Zander? Why yes, Serena, it is. Excellent observation," he mocks.

I ignore his antics. "So, Ophelia has a drawing of it."

"One that she's hiding, in a locked chest, under a rug."

"Who's Helios?" I ask, meeting his eyes as he stands.

"I'd be happy to answer that for you," a deep, confident, masculine voice replies, causing Zander and me to freeze.

Tristan.

Zander's eyes widen. "Quick, make out with me."

"That's the second time you've said that to her." Tristan's heavy boots stomp on the stone as they approach.

The sound is the same as the one we heard earlier in the hallway. It wasn't guards; it was Tristan following us.

Zander and I both turn and face him.

"If your lips so much as graze hers, I'll cut yours off without a second thought," he says, using a velvety, cocky tone.

I pinch my brows. "What are you doing here?"

The confident protector releases a dark chuckle, unnerving me, as his stare runs the length of me.

He tilts his head to the side, watching my reaction. "Watching you two sneak around my mother's chambers."

I swallow at having been caught.

Zander steps forward and narrows his gaze. "You called off the guards?" he accuses, half amused, half annoyed.

Tristan is cool and calm, eerily controlled compared to his mood yesterday. Something has shifted, and he's no longer angered or frustrated. He's back in control and confident.

He's standing so close to me that even in the dark, I can see the sexy scar on his upper lip. My body hums at his closeness, and I curb the desire to fold myself into his arms.

"I had to step away from brunch. When I returned, I noticed you two conspiring and slithering off. I followed you. For being second in command of the queen's army, Zander, you need to work on your stealth skills," he banters.

Teasing? He's joking around?

"What is going on?" I ask again, confused.

"I believe that's my question to ask," Tristan responds.

Zander clears his throat and grabs my hand. "You shouldn't have followed us. Maybe I brought Serena in here to have my way with her," he declares. "We *are* courting."

"So I've heard." Tristan's eyes slide between us and he raises his hands in surrender. "By all means, then, don't let me interfere. Please, woo her."

I lock my gaze on the silver and hematite rings adorning his fingers and blink a few times. "You've been in here this whole time, Tristan, and have overheard our conversation. I know you know we aren't really together," I point out.

He bends down, piercing me with an amused expression. "That is true. I do know. But I've known longer than the past ten minutes. Besides, I know you, and I know your heart. I didn't need to hear the conversation to discern that you're fated to be mine, raindrop."

I still, regarding him for a moment.

"I'd like to be brought into the loop on what it is the two of you think I need protection from, but not here. There are too many eyes and ears at the castle. I also have something to share with you both," he adds. "It has something to do with the *freckle* you seem to know that you have."

Mindlessly, I lift my finger and rub it.

"Your cabin?" Zander replies militarily.

"Yes, but I don't want us followed. Since I can only teleport with one other person, I'll take Serena. Zander, you can meet us there," he directs. "Give us a bit of a head start."

"Will do," Zander agrees without a fight.

Leaning into his brother's ear, Tristan whispers something that even my heightened gargoyle hearing can't pick up, causing Zander's surprised gaze to find mine.

Tristan moves between us, blocking his brother as he steps closer. When his chest touches mine, I stop breathing and lift my gaze. "I won't let anything happen to you—on my honor," he whispers hoarsely.

"That's a pretty big promise to make to someone who isn't your betrothed," I retort.

He swallows and looks over my head, working his jaw as his hands slide around my waist. He takes a soothing breath and he tugs me closer, his eyes finally meeting mine.

"Yeah, that's all about to change, raindrop."

In the next moment, the castle walls suddenly shift, and within seconds we are in the master suite of his cabin. I don't move. I'm not sure I am even breathing anymore. Having him this close is blissful, and yet painful, because I know at any moment he's going to pull away. Ending the wholeness that I feel in his arms.

"Answer me something," he murmurs in my ear, not letting me go. Instead, he tightens his grip on me.

"Anything," I barely manage.

"With our bond severed, do you still feel for me?"

My hands clench the sleeves of his shirt, needing something to hold onto before my knees give out.

"Yes."

He pulls me more firmly against him. "If the bond never existed, would you still want me?" he asks against my neck.

I squeeze my eyes shut, trying to ignore his warm breath tickling my skin. "Want you. Yes, of course."

"And if the bond were still there?"

"Bond or no bond, it doesn't matter to me," I promise.

Then his lips are on my neck, and my breath hitches.

My lower lip trembles and desire explodes through me at his touch. I lean into him. Tristan murmurs something softly against my neck before leaving a trail of small kisses.

He moves upward until he reaches the spot behind my ear, where his insignia is. When he presses a final kiss to it, the mark sparks to life as if it recognizes him.

The slight sting causes me to whimper aloud before the tip of Tristan's tongue runs over it, soothing it back to a calmed state. He pulls back and looks down at me, smiling.

"How are you able do that?" I ask. "We don't share our protector bond anymore; you can't heal me," I point out.

"Because you're mine," he replies, and devours my lips.

His mouth covers mine completely and his tongue slips in, pushing against mine as we fight for control of the kiss. This kiss isn't soft and gentle. It's firm and demanding. Controlling. It's meant to mark me, to make me his again.

My hands reach around his neck and pull him more firmly against me. His hands dive into my hair as he deepens the kiss. I bite down lightly and then suck on his lower lip, causing a growl to escape his mouth as his hands grip my face. I arch up to meet him, needing to be closer to him, and still, I'm not close enough. I pull, tug, and grip, trying to get my body to melt into his as his eager and warm lips glide over mine. Taking and pushing. I just want to rip my clothes off and lose myself in him, branding him as mine.

"Oh, hell no. Get your hands off my girl," Zander says from the doorway before stepping in. "Sorry, am I interrupting?" he adds, not the least bit apologetically.

Tristan pulls away from me, dropping one last kiss on my forehead before turning to his brother. "Yeah, you are."

"Good," Zander announces, and plops onto the bed. "If I don't get to go to second base with her, neither should you."

"You've been to first base with her?" Tristan snaps.

"No," I squeal, and walk over to the bed. Sitting on it, I'm careful to keep at least a foot of space between Zander and me. "By the grace, Zander, would you stop provoking him?" I scold, and blink my eyes quickly—a nervous twitch.

My cheeks flushed, I meet Zander's amused eyes and for the briefest of seconds, I feel a little guilty at being caught kissing his brother, even if our courtship is for show.

"Are you okay? Zander asks. "Are you going to cry?"

"She's fine," Tristan answers for me. His teeth clench as he narrows his gaze on Zander. "Cry? Why would she—"

I intercede. "I'm sorry to break the news to you, but no."

Zander drops on his back to the mattress dramatically as he sprawls himself out on the bed. "Damn."

"You *want* her to cry?" Tristan asks, confused. "What the hell kind of courtship is this?"

"It's nothing," I brush off.

"Someone better fill me in!" Tristan demands.

"No," Zander and I both answer at the same time.

Tristan steps closer, crossing his arms. "Then how about one of you explain the discussion I overheard in my mother's chambers. Why do you feel like I need protection? What were the two of you searching for? And why the hell are you pretending to be one another's escorts? The truth."

I clear my throat and glance down at my hands. My fingers find my bracelet and run over the emeralds.

Tristan makes me nervous. Just being around him is like jumping into a dark abyss—it's terrifying, yet at the same time, I crave it.

"As I said before, we're pretending to court because you banished me from the realm. Thanks for that, by the way."

He smiles. "My pleasure."

"I figured the only way back in was diplomatic," I admit.

"This I know already," Tristan affirms. "What I want to know is why *you* agreed." His focus turns to Zander.

"I, ah," Zander begins, "had this really heartless, cruel answer prepared when she begged me. Then I looked at her, and couldn't do it. I can't explain it—why I agreed. Maybe it's her hair. She has really nice hair. It smells flowery."

Tristan releases a frustrated exhale with a curse as his body tenses. "Zander, I've stopped smoking, which means I have no patience for crazy. The truth, before I start up again."

His brother doesn't move, but he clenches his jaw and the muscle twitches as if he's grinding his teeth together.

"I came across some . . . information a few weeks ago."

"What kind?" Tristan prods.

"The kind that points to treason," he replies cryptically.

Silence falls around us. I remain quiet, afraid to speak.

This moment is tense and the weight of it is palpable as Zander's words hang heavily in the air surrounding us.

Tristan's eyes meet mine, layered with both pain and beauty as the raw reality of the situation hits him full force.

"You both were in my mother's chambers, seeking evidence against her and Oren. Are you accusing the queen of something?" he asks with a sad, knowing smile.

The look he's giving me is too much, and I have to drop my gaze for a moment before lifting again to his hurt one.

At our silence he dips his chin, understanding. He licks his lips, addressing Zander only, but keeping his eyes on mine the entire time. "Did you find what you were seeking?"

"Nothing," Zander responds.

"Have any witnesses come forward?"

"Not yet."

"This is a serious accusation. Do you think the word of a servant, or a piece of paper with my insignia will matter?"

"Perhaps, if the right people believe," Zander replies.

"This is what we were trying to protect you from. Given the delicate situation, we didn't want to bring our theories to you without concrete evidence. Your brother agreed to court me if I promised to help him obtain some," I whisper.

"I believe you. Oren is pushing too hard, which is odd."

"Agreed." Zander matches Tristan's regal tone.

"That said, we protect our family. Spies and treachery are constants in our world and we must be careful which ones to explore, and with whom, if we are to succeed in securing accurate and truthful information to be used."

Zander sits up. "Understood."

"Reach out to Laven. Do so quietly, and seek evidence that way rather than pulling Serena into this and running around the castle looking for substantiation that won't turn up. And for fuck's sake, Zan, stop bribing the staff. Idle gossip is not the way to accuse a queen and an emperor of treason. Facts and testimony are," he states authoritatively.

"Who is Laven?" I interrupt.

"An ancient woodland sprite. He lives among the weeping willow trees, and he's well connected within interdimensional planes as an informant," Tristan explains.

"What about the paper with your emblem on it?" I ask.

Tristan reaches out and cups my face with both of his hands, then leans in and kisses my forehead before sighing.

"I have to tell you something. Hear me out fully."

"Okay." My voice shakes partly because the haunted look on his face is unnerving and partly because he's touching me.

"Should I leave?" Zander asks quietly.

"No. This affects us and the realm's safety and security."

Zander slides off the bed and stands next to Tristan.

"War? What the hell is going on, Tristan?"

Tristan slides his hands into his front pockets. "It's a long, convoluted story. One that I won't go into details on right now. The short of it is," he looks directly at me. "There will be no vows exchanged between Freya and me, and no alliance between the woodland and water realms."

My heart stops.

My breath hitches.

The only movement on my body is coming from my hands, which are shaking uncontrollably.

An erratic pounding grows loud in my chest, echoing in my ears as I stare into his waiting gaze.

"Say something," he demands of me.

I can't. My throat is dry and I can't breathe.

"Serena," he prods, as my world tilts.

"Is this real?" I croak out.

Tristan squats in front of me, brushing a strand of hair off my face before covering my hands with his to stop their quivering. "I swear to you on my honor it is."

"I d-don't u-understand," I push out.

"The Sun of Vergina prophecy has been fulfilled."

"What?"

"There is a symbol, behind your ear. I first noticed it at the Academy, when we were in Chancellor Davidson's office, the day the Diablo Fairies attacked. Today, when I overheard your conversation with Zander, he confirmed that what I saw is in fact my insignia," he speaks in a quiet tone. "You bear my mark on your skin, raindrop."

I remain silent.

"When I was on trial for killing my mother's guard, Gage visited me after finding out I was his son. I sat in the damp, smelly cell, while he wordlessly smoked and stared at me through the bars. When his—," he searches for the right word for Gage's lover, "Nassa came to check on him, her sorceress gifts sensed my insignia was charmed. I gave it to her to check out. She discovered that it was spelled by Helios, the god of the sun. The gods and goddesses blessed the emblem, enabling me to choose my fate. To mark the one my heart wants."

The air in the room shifts as I watch his lips move.

"If you remember, I mentioned that at your uncle's coronation, I touched Abby's stomach. I felt your emotions and read your aura. But that's all I can do as an empath."

I frown. "I don't understand. You said that you had a vision of me. That you thought to yourself how lucky someone would be to get to love me?"

He nods. "*You* showed me the visions. You accepted me. I didn't just bond with you that day, your heart chose mine. *You* chose me. We marked one another. Of our own free will. It's why you were born with my insignia," he rasps.

"I chose you?" I repeat softly.

Tristan releases my hand and snaps off two of the leather bands on his wrist. "And shortly after our link that day, this appeared on me."

He shows me a small black dragon tattoo on his skin.

My dragon—my clan's crest.

"If this doesn't get you to cry, I'm totally screwed." Zander's voice sounds far away, as if we're all in a tunnel.

"That's—" I begin, as my fingers caress the dragon.

"Your mark," he finishes.

My chest tightens, and sudden possessiveness fills my veins. "She can't have you because you're mine," I blurt out.

Tristan cups my face and smiles. "I'm yours."

"And the decree?"

"The gods will not allow me to marry another, because I've already given my soul and heart over to you. Our choice was blessed by the deities. The Vergina Sun is our cessation."

My hands wrap around his neck, pulling him to me.

Leaning down, he nuzzles my ear while whispering in it, "I choose you. I choose to fight for us. You are my fate."

His cheek brushes mine and my skin ignites. His lips trail featherlight kisses over my jawline, leaving me breathless. When his lips meet mine, it's soft and sweet. Just this small tease elicits small shivers of desire within me.

A deep throat clears. "Still here," Zander interrupts. "And by the way, you are still kissing my girl."

Tristan helps me stand and wraps a protective arm around me. "I think we just established that she's *my* girl."

My palms go all sweaty and my heart flutters at being called his girl—I need to get a grip. This is not the time.

"Who else knows about the marks?" Zander questions.

Tristan's stance becomes uncomfortable. "The three of us. But it's not just about the marks; there is more to it."

He holds our focus as he recounts a story Freya shared with him earlier, adding to it what he already knew to be fact. The more he speaks, the more my stomach churns in a combination of fear, confusion, and anger. By the end of it, I can't even decipher my feelings anymore.

Traded. My life has been traded for my aunt Eve's. This is the real reason that the Diablo Fairies are after me. For Asmodeus's own personal revenge against my clan.

I was handed to him on a silver platter by the archangel Michael, my aunt Eve's father, whom I grew up loving. Eve and the rest of my family have no idea of the betrayal set upon them. I realize in this moment that we're all just pawns.

Zander sighs. "This means potential war between not only our realms, but the gargoyles, the deities, the Angelic Council, and the dark army. Hell, the entire fucking world."

"What are our other options?" I go into royal mode.

"We need to take this step by step and consider who knows what." Zander fires back, using his military tone.

"The Diablo Fairies are only a threat to Serena and the gargoyles. If she stays within the woodland realm, they won't attack. For now, they're quiet," Tristan points out.

"How do you know that?" My fingers dig into my arm.

His eyes fall to me. "After my discussion with Freya, I reached out to a friend who got a hold of the secondary treaty. Asmodeus can only attempt an attack on you within human realms, not the supernatural ones. If he tries, it breaks and nullifies the treaty, and the Angelic Council can step in and stop additional attempts."

The hair on the back of my neck tingles as an electrical charge fills the air and my emotions heighten. "If my family knew the treaty existed, they would bait the dark army and end this. It will place them in danger."

"But they don't," Tristan reminds.

"So that's why the dark army never attacks when I'm here," I say under my breath. "They can't, per the treaty."

Tristan gives me a sympathetic look. "Let's just take this one step at a time. First, we need to figure out what Ophelia and Oren are up to. While that happens, we should begin to prepare the woodland realm for war. Once I denounce the marriage decree, the water realm is bound to attack. We'll deal with the rest after we figure out how to secure peace between the woodland and water realms." He turns his focus to Zander. "We need to find a way to alert Asher and the St. Michaels of what Michael did without interfering with their family balance or handling of it."

"Wait," I step in. "You can't. If they find out what Michael did, they will be devastated. My aunt, everyone."

"No, you were right before. If they're made aware, then they can act and strategize appropriately," he suggests.

"That was me thinking out loud. I wasn't suggesting we tell them. We need to handle this on our own," I argue.

Zander scoffs. "No offense, but we're about to walk into our own shitshow. We have treason charges to explore, a potential war to prepare for, and we're about to have one very pissed off water fairy, followed by an even more pissed off nymph princess. Don't even get me started on Ophelia."

I meet Tristan's eyes, pleading. "These marks bind us, which means they tie our realms. If one falls, they both do. You are half gargoyle and bound to their heir, which means both realms' problems deserve our equal attention."

Tristan stares at me for a moment before sliding his eyes back to his brother. "What do you think?"

"Our army can't handle both realms' wars. You're talking about simultaneously fighting off the water realm and the Diablo Fairies. It's just not possible. No matter how strong our army is, and how amazing your commanders are," Zander affirms, "we can handle the water realm only."

"What if together, we were to handle one enemy at a time?" I suggest, and both brothers turn their attention to me. "I'm safe here for now. That means the Diablo Fairies do not need to be dealt with. Any nuisances they cause, my clan and the gargoyles at the Academy can handle for a while."

Tristan pinches the bridge of his nose. "If the water realm declares war on us, I don't want you here in danger."

I roll my eyes. "I am a protector. A warrior. I can fight."

"No." His response is quick.

My brow lifts in annoyance at him.

"I mean, yes, of course you *can* fight. You're strong enough and certainly capable to do so, but this is not *your* battle to wage. It's mine," he counters.

I cup my hand around my hair and push it to the side, showing the emblem behind it.

"This says it's my fight too, Tristan."

"What if we don't fight now," Zander says offhandedly.

I glimpse Tristan's confused look, which must mirror my own, as we both turn to him silently.

He rolls his eyes at us. "I realize that not going to war in the supernatural world is like not having hot dogs at a baseball game." He winces, "Poor analogy. There will be plenty of time for bloodshed later. Right now, what if we approached this in a more—oh, I don't know—strategic and tactical way?" he suggests.

"Go on," Tristan encourages.

"After today, it's clear that Freya knows more than she lets on about matters of realm affairs. It might be best to see what else she knows," he advises.

"About my mother and Oren?"

"In my bones, I know they're up to something. I just need a little more time to figure out exactly what it is. If we declare war, I won't have time. But if we stay the course, we might buy another few days. A week, even," he finishes.

"The course being?" Tristan crosses his arms.

"We keep up appearances," I interject.

Tristan's eyes find mine and his brows drop over them.

I hesitate, trying to form my thoughts. "I'm in no danger in your realm from the dark army. And war is not an issue if Freya and Oren believe that you are still going to go through with the wedding."

"You're saying you *want* me to marry her now?" Tristan asks. "You're giving me mixed signals here, raindrop."

"She's good at that," Zander mutters. "First, she loves you. Then me. Now you again," he goes on.

"I never loved you," I hiss.

"So you say."

"It's true."

"True love, maybe."

"Enough," Tristan interrupts.

I growl and lunge for Zander but Tristan holds me back.

"See that? That is raw, animalistic passion, for me."

I close my eyes and take in a calming breath before continuing. "We need to buy time. The only way to do that is to act as if nothing has changed. Zander and I will continue to pretend to be courting, and you," I pause, my mouth going dry. "You can continue to keep up appearances with Ophelia and Oren. Freya obviously trusts you if she told you this today. Zander is right; you could use her trust to see what else she knows." I force out, pretending to be okay with this scheme.

"It's a good plan," Zander chimes in. "One that lets me go inconspicuously to Laven and secure evidence of treason."

"This plan will also grant us time to figure out what, and how, to tell my clan about the treaty. Their involvement gives you another ally in securing your realm against Oren when you denounce the wedding. Then, we can turn our attention to the Diablo Fairies and Asmodeus."

"Teamwork is romantic," Zander coos.

"Magali is a good lie detector. It's an impressive gift that could help when you question informants," I offer.

Tristan faces his brother, "Perhaps during your nightly visits to the Academy, you could convince her to help us?"

My mouth falls open as I look at Zander.

He's been sneaking back at night to see Magali?

He looks at me sheepishly. "Don't be jealous; you know I like her. I won't apologize for it. You refuse to cuddle with me. I have needs. What did you think was going to happen?"

As he rants, I just stare at him.

"I walked in on you kissing my brother," he fires back, and Tristan takes a menacing step toward him, forcing him to stumble back toward the door. "I'm going. No one declares war until I return." He points at both of us.

"Go. We'll see you later." Tristan shoves him out.

"If I don't see you before I pick you up for the engagement party, wear something revealing," Zander shouts flippantly from the hall, and Tristan slams the door in his face.

Turning to face me, Tristan takes a step in my direction and grants me a wicked expression before reaching me.

I don't back down from his powerful and intense stare.

Instead, I lift my chin and meet it, head on.

"A few more days," he says. "And then you're mine, and this whole tempting fate thing we're doing . . . it ends."

SEVEN
I GET TO LOVE YOU

TRISTAN

I 'M UNSURE HOW LONG I'VE STOOD in the doorway, watching her. Even though it's my house, my prolonged staring is turning into a strained awkwardness. To be honest, I'm so exhausted, I don't even care. She's here. In my home.

Serena takes in a deep breath and I freeze. It's amazing how one being can invoke such passionate extremes from me. One moment she calms me, and the next, I want to tear off her clothes. Tonight, I just need to be near her.

Going back to the castle this afternoon and pretending to be interested in flowers, dresses, and place settings—for a wedding I have no interest in going through with—pushed my limits. Especially when there are diplomatic issues in front of me. Oddly, my mother was not present for any of the meetings, which makes me wonder if Zander is right and she's involved in something bigger than all of us know.

And dinner? It took all my restraint not to tell Oren to fuck off. Thankfully, he took his daughter and wife back to the water realm for the night, allowing me a much needed and desired moment of peace and quiet.

"Twenty minutes of lingering is totally creepy," Serena mutters under her breath, loud enough for me to hear.

A cocky grin tugs at the side of my mouth.

She knows I'm here. It shouldn't surprise me.

Without a word, I step into the bathroom. Her gaze fastens onto mine as I approach, and my vision skims over her, taking her in. Damn, she's beautiful. Blowing out a deep breath, I crouch next to the porcelain basin she's relaxing in.

"You left the door open, again," I point out.

She slowly bats her lashes at me. "I know."

I lift both my eyebrows at her admission and play with my brow piercing, gauging her motives. I like this—our game of chess. My hand slides to her face and trickles over her cheek before I lean forward and press a gentle kiss to her forehead.

"Want to join me?" Her voice is low.

She doesn't look away as I stand, kick my boots off, and without removing any of my clothing, slide in with a groan.

Serena gives me a small grin and shakes her head at me a little, amused. I stare into the endless darkness of her sapphire eyes and it hits me: out of control and obsessive don't even begin to describe how I feel about her.

Suddenly, I'm so fucking grateful that I'm the one that gets get to love her. She gives me security and strength.

Peace.

"This is becoming a habit." I wave at the empty bathtub.

She shrugs. "It turns out, I do my best thinking in here."

"Without water? Or bubbles? Or nakedness?"

The irresistible girl stares at me with a serious expression. "Without water. Or bubbles. Or nakedness."

We fall silent again, and I finally feel so damn relaxed.

A feral smile twists her lips. "Rough day?"

I pin her with a hard glare, because she knows just how rough it was. I close my eyes and drop my head back, allowing an unhappy sigh to escape. "Yeah, raindrop, it was."

My eyes stay closed even when I feel her body shift. She crawls over me, slinking upwards until she finally straddles my lap; her flowery spring scent wraps around me.

When I feel her breath fall across my lips, one by one my lashes separate as my lids open. When I focus, her dark blue gaze penetrates mine. With a mind of its own, my tongue darts out and I lick the curve of my bottom lip, causing her gaze to drop and lock onto my mouth.

A pretty pink hue graces her cheeks and I like it. I like that I get under her skin. Fuck. I'm so infatuated with her.

And when her fierce and wild stare meets mine again, I hold in the animalistic growl that begs to come out. With a knowing smile, one of her soft, delicate hands circles my wrist, while the other undoes the snaps and removes my leather protector bands. I simply watch her, silent.

She places them carefully on the side of the tub before her hand brings my wrist up and in between us. Without dropping her gaze, her fingers caress the dragon and my pulse kicks at her touch. Lusting after a female protector while I am on the brink of war with my betrothed's realm is torture. Pure fucking torture. And not the smartest thing.

Anger festers. I'm furious that either one of us had to be in this situation in the first place. It's getting harder and harder to stay a step ahead of all the lies and backstabbing.

My free hand shakes, as I reach up and use my thumb to tilt her head back so her luscious mouth points at me. At my touch, Serena breathes out a soft little sigh, tickling my lips.

Everything damn thing about her is a test of my will.

"I've missed you," she whispers.

I stare at her lips, knowing they're soft and her taste is sweet. But I don't kiss her, because if I do, I'll kiss her like a woman I want and not one I am trying to resist.

It wouldn't be right being inside her when I'm not free to love her openly. This time, I want to do things right.

"What were you thinking about?" I ask, so I don't tangle my hands in her long auburn hair, pull on it, and use it as leverage to take control of her mouth.

"Everything. Nothing," she replies.

Now that she's this close, she looks weary. Drained.

Her fingers stop moving and she shifts on my lap. I hold in a groan from the much wanted friction she's causing.

Serena sighs. "My energy is depleted. The elements—" she begins, but stops herself, watching me.

"Tell me," I say in a hushed command.

"It hasn't rained since you left," she admits.

Suddenly I feel like I can't breathe. Serena just watches me with sagging, tired eyes. How did I not see this before?

I run my thumb over one of the dark circles and she grants me a solemn smile. She needs the rain to rejuvenate her. Elements give her energy and vitalize her gifts. Shit.

"Oren is holding the rain hostage from the human realms." She adds, waiting with caution for my response.

I blink at her slowly. "He's what?"

Her dark eyebrows pull together. "You didn't know?"

"No." My eyes bore into her. "I'll take care of it. Of him."

Her eyes shift. "It's strange, I didn't start to feel the effects until our protector bond severed." Her voice is quiet.

Serena can't afford to be weak when there are enemies in every realm and around every dark corner, all of them hoping to end her existence. Protectors need strength.

I yank my wrist away from her hand and take her face hard between my hands, forcing her eyes to meet mine.

"Come with me." I don't ask.

I grab her hips, lifting her out of the tub, and then climb to my feet. Throwing my boots and bracelets back on, I grab her hand and drag her downstairs into the kitchen.

"What are you doing?"

"Fixing this shit right now."

Releasing her hand, I storm into the kitchen and start opening and closing drawers, slamming them roughly in the process because I don't know where the hell anything is. My housekeeper, Maria, is the only one ever in here.

"Tristan," Serena says, trying to get my attention.

I ignore her.

When I get to the last drawer, I see the blade.

Taking it out, I turn and face her. Her eyes drift to the steel knife and widen, before granting me a lopsided smile.

"Killing me won't work. I'm too tired to train, or cook."

Ignoring her snark, I motion to the pool table. "Sit."

She tilts her head, assessing me. "Is that an order?"

"Yes."

"I don't take orders."

I press my lips together and wait her stubbornness out.

After a moment of regarding me, Serena shoots me a curious look, walks over and sits on the felt, watching as I approach. With my knee, I push open her legs and step between them, leaning into her space, flustering her.

"Do you trust me?"

"In theory," she fires back.

"Then open your palm."

She casts me a look and hesitates for a moment before presenting me with her closed left fist. One by one, she slowly uncurls her fingers and flattens her hand.

I grab it hard, so that she can't take it back or flinch.

I hold her gaze. "This is going to sting, but trust me."

She nods a little and I lift the knife. I run the sharp point over her palm, the skin spreading and the crimson liquid rising to the surface.

Noiselessly she flinches, but holds my eyes.

I release her hand and flash her a naughty grin. While holding the knife in one hand, I grab the back of my shirt with the other, between my shoulder blades, and yank it off, exposing my chest.

Serena's breath hitches and her eyes drop to my stomach, then roam back up to my chest, landing on my protector tattoo.

Without a second thought I bring the blade up to the two lions outlined within the yin-yang protector symbol and make a small incision on one of the lion's chests.

Placing the knife on the table, I take in the awed look on Serena's face. My thumb runs over her pursing lips.

"Eyes up here, raindrop," I demand.

She gives me a fierce look, which makes me smile because I know she understands what I'm doing and approves. Holding her gaze, I take her hand, now dripping with her blood, place it over my tattoo, and press it down.

Her eyes fall to our hands, as she watches our mixed blood run through the intricate design. The crimson liquid turns it from black to red as our link reconnects.

I ignore the rush of energy as our protector tendrils tether themselves to each other again. My face tightens when Serena's emotions slam into me. Suddenly, she's everywhere in me once more. In every dark corner and crevice, her presence weaves itself around me. Invading.

We are both breathing hard and both flushed. Her eyes turn a deep sapphire, but flecks of cognac dust the interior. When the tattoo returns to its normal black color, our link is complete, finally allowing us both to breathe easier.

Serena releases a little gasp of surprise when the dark gray tendrils we share wrap around us, healing both her wound and mine. A gargoyle gift—once bonded, protectors can heal one another. Normally, you can't see the tendrils, but now, we can, which triggers this fierce desire to protect and claim her. To make her mine and only mine.

I lift my hands and cup her cheeks, running my thumbs over the healthy pink hue dusting them, as I watch the dark circles that haunted her eyes fade away.

"Better?" I rasp out.

She searches my eyes and simply nods.

Things deep inside of me roar and awaken from where they

slumbered as I stare at her lips, wanting to devour her.

All I want to do is stay in this moment—where all I feel, see, and taste is her. Her heartbeat. And her breath.

I lean in to take her lips. My pulse is thundering in my ears so loudly I almost miss what she says. Almost.

"What is that?" she asks, gripping my right arm, pulling me closer and twisting it to inspect my newest tattoo.

A slim, pretty woman adorns my upper arm. She's outlined in black and shaded in grays. Her face is beautiful and her petite body is seated, framed by two large gargoyle wings behind her, lifting to the sky. A flowing dress covers her, but shows her bare legs and arms.

The girl is holding a raindrop in her palms.

I got it when I returned to the realm. It was supposed to be a reminder of Serena, because even though I couldn't have her, I wanted her with me. Always. Now she knows.

I fall silent, letting her inspect the design. The bite of her fingernails presses into the skin and then disappears.

"Is that me?" she asks softly.

Her eyes bore into mine when our gazes lock.

I lift my shoulder and let it fall. Suddenly uncomfortable and nervous. Does she like it, or is she pissed? The damn gargoyle is infuriatingly hard to figure out.

As if hearing my thoughts, she takes my hand and places the palm at the base of her neck, allowing me to read her.

I step closer. Her hips arch to meet mine as she wraps her legs around me. When the fullness between my legs lines up perfectly with the softness between hers, I'm gone.

"It's you, raindrop," I reply hoarsely.

Her eyes drift back to the tattoo of her before sliding over to the protector one, and then rise to meet mine.

One heartbeat. That's all that it takes before my lips touch hers. And before I even consider what I'm doing, I'm kissing her. My hands glide up and tangle into her hair.

The way her mouth moves across mine makes the world falling

apart around me disappear. There is no unwanted betrothal. No realms on the brink of war. No dark army hunting. There's just this fucking amazing woman whimpering as I stroke her tongue with my own.

Serena meets each stroke of my lips. She takes everything I push at her, allowing me to ravish her. Take from her. My hands roughly jerk her hair back, and she gasps, her head falling back farther as I dive deeper into her mouth.

When her hands reach for the button on my jeans, it's like someone doused me with cold water, and I slowly come back to reality. I grab them to stop her, as she sits up.

I stumble back away from her like she's on fire. Both of us are breathing hard as her questioning gaze meets mine.

Catching my breath, I step back between her legs. Cupping one side of her head with one hand, I cradle the top of her head with the other as I plant a gentle kiss on her forehead.

"I'm not rejecting you."

"No?"

"No," I confirm.

Her hands wrap around my waist, guiding me closer.

"Why did you stop? I want you. This. Us," she pants.

I swallow and gather my thoughts. "We just reopened a shared link and our emotions are all over the place. This isn't how I want this to happen this time. Not again."

She looks around, confused. "I don't want to wait."

My heart is racing and I need to calm it down. I take her face between my hands and tilt her head so she's looking at me directly in the eyes. "*When* we do this again, it should be without worrying about our bonds, our oaths, or our uncertain futures. I don't want anything hanging over our heads." I lean toward her neck and brush my nose over it, inhaling deeply. "I just want it to be about me and you."

With a sigh, she slides her eyes closed and unwraps her legs from around me. "I really hate it when you adult."

A dark chuckle escapes me. "Adult?"

"Yes. Make grown-up decisions and leave me hanging."

Not liking her tone, I bend at the knees so I am at eye level with her. "I will never leave you hanging. On my honor."

"Me neither, champ," my brother's voice cuts into our moment. "I leave for a few hours and when I return you're half naked, with my girl sprawled out on the pool table."

"I'm not sprawled out," Serena counters, handing me my shirt. I put it back on, watching as he approaches us.

Zander picks up the blade, waving it between us.

"Kinky."

I snatch it away from him with an annoyed, angry glare.

"You're back early," Serena states.

"Aw, did you miss me?" he coos.

"Back off," I warn, pivoting on my heels to take the knife into the kitchen, and slamming it harshly into the sink.

"You might want to wash that off before Maria gets here tomorrow," Zander suggests.

A frustrated noise gurgles from my mouth.

Zander laughs. "What did you do to him?"

Serena frowns. "Nothing."

"Exactly!" he replies. "This kind of *nothing* leads to alone, naughty shower time. Remember, I'm the brother who actually *will* take you on that pool table. You picked the dark and broody one. Care to change your mind now?"

She hops off the pool table and straightens her shirt. With a pretty smile, she lifts her hand and flips Zander off.

"For the record, Magali is teaching me sign language. That—that is not nice," he pouts.

"Speaking of Magali, did you find anything out?" I ask.

Zander shrugs, sulking. "I learned she loves french fries and mayo. Isn't that gross? I mean, who the hell dips fries in mayonnaise?" he replies. "This might end us."

I don't react, only stare back at him like he's crazy, because he is. He's also pushing on the last of my nerves.

"He meant about Oren and Ophelia," Serena steps in.

"Laven's informant wasn't able to tell us much. Laven suggested we speak to Aoife," he replies, catching my eye.

"Who is Effay?" Serena asks.

"Ee-fah," Zander assists.

"Sorry, who is she?"

"Tristan's ex-girlfriend."

I bristle. Zander's grin is wide and bright. Serena just looks confused, and then irritated.

"Aoife is a magical tree sprite," I explain.

"She's not *just* a magical tree sprite," Zander interjects. "She happens to be the most beautiful creature in existence. Literally. It's what her name means. Her beauty is powered by the sun's radiance."

"Why Aoife?" I ignore the comments he's making.

"Perhaps it's her connection to Helios?" Zander deducts.

"If Laven is sending us to Aoife, she must know something. We have the engagement gala tomorrow night, but in the morning, we'll seek her out. All of us."

Serena turns to face me and hurt flashes briefly behind her eyes. "Great. I look forward to meeting the most beautiful creature in existence tomorrow. Who happens to be your ex-girlfriend. With the hope of finding out that your mother and fiancée's father are committing treason against you. And for sure let's bring your brother, who is in love with my best friend, and whom I am pretending to court."

"Who writes this shit?" Zander asks.

"Whoever it is, they have a fucking dark sense of humor," I reply.

"Tristan?" Freya's voice cuts through the air, stopping everyone. We swing our attention to the front door. "What are you doing here?" she asks, looking around unhappily.

The nymph watches us, her eyes narrowing as her apprehension is replaced with fury. This is bad. Very bad.

I don't flinch as she approaches the group. Slowly her gaze tears away from mine and floats around the group.

"I thought you were spending the evening at home, in the water realm?" I reply.

"I remembered I had a dress fitting in the morning, so I thought I would return this evening instead of in the early hours of sunlight," she states. "Upon my return, your page mentioned to me you'd been gone for hours. I was worried."

My page—who is now fired for speaking out of turn.

"It's my fault." Zander winks at her. "Serena and I got into an argument. She was out of control and enraged. Going on and on about her friend Magali. She thinks I'm still in love with her. It was insane. Women are insane."

Both Freya and Serena throw nasty looks his way.

"What I meant is she was irrational. Violent in a crazed, jealous fit. Can you blame her though? She's obsessed."

Serena snarls at him but doesn't move.

"Her Highness does appear," Freya chooses her words carefully, "enraged. Why was Tristan involved in your dispute?"

Zander's eyes slide to Serena. "She stabbed me."

"What?" Freya exhales.

"With a kitchen knife," he adds quickly.

Freya turns her angered gaze to Serena, who clears her throat, finally finding her voice. "Well, he's an asshole."

"Yes, of course he is, but that does not merit stabbing him," Freya argues. "Gods help us. Where is the knife?"

I walk over to the sink, pick it up, and show her. Grateful that I didn't wash the blood off. "Zander needed my help calming her down."

My brother grinds his teeth at the jab. "My girl isn't just any girl," he fires back with a wicked smile. Zander walks up to Serena and cups her face, looking at her lovingly. "She's a badass gargoyle princess warrior. Lesson learned. Right, champ?"

He leans toward her, as if he's going to kiss her.

Her eyes spark with fire. "Careful. I won't hesitate to stab you . . . again."

Zander smirks at her and backs off.

Serena looks around him to Freya. "He likes it rough."

Freya's face pinches in disgust. "Perhaps the two of you should leave your . . . ," she pauses, "private matters concealed behind closed doors and not involve Tristan. He has more important things to worry over than a simple lover's spat."

Zander moves behind Serena and smacks her on the ass, hard. She and I both flash him warning looks.

"There's no lover's spat here. Just plain old love."

An awkward silence falls around us before Freya speaks.

"Tristan, perhaps we should return to the castle. We should discuss our plans for tomorrow evening." Freya tilts her head toward Zander. "That is, if you are now feeling safe to be alone in your love's presence."

"Oh, I am. Thanks for checking," he quips.

I turn to them both, keeping my face unreadable. Hating this fucking charade. Even more, hating leaving Serena.

"Zander, tomorrow we need to speak regarding the army. I'll be here early. You can take me to meet," I try to find a way to speak of Aoife without Freya discovering what I'm doing, "this new commander you feel is of value."

Catching on, he nods. "Perfect."

My eyes slide over to Serena. There is no sadness in her expression, only irritation that I'm leaving with Freya.

And I fucking hate it.

"If I see you holding a knife again," I begin, "I will not hesitate. There will be a repeat of what happened earlier," I threaten, and my eyes slide to the pool table, hoping she understands I'm referring to kissing the shit out of her on it. "And next time," I lean in, attempting to seem menacing for Freya's sake, "I won't show restraint." I give her the smallest smile before stepping toward the door to leave.

She frowns, but a glint of excitement and desire flickers in her eyes. "While I can't promise that I won't threaten him, you can be assured that I won't lay a finger on your brother this evening."

Relief floods me for some ridiculous reason. Our eyes latch on to each other before I give her a slight nod and follow my fiancée out the door.

A few days.

A few fucking days until I get to love her.

EIGHT

THE GARDEN OF THE DEITIES

SERENA

S UNLIGHT WARMS THE REALM. ITS YELLOW rays bounce off the lake, causing the clear water to glisten and shine with each movement it makes. A cloudless, expansive blue sky stretches above, its azure tint reflected in the liquid.

The trees and plant life here are so lush and vivid, it is hard to focus because you just want to look at everything and become one with the realm's beauty.

My stomach clenches with apprehension as I listen to Zander and Tristan speak in hushed voices.

Tristan paces behind me, and when he stops, I watch his mirror image frown at me in the glass.

When our eyes meet, his frown deepens as he listens to his brother. I pay no attention to what Zander is going on about, because I can't keep my eyes off Tristan.

The creases between his brows deepen and the need to smooth out the furrow surfaces within me. Something has caused him to worry, to change. He's anxious about our uncertain future. More so than he was yesterday. His lips straighten in a grim line before he turns toward Zander.

"Laven will keep me informed." Zander's words are final and meant to end their conversation just as I tune in.

I twist and see Tristan staring at nothing at all, lost in thought. A moment later, his eyes connect with mine, causing my heart to stutter. He shoves a hand through his hair and glowers at the bookcase in the living room.

"What's going on?" I ask in a soft tone.

"A complication," he replies, then curses and begins to pace back and forth again.

My eyes slide to Zander, who is watching me solemnly. "Chancellor Davidson was murdered last night. He was found in his office this morning. Beheaded," he explains.

When his words finally sink in I feel as though I can't breathe. Henry wasn't just the head of the Royal Protector Academy, he was also a close family friend. I look at Tristan.

He's gauging me in the same way I'm gauging him.

"Henry is dead?" I ask, needing confirmation.

"Annabelle too. She was with him last night," he replies.

"Late at night?" I repeat, surprised.

"As in, *with him* with him," Zander alludes.

A blush heats my cheeks; I knew they were fond of one another, just not in a *physical* manner. She was so lovely.

"What happened?" I question.

"We're not sure." The edginess in Tristan's tone is unsettling. "Gage and Nassa are attempting to find out."

Gage. He was extremely close with the chancellor.

My eyes roam over Tristan. Although it's subtle, it's apparent to me. He may not be sure, but I can see he has an idea of what happened and isn't going to share it right now.

"Is Gage . . . um . . . okay?" I ask Tristan cautiously, knowing how he feels about his biological father.

"No. He's not. He's devastated."

"Your clan knows, too," Zander points out. "They've asked that we keep you here under our protection. The Academy's security has been breached, which means it's unsafe for you to return for any reason, Serena."

"You mean they want me to hide," I counter.

Tristan's eyes follow me with a protective possessiveness. "You will stay in this realm where I can protect you. I'm sorry for your loss, I am, but whoever did this was able to bypass an entire school of protectors, which means it was either an inside job or the demons are getting smarter and are able to use dark magic against gargoyles."

Sadness sinks in. I was very fond of the elder gargoyle who ran my family's school. I'll miss him terribly.

Tristan approaches me with a prowl, stopping so close in front of me that I'm forced to tip my head back to see his face. His stance is confident and controlled.

"Please," he adds, and my heart sinks.

The plea is unlike him. I study him, noticing he looks even more formidable than normal. He's worried. "Okay."

Zander shifts. "Even with everything going on, we'll need to keep up appearances today and go through the motions. We're expected to meet with Aoife shortly."

"We'll be right there," Tristan answers for us, his eyes never leaving mine.

Zander disappears as Tristan moves closer and entwines his fingers in my hair. My breath catches as he leans in, inhaling my scent. When he pulls back, his cheek skims mine, and I shiver. His soft breath falls on my ear.

"You okay?"

I nod, shocked and saddened at the news. "Do you really think it was the dark army? I mean, Henry was smarter than to let his guard down. If they can get to him, then—"

His thumb brushes over my cheek, but he doesn't answer my question. "On my honor, it's you and me from this moment forward—whatever happens." His deep voice vibrates throughout my body, sending waves of desire through me. "There is nothing for you to fear."

I pull back from him so I can read his expression.

"I'm not afraid. I'm sad and worried. I don't want anyone else to get hurt because they're protecting me."

He exhales slowly. "I can't promise that won't happen."

"This is really bad, isn't it?"

"Yeah, raindrop, it's really fucking bad."

Taking in a few deep breaths, I try to calm my racing heart. "Henry and Annabelle weren't just friends, they were gargoyles. That made their lives my responsibility. Their blood was spilt while I was here—in your realm."

"Stop. You are not seated on the throne yet. Don't take this on," he hushes. "Understand this, though: when you are on the throne, blood will be shed for your protection. That is our curse. You must accept this." He looks me in the eyes.

I stand straighter and lift my chin. "You're right. And as the future heir, I will fight off whatever it is trying to destroy my world and race. Or yours. And I'll succeed."

He leans forward and brushes my lips with his own for the tiniest of moments. "You're incapable of failure."

I blink at him a few times. "I'm incapable of escape."

One hand travels down my back, as the other strokes my hair. "We should go. Aoife isn't patient."

I nod slowly and square my shoulders. He takes my hand and teleports us into the forest, under a canopy of emerald green leaves that appear to glow when the sun kisses them. Zander stands waiting for us in front a tree.

"About time," he complains.

"Afraid of Aoife's wrath?" Tristan asks as we approach.

"She bites," his brother teases.

Moments later, we stand with him before the large tree. I look up. It soars higher than any tree I've ever seen.

"It's a sequoia tree." Tristan steps up beside me. "This particular one surpasses the height of the Hyperion tree."

"Hyperion?"

"The humans' tallest tree on the earth realm, standing over three hundred seventy-five feet tall," he answers.

"By the grace, how colossal is this one?"

"Four hundred eighty-two feet."

My lips part in awe at the sheer elevation.

"Huge, right?" Zander's gaze is playful.

"Ginormous," I push out on a breath.

"I knew you'd be impressed by size," Zander banters.

I sigh at the underlying meaning behind his statement.

My voice is calm. "Must you turn everything sexual?"

"Once again, I. Am. A. Nymph. Sex is who and what I am," he answers honestly. "And why is it that you are not affected by me? I'm designed to seduce you. But with you, nothing. No doe eyes. No weakness in the knees. Nada."

I glance over at Tristan. "You're just not my type."

"You two are becoming annoyingly love-struck and as the third wheel in this little faux triangle, I don't like it."

I turn away and look straight ahead again at the tree. Its brownish-reddish bark is smooth, yet aged, with deep creases between the dips and valleys that adorn the trunk. There is no arch, just one lanky, strong column of bark that reaches skyward, climbing higher than the eye can see.

Tapered limbs cluster in certain areas and stretch outward from its core, like arms reaching out. A perfectly formed green triangle of leaves sits on top. The sun shining on the peak makes it appear as if it's on fire.

At the base, strips of green and brown moss grow in a patchwork, like a dress, over the cracks and crevices of the trunk's even lines. There are no branches that are dry, cracked, or broken.

It's the most perfect tree I've ever seen.

"Would you like to greet her?" Tristan asks.

My gaze bounces between the tree and him. "Her? I-I don't know . . . I mean, I don't know how to," I stammer.

Tristan smirks at me, and there's something in his eyes as he assesses me—it's like he's never seen me before.

He steps behind me, his chest touching my back as he wraps his fingers around my left wrist. At his touch, my heart drums frantically in my chest and pounds in my ears.

Tristan guides us forward and I keep my eyes straight ahead, on the tree, even though I can feel his attention on my face.

He lifts my hand and places my palm upon the smooth-skinned trunk, his hand on top of mine, gently pressing.

Glancing upward, he whispers something in Greek.

Within seconds, an outline forms within the bark, startling me. Tristan lightens his grip and we take a step back. Long, lean legs lift and stretch out of the trunk, followed by an extremely tall outline of a curvy female body.

Two arms and a stunning face emerge last. The being's skin color is similar to that of the tree trunk. It's as if she morphed directly from the tree's soul. She's stunning.

Her back is still attached to the tree, making her appear as an extension of the trunk, like a naked tree hologram.

Both Tristan and Zander take a knee, leaving me standing awkwardly in awe and unsure what to do.

"Lady Sequoia," Tristan greets.

The tall figure tilts her head. "Your Royal Highnesses," she replies. Her voice sounds as if it's being projected.

Both brothers stand and flank my sides.

"We have an appointment with Aoife," Zander states.

"I am aware." Her words echo in the quiet of the forest.

The sound of tree branches bending and twisting follow the motion of her head tilting in my direction. It's eerie.

"You have brought the princess of the gargoyle race with you, have you not?" Lady Sequoia questions.

"We have," Tristan replies, appearing apprehensive.

"Come closer, child," she calls to me.

My mind whirls and I look to Tristan for approval. He dips his chin in consent, so I take a step closer to her.

"That is far enough," she shrieks, panicking me.

Confusion sweeps through me at her sudden distress and I freeze, thinking I must have offended her somehow.

"You have not," she replies, reading my mind.

My eyes widen, alarmed she overheard my thoughts.

"You heard me?"

"I am a tree spirit, I listen to everything."

I remain silent.

"She has been marked." Her words come out as a statement spoken in dread, not as a curious question.

Tristan stiffens next to me. "No," he lies. "Our protector bond was severed. You may sense our lingering link."

"Perhaps, Your Highness. Or perhaps, it is not old but new."

A cool breeze lifts around us. I try to calm my emotions so the wind will settle down. It's obvious he doesn't want her knowing about the rekindling of the bond. Why is that?

Lady Sequoia's leaves shift in the gentle wind, and her eyes slide to me. "An elemental gargoyle. How interesting."

Her gaze cascades down on me in a judgmental manner.

"Can you make it rain?"

"I can manipulate and pull energy, not control or force."

"What a shame," the tree spirit tsks. "I'm so very thirsty, and the gesture would go a long way with my favor."

Is she asking for a bribe? If we provide rain, she won't speak of the bond she senses? She seems annoyed at my thoughts and I scold myself, because she can obviously read them.

My two escorts shift nervously next to me.

"We apologize for the lack of rainfall, Lady Sequoia. When I return, I'll see to it that Oren allows for more storms." Tristan appeases her using his formal prince tone.

She stands tall and casts a glare down at him. "I should hope so,

Your Highness. The emperor's interests seem to lie elsewhere these days. Outside of the woodland realm."

"How so?" Tristan inquires smoothly.

"As I told Queen Ophelia, on several occasions, he has crossed the border into the earth realm," she replies.

Tristan ponders her words. "Are you sure?"

"I am." The tree stares back at him.

Tristan's nostrils flare. "Thank you."

A ringing sound appears out of nowhere, almost like a bell chiming, and on the side of the tree's bark, a rainbow-colored ripple appears and shimmers. The portal gateway.

Lady Sequoia inclines her head toward it. "I bid you safe passage to and fro, Your Highnesses. Princess Serena."

Zander and Tristan dip their chins. "Peace be with you," they say in unison, and guide me toward the gateway.

We step through and enter a tunnel that seems made of a rainbow, walking at a fast pace toward the other side. The colors twist and turn, causing me to become light-headed, and I squeeze my eyes a few times to regain my center of gravity.

"Does every tree have a spirit?" I ask Tristan.

"Just those within the woodland realm. They protect our borders. Only certain woodland nymphs can see them."

I grab his elbow, forcing us to stop. "I saw her, though."

He frowns. "You wear my mark, so you carry the gift."

"Is that what Queen Ophelia meant the last time we were here in the realm? When she said the forest has eyes?"

Tristan's frown deepens. "Yes. The trees are part of our army, Serena. They see, hear, and report on everything."

I chew on my lip. "Does Oren know this?"

"No. Only woodland nymphs know."

"And now you do too, champ," Zander adds.

"Why go to Laven then? Why not just ask the trees if they've seen Oren and Ophelia conspiring?" I pose.

Tristan and Zander share a knowing glance before Tristan shakes his head no at me in some type of warning.

My brows pull together before I remember that we're still inside the tree trunk. Which means she can still hear us.

I nod my understanding and we take the last steps to the other side. Tristan leads me into a new realm, which is so blindingly bright, I'm forced to squint and lift my hands to cover my eyes. Behind us, the portal shrinks and closes.

"Daphne will open it when we return," Zander states.

I throw a confused look his way, not knowing who Daphne is. I really should learn more about other realms.

"Daphne is the tree-morphing nymph on this side. She guards the gateways into and out of this realm," he explains.

My lips part to say something, but he holds his finger up to his lips as we move farther and farther into the realm, away from the sequoia tree.

When we reach what appears to be a border, Tristan leans close to my ear. "My mother controls the woodland realm. The trees report to her daily. We must watch what we say."

My brows pinch. "Wait, you lied to Lady Sequoia about our bond, then confirmed that I am marked while inside the tunnel," I point out. "Wouldn't she have heard that?"

"I only said you wear my mark, not that you bear it on your skin. If asked by the queen, I'll say I gave you my necklace for protection while we visited Aoife. And if asked by the queen, then we know my mother is inquiring about my comings and goings with the tree spirits," he adds.

"Meaning she's having you watched," Zander speaks up.

"Exactly."

The two brothers exchange a look of understanding.

My gaze shifts to our surroundings. The lush forest continues for a few more feet, but then changes into something less wooded and more orchard-like in appearance.

Large, white, billowy clouds creep slowly over the new realm's floor and float in an unhurried manner among the beautiful flora, which is sprinkled between spindly trees and twisted vines. It almost feels like a grove in the sky.

"This is the Garden of the Deities," Tristan murmurs, his eyes focusing on mine. My pulse races as I stare into his gaze. Not out of fear, but out of pure need for him. Even here.

"Oh," I manage to reply, forcing myself to tear my eyes from his, ending the surge of desire running through me.

Focusing, I recall my studies about this plane; it's a realm dedicated to the gods and goddesses, allowing them to express themselves sexually and explore their cravings.

Swallowing, I focus on a golden pathway that disappears within the fluffy patches swirling throughout.

"Welcome to the *naughty* playground for the gods, goddesses, nymphs, and sprites." Zander wiggles his brows and rubs his hands together. His excitement is palatable.

"Or heaven to you," I tease.

His grin grows. "This *is* my favorite dimension, champ."

"I bet it is." I return his smile.

We follow Zander through the winding grove. I notice it's filled with plants and flowers indigenous to Greece.

Large almond and apple trees shade certain areas of the flowery patches from the too-bright sunshine, filling the realm with an angelic golden glow, giving off a divine feel.

"Why is it so bright here?" I ask Tristan quietly.

"The deities' powers increase nearer the sun. The closer to it they are, the more powerful they can become. It's why Aoife lives here even though she is a nymph. Her beauty is powered by the sun, thanks in part to Helios. That, and she adores apple trees." He smiles fondly, seeming to recall a pleasurable memory. I try not to stab him with my daggers.

"I'm more of a banana person myself," I mutter under my breath, slightly jealous and annoyed.

Tristan tries not to smile. "Why is that?"

"Apples are either too sweet or too sour. I don't trust them," I reply in a frustrated tone. "You never know what you'll get until you bite into it. They are deceptive. With a banana, it's always the same flavor. Loyal. Trustworthy. Nontoxic."

"Nontoxic?" He releases a chuckle. "Bananas are safe."

"And yellow," I add quietly. "One of my favorite colors."

"Noted."

"I like bananas," Zander interjects from in front of us. "In smoothies and sometimes mixed with strawberries."

"What about you?" I ask Tristan.

"I like apples. They're unpredictable."

I internally roll my eyes. Of course he does.

"Tell me more about Helios," I say sharply, trying to change the subject as my resentment of Aoife rises.

"Helios is the sun god." He looks away. "He spends much of his time in the earth's sky each day, looking down upon the realm. This makes him an excellent resource, since he hears and witnesses everything in the human domain."

"He spies on them?" I accuse. "Isn't that against some sort of supernatural code of ethics?"

"He's a god. Moral code doesn't apply to deities. Besides, they don't view it as spying, more like ruling."

"Is Aoife his mate?"

"No, he's already mated. Aoife is his consort."

"His lover? And she knows he's married?"

"She's a nymph, Serena. It's her calling to be his for pleasure only. As it is your calling to protect human souls."

"Does he love her?" I ask, forcing myself to sound normal, because sometimes my world angers me.

One where treating nymphs as property is considered normal—expected—and treachery is child's play.

"I suppose in his own way he does. She is his favorite. Allowed to reside in his home and stand by him as his wife does. He powers her beauty and in turn, she is a trusted confidant. Respected. Well taken care of, I assure you."

"Is that why Laven suggested we speak with her?"

"Helios might know what Oren and my mother are up to, given Oren's recent visits to the earth realm. In that regard, he's most likely shared information with Aoife."

"And you think she'll share with you?"

"Given our history, yes, I do."

"Right." I pick up my pace to catch up to Zander, and Tristan follows suit. "Why not just meet with Helios?"

Zander's shoulders tighten in front of me, but he keeps walking forward. Tristan grabs my arm, stopping us.

"I may have a royal title, Serena, but gods don't meet with my kind. I'm half satyr which means in this realm, I'm nothing more than a being to be used for pleasure. A second-class citizen. Do you understand?"

My heart contracts painfully at his words. "No. You are half gargoyle. Which means you are equally as worthy."

"That makes it even worse. I'm not even a pure nymph. I'm tainted. I have a polluted bloodline," his tone is sullen.

I take his face in my hands and look him in the eyes.

"You are not tainted. Nor are you a second-class citizen. You are perfect. And you are mine," I say breathlessly.

His hand reaches up, cupping my cheek, pulling my lips to his as he breathes against them, "We should keep going."

Tristan pulls away from me, letting go of me completely before trying to catch up with Zander.

My footsteps are quick as I follow them in silence before I speak. "There are so many places I've only experienced in books." I run my hand over a purple flower, admiring it.

"That is aconite," Tristan states.

"I think you mean asinine."

"No. The flower you're touching is called aconite. Its leaves and roots are extremely toxic. The gods and goddesses apply it to the tips of their arrows when hunting."

I remove my hand quickly and wipe it off on my pants. A small, amused smile graces his lips at my ridiculousness.

"See what I mean? Unprepared and sheltered."

"You're learning now, Serena. That is what matters."

We continue through a canopy of white flowers resting on trees that line each side of the pathway. The spring blooms are in small clusters, looking like beautiful, draping cotton balls.

Tristan plucks one and hands it to me. "This is a melia tree. It secretes a sweet sap known as manna. It's like honey. These trees are the first to have appeared in this realm. They are rumored to carry the blood of Heaven, which the gods and goddesses are said to drink in their tea and water."

Bringing the flower to my nose, I inhale and meet his sparkling eyes. "Is it weird that it smells like my hair?"

He leans in and breathes in my scent. "No, because I think you smell like pure fucking heaven, raindrop."

I shiver, reacting to him. My gaze falls onto his lips as I recall how they feel against mine. Heat rises to my cheeks.

His fingers brush over the color with a gentle caress before he takes my hand and guides me forward.

The path stretches over a small pool of deep blue water. Abundant waterfalls gently flow into it and beautiful white petals float on the water's surface.

Naked female and male bodies inhabit the azure pool, kissing and caressing one another without a care who sees. Zander throws a smirk over his shoulder at me, and I roll my eyes. Of course, he'd love the orgy scene around us.

We finally make our way up several stone steps. As we climb higher, I can't help but notice that the clouds rising and surrounding us are even thicker and more prominent.

Once we reach the peak, the path opens into a beautiful lush courtyard with small, pallid palaces built out of white clay surrounding its outskirts.

Zander stops and turns to face us. "A couple things to remember, Serena. First, the deities rank higher than all of us, so you must show them respect. Second, sprites and nymphs serve the deities. Whatever a god or goddess requests, they will fulfill it. That is their purpose on this plane, as yours is to protect humans. Do not judge outwardly what you do not understand. They don't like it."

"Anything else?"

"Yes. Aoife angers easily. Don't piss her off."

NINE

BREAKING YOUR HEART

TRISTAN

S ERENA'S LIPS PART, MOST LIKELY TO shoot off a snarky response at Zander. I place my hand on her lower back and she cuts me a hard look, but immediately relaxes at my touch. "Just be you . . . only respectful," I whisper in her ear.

Her eyes drift to my mouth, focusing on the slight scar above my lip. I notice she does it when she's trying to calm herself down. And I can't help but like that she does.

I move aside, stepping in front of her, snatching her hand and dragging her toward one of several Greek-style homes.

We pass between the large columns, and the two motionless guards standing outside the open entrance ignore us as we freely make our way inside, into the expansive interior marble courtyard of Helios's palace.

Four more large columns frame an ancient, stone water fountain. A statue of a nude decorates the middle of the entryway. Water spills from its mouth into a pool below, where tiny water sprites frolic around, splashing and playing. Their delighted laughter echoes off the marble.

Sun filters into the room through an opening in the ceiling, above the fountain, allowing natural light to highlight the ancient paintings and drawings on the walls.

"I've been expecting you," a sultry voice greets us.

We all lift our gazes to a golden curved staircase in the back of the entry. Aoife moves down the stairs, taking slow, methodic steps.

I'd forgotten how blinding her beauty is. Light radiates from every part of her body, shimmering off her skin and glowing out through her completely translucent white chiton.

She wears the elegant dress in most tasteful manner, dipping low in the front to show off her stomach and dragging on the floor behind her as she takes each step.

Gold-plated sun bands decorate her arms, attached with dainty chains to the rings on her fingers. A copy of Helios's gold-leafed crown adorns her head, marking her as his.

As she descends the staircase, her familiar honey eyes devour every inch of me. I shift under her gaze.

"Tristan," she says, when she reaches the bottom step.

"Aoife," I reply, inclining my head in a civil greeting.

"Zander. Delightful to see you," she greets.

Aoife takes the last step before holding her hand out for someone to take. Zander steps forward, dropping a kiss on it before placing it on his arm to escort her to where we are.

I place my hand on Serena's lower back again, hoping to keep her calm, knowing how Aoife can be. "May I present Serena St. Michael, princess of the gargoyle race."

"You may," she encourages, with an intrigued look.

Serena blinks away her annoyance as I watch her take in Aoife's perfect tan skin and long platinum-blonde hair, braided on each side and pulled back.

"It's nice to meet you."

"Of course it is," Aoife replies haughtily.

Ignoring Serena, she releases Zander's arm.

Approaching me, she looks me directly in the eyes with an alluring self-confidence.

Serena holds her breath next to me as Aoife's eyes shift to hers seductively and the nymph moves into her personal space.

Aoife takes Serena's face between her palms and pulls her closer, her lips brushing the gargoyle's as she sensually kisses her.

"Holy shit, that is hot," Zander blows out.

In an instant, I pull Serena away. At my reaction, a strange glint crosses Aoife's eyes and a secretive smile appears on her lips. Every hair on the back of my neck stands at attention watching the two of them. This is bad.

Aoife's eyes narrow and slide between us. "She tastes familiar, Tristan." She licks her lips again. "Ah, there it is," she goads. "Your scent. Your taste. She's yours. Marked."

Serena's sapphire eyes turn fiery at the statement, and I step between them. "Aoife," I say her name in warning.

"Do you want me to teach your little gargoyle princess how to please you properly?" She whispers enticingly.

Serena angers behind me, but Aoife's cautioning eyes slide to the guards in forewarning. They're watching us.

Fuck. I look to Zander, who inclines his head in understanding. Serena—I don't have time to explain to her.

I slide my eyes closed, hoping she doesn't freak the fuck out, but instead, that she will follow my lead and play along.

"That would be most kind of you, since it is the reason for our journey," I reply, and Serena growls behind me.

I spin quickly, grabbing her face and looking her in the eyes, the action happening so fast, her eyes widen in a startle.

"Do not argue with me, princess," I warn, her eyes narrowing at the nickname, "or I will strip you naked right here, in front of the *guards*." I emphasize the last word, hoping she catches on. Her gaze slides to the open door where they stand, and realization crosses over her expression. "And then I will allow Aoife to show you, out in the open, where all can *see* and *hear*, how to properly please me. Now, go with the nymph to her chambers, where there's *privacy*."

Serena's anger doesn't dissolve, but at least she gets it.

She yanks her head out of my hands, and Aoife clasps her hand, pulling her toward the stairs. "There is an art to hosting two lovers at one time," Aoife explains loudly, so everyone can hear. "I will show you. They will follow."

Annoyed, Serena allows herself to be dragged up the staircase.

Zander and I share a glance before following. The deities spell the realm so other supernatural beings can't use their gifts. Therefore, we're powerless here, which means we need to be on guard and follow Aoife's lead.

Once in Aoife's chambers, she closes the door tightly, turns, and addresses us. "Helios has become overly concerned for my safety recently. His visits to the earth realm are longer and longer. The guards, while silent, are always listening and watching. Is that why you are here?"

"We're here because of the Sun of Vergina. The sixteen triangular rays are his signature." I pull my necklace out of my shirt to show her the emblem. "My insignia was charmed by Helios himself, at my mother's bidding."

Her honey-colored eyes lift to mine. "I love Helios. I won't break his confidence, Tristan. Not even for you."

"I would never ask that of you. But you hold answers."

"Serena bears the insignia on her skin. I feel its power from where I stand, exuding off her. You must already know of the prophecy, since you fulfilled it. What other answers do you seek that I could possibly be safeguarding?"

"Helios spends a lot of time on the earth realm. He sees and hears things," I tread lightly. "Treacherous things."

The nymph stands straighter, understanding my meaning. "Serena smells like the humans on the earth realm. Why can't she help?" she asks in a strained voice. Fearful.

"Did you just insult me?" Serena interjects, and Zander steps in front of her slightly. Protecting both her and Aoife.

I throw my brother a pleading glare, asking him to help keep Serena calm. Aoife won't help if she's angry.

"I understand you've spend most of your life, *princess*, living among the humans in their dingy realm, while we all enjoy the luxury and beauty of the supernatural realms."

"The earth realm is equally as beautiful," Serena retorts.

Aoife laughs. "I doubt that. If humans set their eyes on our worlds, they would never return to theirs. It's why we keep ours hidden. Theirs is full of ugliness. Darkness and deceit. Treachery. Earth is where our kind goes to slum it."

"That's saying a lot coming from a nymph mistress." Serena fires back, and I snap a cold angry gaze at her.

She lifts a challenging eyebrow at me and narrows her eyes a fraction, making her displeasure with me known.

Anger and tension hang in the thick air and Aoife presents me with a hurt look, one that will haunt me, but can't be fixed now.

I shift my stance so that I'm only focused on her, giving Serena my back. I know it will only piss her off further, but right now, I don't care. We need answers and I need to leverage my previous relationship with Aoife to get them.

I breathe out a heavy sigh and move closer to Aoife, softening my tone. Hoping our past will persuade her.

"I need your help. I'm not asking you to betray him. Just share with me what you know to be factual. That's all."

The nymph frowns. "You've made a fatal error by marking Serena. Helios never meant for it to be this way."

"How was it supposed to be?"

"When Helios discovered what Michael promised the dark army, all those years ago, he was disheartened. But when he found out that Michael forced the queen's hand and bound you to Serena, he was enraged and stepped in."

"Why would a god be upset?"

"The gods and goddesses enjoy the company of the woodland and water nymphs and sprites. If the two realms go to war and the beings cease to exist, the deities will be lost without them. The senate wanted Helios to unite the realms, keeping the nymphs and sprites safe. The Sun of Vergina was meant to connect you and Freya. But you changed your destiny, rewrote your fate. And because of this, war is on the horizon at your and your love's hands."

"And Oren?"

"Helios has returned on several occasions troubled by what he has seen while on earth. Oren is working with the dark army. Regardless of whether you marry Freya or not, Oren now seeks war and has made agreements that cannot be changed or withdrawn. He wishes to rule both realms."

Cold sweat breaks out across my skin at hearing the confirmation. "How is he planning to do this?"

"Your realm is sheltering Serena. The dark army can't attack on supernatural soil, per the treaty. However, Oren has agreed to open his borders to Asmodeus, granting his army access during the wedding. In exchange, Asmodeus has promised to extinguish everything in your realm, including you and the royal family. Your planned deaths are meant to look like casualties of the unforeseen attack. This is the reason he moved up the date, knowing Serena's love for you would bring her into the realm. You've played right into his hands," she scolds. "Marking her sealed your fates."

"FUCK!" I bark out.

The look on Aoife's face is tense as she falls silent.

"And Helios?" I grind out.

"He's displeased and has made his own arrangements to protect the nymphs and sprites during the war. The gods and goddesses will offer no assistance to you now. If they do, the nymphs and sprites will be caught in the cross fire."

"This is fucking amazing," I growl.

"I'm sorry," she whispers. "I know it's not what you wanted to hear, but as my future king, you should know."

I give her a small smile and pull her into my arms.

"What will you do?" she asks.

"I am a fighter who refuses to be intimidated by any being," I reply, pulling out of her embrace. "I'll fight."

Over my shoulder, I glance at Serena and Zander.

Serena's eyes have darkened several shades.

Zander just looks pale and at the same time, ready to go into battle and murder someone. I know he's ready for war.

I turn my attention back to Aoife. "Thank you, for telling me this. On my honor, I'll protect our kin," I vow.

The woodland realm was her home before she chose to live with Helios. She is a nymph. She's worried for her kin.

"Peace be with you," she murmurs in my ear, and plants a gentle kiss to my cheek. "Go now, before Helios returns."

THE RETURN INTO THE WOODLAND REALM is silent and tense. My gaze slides to Serena. She gives me a hard look, still pissed off at the way I spoke to her earlier. Warranted, but annoying as fuck right now. Zander slips past us and stops, turning to face us. The look on his expression says it all.

"What's the next step here, Tristan?" he asks.

Exhaling, I run my hand through my hair because honestly, I have no fucking clue what to do next. This whole thing is a shitshow at this point. And trust is nonexistent.

"The only thing on our side right now is that we know what their plan of attack is, allowing us time to prepare," I reply in a clipped tone.

"Why not just show our hand to Oren? Then there is no need for the wedding. I could leave. Return to the Academy. The dark army only wants me. If I'm not here, they don't have to charge into the realm," Serena suggests.

"It's too late. Oren has made his deal with the dark army. Regardless of whether the wedding happens or not, or if you are or are not present in the realm, they'll attack," Zander answers. "No offense, but he couldn't care less about you, Serena. You're simply the bait. He wants the realm. Your leaving won't stop that. At least with the wedding in place, we know when and where to expect the attack."

The chatter around me is starting to grate on my nerves, making me more tense. "Then that is what we do. We give the appearance that we are going to go through with it and allow them to invade. When they do, we'll be ready," I reply.

Zander doesn't say anything.

Neither does Serena.

Which is good, because the feeling that this is all my fault is settling in the pit of my stomach. It's killing me.

I should have walked away from her months ago.

I can't protect her.

Or my realm.

Or anyone I care for, for that matter.

And it is my fucking fault.

"We need to be careful who knows. The last thing we want is our knowledge getting back to Oren or Asmodeus."

"What about Rionach?" Zander asks.

"No. I'm still unsure of my mother's role in all this."

"He is the commander of your army, Tristan. And our father. A planned attack on the realm is not something we should keep from him," Zander counters.

"We need to. For now."

"What about my clan? Maybe they can help—"

"No. If they start pulling resources from the Academy, or simply show up in this realm without a reason, it might alert the dark army that we know something. We keep this between the three of us," I order, and face Zander.

He sighs. "You want to prepare for war behind the back of the commander of the queen's army, and not tell a king that his future heir is about to be placed in danger? This has disaster written all over it. We should bring Rionach in on this."

"Business as usual. Prepare our army, quietly."

"SHIT!" He yells out, frustrated at me. I get it. I'm pissed off with myself. "I'd better get to work then. Serena, I'll pick you up around six for the gala," my brother says, and vanishes.

"You're putting him in a terrible position, Tristan."

"I fucking know!" I lash out at her. "What the hell do you want me to do here, Serena? Everyone is vying to hurt us. I trust no one, not even my own mother at this point."

I wasn't being tactful or kind. I don't have it in me anymore and I know she knows it, because she looks at me with a regal edge to her, unruffled. Strong. Fierce. A future queen.

"I understand you are frustrated. I am too. But this is the world we live in, Tristan. It's shitty and dark and full of lies and deceit. But there is good in it, too. There is us. I get that you are trying to protect what you love. Those are honorable and good traits, not bad. But you aren't alone. I am here, by your side. I will fight for us with you."

"Just because I protect, it doesn't mean I'm good. Don't confuse my purpose with other emotions."

"I'm well aware of your purpose."

"Oh, yeah?"

"You want to protect the princess, lock her away for safe keeping. The problem is, you didn't choose a princess who needs a knight in shining armor, Tristan. You chose one who protects. Who fights. Who speaks her mind. You can't push me away under the guise of safety. I won't let you."

She crosses her arms over her chest and her sapphire eyes narrow at me in challenge. I rub my hands across my scruffy jaw, watching her. She's right. It's time we both accept our fates. Which means I need to stop treating her like a fragile doll and start treating her like an equal.

"You are brave. And beautiful. And irritating as hell. You're strong and can be extremely violent at times. And goddamn if you aren't too smart for your own good—"

"You done?" she interrupts, her breathing heavy.

I sigh and let my head fall forward so I'm looking at my boots and the forest's moss-covered floor underneath them.

"Aequus." I whisper the word.

"What?"

"It's what we've become. It means equal," I lift my gaze and hold hers, feeling like I'm drowning in the depths of her stare. "I will never stop protecting you or trying to keep you safe. But you're right. You're not a princess who needs saving. You are my equal. A future queen who is ready to save her kin, and mine. We've rewritten our fates. Now, we face the consequences, together. Whatever may come."

She opens her mouth, and then closes it.

"In the real world, good doesn't trump evil, because evil doesn't play fair. So I am asking you, as my equal. Stay the course, or reach out to Rionach and your uncle?" I pose, backing away slowly with my eyes locked on hers.

She returns my stare, and I can see her running through all the possible scenarios and outcomes in her mind. I've almost decided she isn't going to answer, when she suddenly blinks and gives me a small, curt nod.

"Stay the course."

TEN

DANCE WITH ME

SERENA

ALL I CAN THINK OF IS how good it would feel to stand under jets of hot water from a shower. My shoulders are tense and my body aches from today's realm jump to see Aoife.

At the thought of the nymph, I growl and storm into Tristan's master suite, yanking off each piece of my clothing with angry annoyance. How is it possible that one being could be so beautiful and so cunning at the same time?

I throw my jeans onto the floor and give them a dirty look before I curl my fingers around my shirt to yank it off, tossing it next to my pants with a force driven by irritation.

And how dare Tristan turn his back to me?

I make a vow to myself that if he ever does that again, I'll throw my daggers at his back. Without a thought.

Resolved, I take off my socks, placing them next to the pile. In only my white lace bra and matching panties, I make my way over to the bathroom.

I turn the hot water on and allow the steam to fill the spacious room before I look at myself in the mirror. I look as exhausted as I feel. I really need to energy source, but rain isn't likely anytime in our future if Oren is focused on killing us. Sighing, I run my fingers through my hair before pulling down one of my bra straps to remove it.

A warm breeze floats over me, and suddenly a hard body is pressed against my back, pushing me into the vanity.

My eyes lift and lock in the mirror with Tristan's. Desire is evident on his face, stirring a hunger for his touch within me. One that I can't deny, but also can't act on.

Neither of us move.

We just stare at one another in the mirror.

Our eyes locked.

The only sound filling the room is the water pouring out of the rain shower head. My heart is beating wildly in my chest and breathing is becoming more difficult with each moment that passes. Steam billows around us, causing my body to glisten slightly as the mist settles on my bare skin.

A vision of our bodies intertwined in pleasure hits me, causing my lungs to clench. The lower portion of Tristan's body hardens under his soft jeans and settles in the crevice of my backside. I breathe in deeply though my nose at the connection. Tristan moves even closer, pressing into me farther, and I release a soundless gasp.

Holding my eyes, he moves his hands up to my shoulders, an inch away from my bare skin, as if he's afraid to make contact. His right palm glides across the top of my chest, settling on the base of my throat. My pulse beats erratically under his touch as he reads me. One finger on his other hand slowly pulls the other strap down on my bra, so both are hanging on my upper arms.

Tristan's eyes darken in the mirror as he stares at me. The heat and energy vibrating off him feels like a thousand tiny pricks against my skin. I want to tell him to stop, to move away because I can't breathe, but the words catch in my parched throat.

The soft cotton of his tee moves slightly against my bare back and the oversensitive skin tingles, feeling every hard plane of his muscles through the material. His scent fills the room, mixing in with the warm, light spray surrounding us, now fogging up the mirror, shadowing our outlines in the condensation.

The fingers on his left hand trail along the back of my arm as the tension between us builds. My knees shake from the slightest caresses, and a soft whimper escapes my lips.

The hand on my throat tightens the slightest bit as he curls his free hand in my hair and pushes the now-damp strands over my shoulder, exposing one side of my neck.

My heart kicks up a notch as he leans down, his lips grazing the sensitive area behind my ear, over his mark. At his touch, it awakens with a burn, causing a pleasurable pain to float through my veins and a heavy breath to push through my lips.

His hand goes to my thigh, skating up it, leaving a trail of goose-bumps, as he continues to my stomach, circling around my belly button before the hand on my throat squeezes and the other slides into the front of my panties.

My head falls back to his shoulder. His heavy pants filled with desire tickle my ear as his hard, wanting length is pressed against me. I curl my fingers around both his wrists in anticipation, my muscles shaking. One touch and I know I will explode.

His fingers push away the lace fabric and I hiss through my teeth. Tristan's knee slides between my legs, holding up my weight and pushing them open farther as his fingers find their way inside me.

I moan and grip his wrists harder. My breath quickens as he moves faster, building friction within me. His movements are vigorous as he slides inside me, pleasuring me to the point I am forced to squeeze my eyes shut. His thumb works the most sensitive part of me, pushing me to climax.

Just as I am about to shatter, he spins me around forcefully, one hand still at my throat and the other inside of me. His mouth devours mine, swallowing the deep cry that bursts from me as he pushes me over the edge.

I grip his shoulders for support as my body shakes uncontrollably and pleasure exudes from every pore.

With a whimper, the last shudder runs through me as Tristan gently takes my face between his hands. His thumbs wipe away the moisture on my skin from the steam and my sweat. I steady my legs and try to control my breathing.

A cocky smirk appears on his lips as he releases a deep rumble from his chest, before taking my mouth one final time in a deep, sensual kiss that leaves me breathless.

He drops his forehead to mine, whispering across my swollen lips, "Tonight, dance with me."

ELEVEN
SECRETS AND DECEIT

SERENA

ZANDER'S CURIOUS GAZE FOLLOWS ME AS I carefully move down the staircase. My gown is floor-length, and I'm afraid it will get caught on my heels and I'll trip, planting myself face-first at his black dress shoes.

My fingertips lift the bottom of the light blue dress as I take the final steps and move toward him. Nervously, I wipe my palms on the top layer of lace with white and silver beaded flowers.

I flatten my palm over my stomach where it pulls in at my waist. Two thick straps of fabric fold over each of my shoulders, connecting the material. A large V dips low in the front and a matching V shows off my back.

My hair is pulled up, but still covers the mark behind my ear, and my body is devoid of jewelry or heavy makeup.

Zander blows out a low whistle through his lips as he motions for me to twirl, which I do.

"You look stunning," he grins. "Tristan is so fucked."

"Did you just give me a sincere compliment?"

"I did. I can act like a grown-up, on occasion."

I smile. "Thank you. You clean up nicely too."

He looks down at his elegant, tailored black tuxedo.

"This old thing?" he waves me off with a wink. "The cleavage is a nice touch as well," he points to my chest.

"Um, thanks."

A strange gleam crosses his eyes. I drop my gaze from him, feeling like he can see right through me.

"That sex blush looks good on you too. It relaxes you."

"And there it is."

"Did you think I wouldn't notice?"

"I think the polite thing to do is not mention it."

"I never claimed to be polite. Just wildly handsome," he says arrogantly, presenting me with his hand.

When I take it, he places mine securely on his arm.

"Let's go dance the night away and drink too much."

And with that, he teleports us into the entryway of the castle, where Rionach and Ophelia are greeting guests.

While in line, I attempt to muster my courage and straighten my spine. Zander leans in and whispers, "I've got you, champ."

We are announced, and as we approach the queen and Rionach, fear shines in Ophelia's eyes. She quickly recovers by plastering on a fake, uncomfortable smile.

Stepping closer, she dips her chin. "Princess Serena, Prince Zander," she greets us formally, with a shaky tone.

I curtsy and Zander bows slightly.

"Your Majesty, Commander," Zander returns.

"Well, don't you both look lovely this evening," the queen adds politely, still shaken.

"Thank you, Your Majesty. As do you," I motion to her exquisite floor-length dress.

It's nude in color, tight-fitted and long-sleeved. Black sparkly branches are strategically placed throughout the design to resemble a tree. Fitting for the queen of the woodland realm.

"I agree, you look stunning." Zander kisses her cheek.

"I second that." Rionach states, inclining his head to us.

He's dressed sharply this evening in a tuxedo.

"What a wonderful and happy occasion," he announces.

"Yes, well," the queen glances at her husband before looking suspiciously between the two of us. "I do trust this evening will be one of cordialness with focus only on the bride and groom to be." Her tone is a blithe warning.

"Of course," Zander answers. "Love is indeed in the air."

He leans toward me, kissing my cheek, lingering a moment for effect before pulling away and winking.

"Now, if you'll excuse us, Your Majesties, there is a room full of people I am anxious to introduce my love to." Zander pats the hand I have on his arm, and guides us into the elegant ballroom.

Tonight, it's decorated in purples and creams. If this weren't a celebration honoring the man I love and his fiancée, I would envy the simplicity and beauty of the room.

"Drink?"

"Yup," I pop my *p*.

Zander grabs two glasses of champagne from a silver tray being passed and hands one to me with a smirk.

Raising his glass, he toasts. "To fate."

I clink my glass with his. "To fate."

We sip and he winks at me. "I like that you drink. Now, if you'd just let me feel you up, you'd be the perfect date."

"Not a chance. Snag me one of those bacon thingies, would you? I am starving," I motion to the tray of passed hors d'oeuvres and Zander grabs a few, handing them to me.

I moan in pleasure biting into one as he watches me.

"What?" I ask.

"This afternoon's activities leave you a little hungry?"

I roll my eyes and shove another bite in my mouth.

"Tell you what, you keep feeding these to me, and I'll let you grab a boob," I tease.

Zander's eyes light up. "Really?"

I swallow the bite in my mouth. "Ah, no."

He pouts. "I dress up for you. Take you somewhere nice. Throw expensive champagne down your throat and feed you bacon. And what do I get? Nothing. Not even a, 'Hey Zander, it's true. You *are* devilishly good-looking.'"

Feeling bad, I exhale. "Fine. You are, like, good-looking."

"FINALLY!" he throws his hands in the air dramatically, causing me to laugh—really laugh—for the first time in what feels like forever. Zander is good for the soul.

He winks, and we both freeze when Oren and Lily make their way through the room. Both are formally dressed, Oren in a tuxedo and Lily in a lovely, blush-colored, one-shouldered silk gown. They greet guests with smooth, casual smiles.

"Looks like it's showtime," Zander whispers, and clasps our hands, giving me an encouraging squeeze.

My eyes lift to Zander's and I'm suddenly nervous. I flatten my free hand on my stomach, where the half-dozen bacon things I ate are proving to have been a bad idea.

Oren gives me a calculated smile as he and Lily approach us after making their way around the room.

"Prince Zander," he greets first. "Princess Serena, I'm surprised to see you here this evening."

Refusing to let him intimidate me, I lift my chin. "Is that so?" I attempt to hide the note of irritation in my voice.

"It's funny how you've recently begun to turn up in the most unexpected of places. If I may be so bold, why are you *really* here?" He asks me point blank.

I smile, not taking his bait. "Whatever do you mean?"

"I mean, you must be a masochist to watch your true love marry another," he throws out with a cruel smile.

He's right. And if this were real, my heart would be shattering into a million pieces. But it's not. It's for show.

"I'm here for Zander, and Zander only." I continue to fake-smile as a tense vein shows itself on his forehead.

"What can I say? Serena is impressed by size, which is why she has chosen me over Tristan." Zander steps in, sliding his gaze to mine before his expression turns serious. "Oh, my apologies, I suppose that bit of information is bad news for your daughter. Regardless, Tristan is hard-working. Rest assured his try-hard attitude will make up for his lack of girth when producing offspring," he adds.

At his statement, I almost spit out the sip of champagne I took. Instead, I begin to cough uncontrollably. Zander rubs my back and I wave him off. "I'm fine. Wrong pipe."

When I'm finished, he pinches my chin between his fingers, looking me over. "Are you sure you're okay?"

I nod, unable to speak as the last of my coughs leave me.

Zander faces Oren and Lily. "Apologies, what I meant to say is it's an honor to be here on this joyous occasion."

Annoyed, Oren places his hand on his wife's back, pushing her forward. "Serena, I don't believe you've been properly introduced to my wife Lily, Freya's mother."

"I have not." I dip my chin. "Empress Consort."

A cold glare greets me as she slides her stare over me before granting Zander a warm, friendly smile.

"Zander, as always it's lovely to see you," she coos.

"You as well, Empress," he blushes under her stare.

I narrow my eyes at the action, which is weird for him.

With a worried expression marring her face, Ophelia and Rionach approach. "I do hope everything is all right. I noticed you choking, Serena."

I clear my throat and nod. "Yes, thank you, Your Majesty. The champagne simply went down the wrong pipe as I was being introduced to the empress consort."

The doors to the ballroom close and a loud trumpet is sounded, announcing Freya and Tristan's arrival.

I stiffen and inhale through my nose.

As all eyes focus on the doors, Rionach moves behind his wife, to my free side. His hand slips into mine, squeezing once before letting go. I raise a curious glance to him, and he simply smiles down at me paternally, granting me a look of understanding. I really need to work on hiding my feelings much better. My nerves jump sky high.

The butterflies come alive when Tristan walks in wearing a tailored black suit and crisp white shirt with the top button open. Freya dazzles the room on his arm in her deep-ocean-blue gown. Everything on it sparkles, like her, including the thin straps holding it up. The breathtaking material glides along the floor, cascading like water.

They stop for a moment while the throng of guests clap and toast to their faux happiness. A bright smile graces Freya's lips as she enjoys her moment in the spotlight.

Tristan looks dangerous, his jaw tense as his eyes shift around the room. When his eyes land on me, he relaxes.

I incline my head to him, and he returns the gesture. Feeling solemn watching the scene play out, I lean into Zander, who puts his arm around my shoulder for support and squeezes.

Tristan's cognac eyes narrow fiercely on Zander's arm, and his nostrils flare in anger. I shake my head in warning just as Oren looks over his shoulder at me, and then back to Tristan. Tristan notices Oren, and tilts his head toward Freya, offering her a bright, happy smile as he takes her into his arms and moves her around the dance floor.

Dismissing the scene, I turn to Zander, who, for the next hour, leads me around the room, introducing me to the important dignitaries in attendance. After each introduction, he makes sure to explain what each person's role is, and how it affects the monarchy and state of the realm. It's the perfect distraction and honestly, educational.

The entire time Zander is parading me around, I feel the weight of Tristan's eyes on me. Even with the french doors open to the balconies, the air in the ballroom is so heavy and tense that it's hard to breathe.

A glass of champagne appears in front of me as Zander leads me out onto the balcony into the evening air. I inhale deeply, relishing the flower-scented breeze.

That's the thing about Zander: he always knows what you need before you do. He grins at me; it's a smile that makes you think he'll promise you everything under the sun, including dirty, sexy things. It's easy to see how he gets his way with little to no effort.

My response is to roll my eyes at his attempt.

"I paid extra for the moon in the hopes you'd kiss me."

"Oh?" I giggle. The champagne finds him charming.

We both lean against the railing, facing one another.

"How are you holding up, champ?"

I shrug. "It is what it is."

Awareness dawns on his handsome face that I'm struggling. "Well, you're not all shouty and punchy, so . . ."

Feeling brave, I ask, "What did I witness between you and Lily earlier?"

He feigns innocence. "What do you mean?"

"The awkward exchange; you blushed."

"I don't blush."

"You did."

"No."

"You totally did."

"Fine. So, what if I did?"

"Well, now you need to cop to it."

"What I need is to cop a feel."

I growl. "My fault. I walked right into that one."

"Yeah, you did," he laughs, and becomes quiet, lost in thought.

"Do you think Oren will ever let the rain fall?"

"He wants you weak when they attack. They know you source the rain's energy, so my guess is no."

I sigh heavily, suddenly tired and sad.

Zander taps his shoulder with mine. "Does the frowny face work with Tristan?"

"Sometimes." My eyes float out to the realm. "Sometimes my sexy eyes work too."

"Now those I would like to see," he teases.

"Keep dreaming, pretty boy."

He smiles brightly. "You have a nickname for me."

"What?"

"You called me pretty boy."

"I did?"

"Yup, so either you think I am actually pretty, and want to make sexy eyes at and with me, or you have a nickname for me now, which makes us the best of buddies," he retorts.

"Nickname," I reply quickly.

"Fair enough."

"Unless you want to share a secret with me. Then we can be best friends forever." I stare into the inky night.

His gaze follows mine.

"When I was a teenager, I had this huge crush on Lily."

"What?" My tone goes high.

"Shhh," he scolds, and looks around before returning his focus onto the darkened land. "Like, this ridiculous crush."

"Are you telling me this so we'll be best friends?"

"I'm telling you this because you look all sad and shit. And trust is important between us. So I'm sharing. Even Tristan and Magali don't know this," his tone firm.

My eyes widen and I zip my lips with my fingers.

"She was my first."

I pinch my face. "First what? Girlfriend?"

He gives me a sharp look. "I think you're smart enough to know I didn't send her flowers and court her."

"First crush then—oh, wait, are you saying that she took your virginity?" I prod with my mouth open.

"Would you stop?" he grabs my hand and pulls me into the corner where no one else is. "How old are you?"

"Tristan always made it seem like you liked Freya."

"I pretended to, to throw him off track. For years, Lily and I were—"

"Lovers?" I finish for him, and he winces.

"Yes. As I got older, I realized that I suffered from just a simple teenage crush. And on her part, she was attracted to my satyr gifts. Like most women who use me."

He smiles sadly and my heart sinks.

"You are more than just a nymph, Zander. You're smart, funny, charming, devilishly good-looking, and any being would be more than lucky to have you. I know Mags is."

He pulls me into a tight embrace and I go willingly, allowing myself to relax in his arms. I hadn't realized how much I needed a true friend with me during all this, until now.

Movement from the corner of my eye has me stiffening. I look up to see Freya and Tristan rounding the corner and approaching us. Freya wears a happy grin, and Tristan, well, given how it looks—Zander and I in a dark corner, embracing—he looks murderous.

I try to push away from Zander with a wide-eyed stare.

With a huge sigh, he reaches for my hand and picks it up, squeezing, and refuses to let go, even when I try to escape.

"There's the happy couple," Zander's voice sounds light.

"Are you referring to yourselves or us?" Freya counters, delighting in what she thinks she sees.

"I was hoping to have a moment alone with Serena," Freya says, her gaze sliding between Tristan and Zander.

Everyone falls silent until I clear my throat.

"That would be lovely."

Both brothers' expressions turn guarded and worried.

"Don't fret, gentlemen. We'll just be right over there in plain eyesight." Her voice is calm and childlike.

Zander dips his head in acknowledgment. "Ladies."

Freya is a xana, which means the water nymph can easily become angry and violent, if pushed too far.

She shoves up on her tiptoes and places a kiss on Tristan's cheek; I curb my desire to smash her pretty face into the wall over, and over, and over again.

"Shall we, Your Highness?" She motions to the other side of the balcony, which is empty, and I follow.

"To what do I owe this great honor?" I feign politeness.

"I do believe I owe you an apology, Princess Serena."

Her voice and face are calm, despite the uneasiness emanating off her in palpable waves. It's nauseating.

"How so?"

"With all that is going on, sadly, you and I haven't had a simple moment to become reacquainted." Her tone is eerily civil. "Since our first meeting in the forest, I mean. When you came upon me during my melancholy moment."

I guess she wasn't referring to the time when Queen Ophelia outed her and Tristan's engagement after dinner.

"Your apology, while most gracious, is unnecessary."

"I appreciate your kindness," she replies with grace.

"I am curious, though," I begin. "I mean, if you'll indulge me for a moment, I have a question regarding that day."

"Of course, Your Highness, ask me anything."

"Did you know who I was that day, and that Tristan was protecting me?" The branches on her brows pull together. "I mean, is that why you kept his name from the conversation?" I ask, trying not to look at him.

"You summoned me, by turning the stream vernal. It was an invitation, was it not?" Her tone sharpens as she attempts to twist the conversation while maintaining her well-bred manners.

I take in a deep, calming breath. "You are correct. I summoned you because I thought you were hurt. I was trying to help you. My intentions were kind in nature. Do you want to know what I believe your intentions were?"

She glances at me, clutching her small platinum comb. "I would be happy to listen to your thoughts on the matter."

Polished. She's always so polished. I smile respectfully.

"I believe you knew who I was. I also believe you knew Tristan was assigned as my protector. I don't believe that our meeting was coincidental that day. *You* released the amethyst hue, and the cries, so

I would come to you and summon you," I state in a poised manner.

"Why the water realm would I do that?"

"So you could warn me off with your story about love. You shared your feelings with me that day, helped me feel love and then loss, as a warning. Am I incorrect?"

She regards me, considering my words. "Your Highness, you are quite astute. I shared a cautionary tale, which sadly, you did not heed. And now, we are in this most ungracious position."

"And what position is that exactly?"

From my peripheral vision, I see Tristan lean closer. I know that with his gargoyle hearing he can hear the conversation and is listening to every word while sharing it with Zander. Freya seems to have forgotten he has this gift.

Freya's eyes turn cold and her voice becomes cross. "You were banned from this realm for a reason. Yet, here you are, on Zander's arm this time. That day in the forest, I expressed to you how deeply I love Tristan. I even showed you my love for him through a shared connection, and yet, even after discovering he was betrothed to me, you tried to take him from me." She begins to comb her platinum hair, a nervous habit of xanas. "Since you've returned, he has gone missing for hours at a time. I'm not stupid or blind. I know he's with you. I see the way he looks at you, Serena."

"This conversation should be between you and Tristan, Freya. Not me. I have nothing to do with it."

"NO!" She becomes unglued, her face immediately morphing into a mask of rage before going blank. She shakes her head, smoothing her dress with her free hand before meeting my eyes with her icy ones. "I have tried to be kind. I warned you and you didn't listen. Tristan banished you from the realm and you've reappeared. I even went so far as killing Henry and Annabelle so you would be forced to return to the Academy to mourn them, and yet, you are still here. What else is it going to take for you to just . . . *disappear?*"

My body runs cold at her words, and my eyes lift to Tristan, who looks shocked. "What did you say?" I whisper.

Realizing what she let slip, Freya straightens her spine.

All the air escapes my lungs and my world tilts. She killed Chancellor Davidson and his secretary. Freya. Not the dark army, or another gargoyle. A jealous water nymph.

"That's how someone got in undetected. You came in through the water in the faucets." My eyes fall to her comb, and she slowly moves her hand to her side so it's out of view. "They were beheaded. How did one tiny nymph take on two skilled gargoyle warriors?"

"I drugged their tea," she answers, in a kind tone that doesn't match her words, as if this will make it all okay.

My eyes lift to hers. "That's why the protectors didn't fight back. They couldn't. You paralyzed them with a drug?"

"Aconite. It's easily absorbed and untraceable, which is why Gage and Nassa have come up empty-handed. It causes asphyxia and arrhythmic heart failure, leading to suffocation, which is why I had to behead them. Their throats swelled and I didn't want any traces of the flower. I believe you came across the bloom on your recent visit to the Garden of the Deities." Her tone is quiet, but her words are a challenge. She knew we went into the realm that day, which means she's following us or having us followed.

Without a thought, I lift the bottom of my dress and yank out my daggers, pointing them at her throat. Her eyes widen in fright as she backs up to the wall. In an instant, Tristan and Zander are both at my sides as I seethe.

"You killed my kin. You spilt gargoyle blood."

"Serena," Tristan says my name calmly.

"In my world, when you take a protector's life, we show no mercy. An eye for an eye," I spit in her face.

"Serena," Tristan speaks my name again.

"Did you hear?" I ask him.

"Yes. I heard everything. Put down the daggers. This isn't the time, nor is it the place," he says slowly.

"Give me one good reason not to end your life right here and now." I dig the points of my knives into her throat.

A defiant smile crosses her lips. "Go ahead, Your Highness," she spurs me on. "But know this: if I don't check in with my helpers at the Academy, Magali will be next. Followed by Ireland, and then Ryker. I also have a team watching Ethan and Lucas in Paris. They won't hesitate."

I yank my daggers away from her throat, but slap her hard with the handle of one of them. "You bitch."

Her shaky hand goes to her bleeding mouth. "I am simply claiming what's rightfully mine. I don't care why you went to see the gods and goddesses. I couldn't care less what you three have been doing secretly behind Ophelia's back. All I want is Tristan. That is it. You go. He stays. It's that simple."

Tristan's jaw clicks. "Serena, stop." He grabs my arms, pushing me back. "Both of you. Stop."

I take a step back and he steps in front of me, bending down so we are at eye level. "This isn't the way to do it."

"Listen to him, Your Highness," Freya adds, and I lift my daggers again.

Tristan's hands grab my upper arms and tighten, walking me away from her.

"Let. Me. Go."

"No."

Suddenly, I am being lifted and dragged away.

"Calm down," Tristan whispers in my ear.

"No," I mutter, pushing him away.

My chest heaves with hatred and adrenaline.

Zander walks between us and cups my cheeks.

"Champ, we will take care of this. On my honor. If you kill her tonight, you will start a war that we are unprepared for. Do you understand?"

My eyes glide to Zander, and I breathe in and out. With teary eyes, I nod and curl into the safety of his chest.

After a moment, I step back.

Hurt crosses Tristan's expression as he watches us.

"We're done, Tristan. He's all yours, Freya. You can call your team off my friends," I state, my voice void of emotion.

"After the wedding, I would be happy to," she replies.

Zander and Tristan exchange a look before Tristan steps away from me, allowing Zander to guide me away.

"Oh, Your Highness," Freya's voice stops us. "Please consider yourself having declined Tristan's earlier request."

"Which was?" I ask over my shoulder.

"He wanted you to dance with him tonight."

TWELVE
OLD FRIENDS

TRISTAN

SERIOUSLY? FREYA WAS WATCHING US IN the bathroom? I drop my arms and whirl around on the nymph. I stare at her, fury raging under my skin. She's holding her jaw where Serena smacked the shit out of her. The bruise is appearing quickly under her silver skin, as drops of blood fall from her cut lip.

Without another word, I spin around and stomp away from her. I can't even look her in the eyes right now.

"Tristan, wait!" she calls after me.

I turn and lunge at her so fast that she startles, scrambling back, and hits the side of the wall. Fear is apparent in her stare as I seethe at her, my teeth bared in an animalistic expression.

"What the fuck do you want?" I bark.

"YOU!" she shouts. "All I've ever wanted was you."

"And you think killing two gargoyles, threatening five others, and following me around is the way to get me?" I yell in her face, not caring that I'm scaring her.

"No, I don't."

My eyebrows furrow, confused by her answer.

"I think it's the only way to *keep* you."

My angry stare drives into her, my hands twitching and flexing with my wrath. Automatically, my arm snaps out, my hand grabs her throat, and I push her hard against the wall. My rage is so palpable I can feel it coming off my skin.

"If anything happens to Serena—or Magali, Ireland, Ryker, Ethan, or Lucas—I will end you. Without batting an eyelash, I will personally kill you myself." I lean into her. "You think you can threaten me? Kill two of my kin? And that will keep me in line? If so, you're so fucking wrong. If I were you, I would start sleeping with one eye open." I release her hard and she falls to the stone ground.

Within seconds, I vanish, reappearing in the one place I may not be welcomed, but know I'll be safe and understood.

THE LOFT IS DARK WHEN I arrive. Then again, it's always dark. The fireplace is lit, providing a warm glow, and the amber lights from the Eiffel Tower outside the large, floor-to-ceiling windows offer a small amount of ambience.

On the stone coffee table, two crystal tumblers sit, filled with amber liquid. As I approach, the dark figure on the L-shaped couch shifts. A lit cigarette dangles from his lips as he watches me grab one of the glasses and fall into a chair across from where he is with a heavy, tired sigh.

"Tristan."

"Gage." I lift the glass to my lips. "Expecting me?"

He sits back, eyes on me, inhaling the nicotine from the cigarette before blowing out a trail of smoke at me.

"I found out who killed Henry and Annabelle," he says around the cigarette, and leans over to snatch his glass off the table, swirling the liquid as he stares at it. "I figured it was only a matter of time before you showed up."

I tip my glass toward him and he mirrors the gesture before we each toss a shot of brandy back in one swallow.

With the burn of alcohol flowing down my throat, I ignore how similar our mannerisms and appearances are.

He takes another long drag off his cigarette before releasing out the smoke in a slow, methodical, calm exhale.

Sea-green eyes meet mine. "The London clan will find out. And when they do, they will kill her. Regardless of whether she's your mate or not." Gage speaks in a bored, detached voice.

I fall silent. Dropping my head back on the leather chair, I focus on the dark wood beams running across the ceiling.

"I'll take your silence as an 'I don't give a fuck, Gage.'"

I grunt. "Apologies. I don't give a fuck, Gage."

Watching me, he places his glass back on the table, then pinches the last of his cigarette between his fingers as he runs his thumb over his bottom lip in contemplation. "Freya is to be your wife. Her death doesn't affect you at all?"

"No." My answer is clipped.

"Why are you here then, Tristan?" he asks in a low tone.

I drop my chin and look him directly in the eyes, so he can see just how fucking serious I am. Because when it comes to Serena St. Michael, apparently, I'll make a deal with the devil himself—my biological father—to save her.

"I need your help."

Wordlessly we hold one another's gaze, allowing a few tense moments to pass between us before he speaks again.

"You must be desperate if you're asking for my help."

"I am."

"But not with Freya?"

"No."

He waits quietly.

"Serena."

"Ah. The London clan's princess." He falls quiet again as his eyes search my face. After a few moments of assessing me, he inclines his head. "Lay it out for me," he demands in an even tone. "Make it short and sweet. Simple. I have a very low tolerance for bullshit and lack of clarity."

That makes two of us—it must be another inherited trait.

"The Sun of Vergina prophecy has been fulfilled. Not with Freya. With Serena. Oren made a deal with Asmodeus, granting him access to my realm during the wedding, so he can get to Serena and murder my family. Oren wants to rule both realms. Freya has nymphs stationed at the Academy, targeting Magali, Ireland, and Ryker, as well as here in Paris, at Notre Dame, on Ethan and Lucas. Should I decide not to marry her, those protectors will experience a fate similar to Henry and Annabelle's—death by aconite."

"Christ. Is that what she used on them?"

"Yes."

He sits back, studying me. "Nassa has no pull with her uncle. If a deal was made with Asmodeus, it's set in stone."

"I figured. That's not what I need your help with."

"I disagree, but go on."

"I want to know who the nymphs at the Academy are."

"Easy enough."

"And I require—I need them not to exist anymore."

"That shouldn't be a problem."

"They're my kin, so it can't be traced back to me."

"These nymphs threaten to spill protector blood, which also runs through your veins. Your hands are clean," he assures me.

"We need to find them before the London clan does."

"Is Ophelia aware of any of this shit?"

"No. Neither is Rionach. Let's keep it that way."

He ponders my words for a long moment, before leaning forward and resting his elbows on his knees. "How are you planning to deal with Asmodeus and the war Oren is bringing into your realm if the queen and commander of her army are unaware of the dangers?" His voice is hard.

"I don't know yet."

He throws the last of his cigarette into his empty glass.

"I do." The protector stands. "Follow me."

Gage guides me down a short hallway before opening a door that leads into a dimly lit room. From the small amount of light coming through the large floor-to-ceiling windows, and the several burning candles, it looks as if the room might have been an office at one point—but it's not anymore.

The smell of vervain incense, used by sorceresses to ward off vampires while they do magic, fills the air. A large wooden table, covered with sorcery engravings, has been pushed against one of the walls. On the table are various candles in different sizes, shapes, and colors. Gemstones and old books are scattered around the candles.

My questioning gaze slides to Gage, and he grunts.

"This is what happens when you give a sorceress an overnight drawer. Her shit shows up everywhere. It was only supposed to be floss." He runs a frustrated hand through his golden-blond hair. "Now, it's fucking candles, and a squawking crow," he yells the words at the bird.

On cue, a black, beady-eyed crow caws from its perch in a cage located in the back corner of the darkened room.

"Nassa's familiar?" I question.

"Tristan, Noir. Noir, Tristan."

The bird screeches again and ruffles its raven feathers.

"Fucking crow."

"Watch it, Gallagher," a deep, raspy voice warns.

Nassa, sorceress of prosperity and Gage's significant other, approaches us from behind. I turn, meeting her deep emerald eyes. Her face is pretty and delicate—unlike her personality, which is hard and tough. She flicks her long, straight, plum-highlighted, black hair over her shoulder.

Narrowing her gaze at me, she points a black-manicured finger in my direction. "I've heard of runaway brides, but not grooms. Why are you in my spell room and not marrying the water-princess-nymph-being-thing?"

"It's not your spell room. It's my office," Gage snarls.

A hard glare is thrown his way. "Why are you in here?"

"Because," Gage's tone is irritated, "it's *my* office."

One of Nassa's perfect brows arches as she ignores Gage's moody personality and turns her focus onto me. "Tristan?"

I shrug. "Honestly, I have no fucking clue."

She rolls her eyes. "Like Gage, you curse a lot."

Gage exhales and runs his hands over his face, calming himself down, and his voice turns stern. "Looking for you."

"I didn't hear you. You're doing that *mumble quietly so she doesn't hear me* thing you've been doing lately."

"I was looking for you!" he shouts.

"Me?" she asks, not believing him. "Why?"

"We need Branna," he states simply.

An unreadable expression crosses her face. "For?"

"It's complicated," he answers.

She crosses her arms and toes her Converses, annoyed.

"Everything with you always is, Gallagher," she rasps.

"I need her in the woodland realm. Tomorrow," he adds.

She sends him a death glare. "Branna isn't at your beck and call, Gallagher. You just can't command things of her."

"I can. Find her. Get her there," he fires back.

The two of them stare at one another in some sort of standoff. It's apparent there is more to this heated discussion than I'm picking up on. And truly, I don't care.

"Who is Branna?" I end their confrontation.

Watching the two of them interact is strange and fascinating. Like watching animals use utensils. It's wrong on so many different levels, but you just can't stop looking.

Nassa clears her throat. "She's an old friend of mine."

"An old friend." My eyes glide between them.

"Of both of ours," Gage snips, and she flinches.

"Is she a sorceress of the Black Circle?" I ask Nassa.

"No. Branna is a Maleficium witch," she responds.

"What is Maleficium?" I ask, never having heard of it.

"A form of dark and powerful sorcery," Nassa replies.

"Dark magic?" My eyes slide to Gage.

"To fight darkness, you need darkness," he resolves.

THIRTEEN
END GAME

TRISTAN

ZANDER CROSSES HIS ARMS OVER HIS broad chest. He isn't as imposing in stature as either Rionach or myself, but there is a severe elegance about him that seems just as threatening while he considers me silently for a moment.

"I want to know what the endgame is here, Tristan. What happens when Branna enters the realm? And what about Serena? I know you well enough to know that if she's in danger, your focus will be on her and not on taking out the realm's risk. Don't even get me going on Freya's threat against Magali and the rest of the protectors at the Academy. So what is the real reason you've agreed to bring a Maleficium witch into the realm? Keep in mind, I'm not just your brother, but I am second in command of our army. I have no problem leveraging my position if you don't want to be honest with me."

Begrudgingly, I tell him the plan I agreed to last night with Gage and Nassa. His dark eyes become slits and his jaw clenches as he listens, until awareness dawns on him.

I lean back into the kitchen counter and watch him as things start to shift in his gaze as he puts the puzzle pieces together. When he has everything figured out, he takes a step closer to me and scowls. "And you trust this witch?"

I push off the counter and match his stance.

"I have no choice."

He nods his agreement. "If this doesn't stop Oren for good, our army will step in and finish the task, at my lead."

I breathe out a sigh of relief. "I need to tell Serena."

Zander releases a bitter-sounding laugh and lifts his hand, rubbing at his jawline. "Yeah. Good luck with that."

"How is she?"

"Worried. For her best friend, as am I. And the others. Serena is convinced Henry and Annabelle's blood is on her hands," he sighs. "She's a royal protector. Her DNA is programmed to save lives, not end them. Especially her kin. Something your gargoyle half should sympathize with."

I ignore his taunt. "Where is she?"

"Upstairs." He steps in front of me, blocking my view of the staircase. "You should know something." He pauses.

"What?"

"She's convinced herself that until the risk against her friends at the Academy is gone, you and she can't be together."

The fuck we can't. I don't wait for him to continue; instead I step around him and storm up the stairs, taking them two at a time. My brother's dark chuckle follows me. Once at the top of the landing, I march over to my bedroom doors and slam them open, seeking her out. They hit the wall with such force, the house rattles as I step in.

Serena is by the bed, packing her suitcase. She glances over her shoulder at me for a quick second and with an annoyed huff, she swings her focus back to the bed and continues to throw her clothes into her luggage.

"Why aren't you with your betrothed, Tristan?"

"Because I am here—for you."

Her hand freezes in mid-motion before she shakes off my words and keeps packing. Her tone is cool when she says, "You shouldn't be. Your wedding is soon. And . . . I don't want you here. For me, or for any other reason."

I snap. Her attitude in this moment, her words, and everything I've been through over the past few months with her finally comes to a head, and I completely lose my shit.

Once in my room, I slam the doors shut, storm over to her, grab her elbow, drag her to the chair, and throw her into it with a forceful push. Serena curses at me and fire ignites behind her eyes. She stands and steps into my space.

"By the grace. What is your problem, Tristan?"

"My—" I make a pained sound. "*My* problem?"

"Yes, *your* problem," she snaps back.

"YOU!" I shout. "You are my fucking problem."

She rears back as if I slapped her, and falls silent.

My footsteps echo in the room as I pace in front of her trying to control my temper and erratic behavior.

"I'm sorry. It's just after last night . . ." I trail off.

"Last night," she spits out. "Are you referring to the moment when your batshit crazy fiancée threatened the lives of my friends and admitted to killing my kin because she is in love with you? And then, you ran away. Again."

"I didn't run. I had an appointment."

Her eyes close as she tries to control her own temper.

"Look at me," I demand, and she does. "I'm sorry. I'm not handling all of this very well. You. Freya. Any of it."

Defeated, she drops back onto the chair and inhales.

"I'm leaving. I need to return to the Academy to protect Magali, and everyone else," her voice shakes.

I crouch down in front of her and take her chin between my fingers, looking her in the eyes. "Who's running now?"

She swallows, searching my gaze. "I won't—can't watch you marry her, even though I know it has to happen. Seeing it will kill me,

Tristan. And in turn, I will kill her."

Serena pulls her chin out of my grip, as her fingers brush and fiddle with the emeralds on her protector band.

"Don't push me away."

"She threatened me, here at court."

"I know."

"I don't have your realm's protection."

"You do."

"If you protect me, you go against your vows."

I take her face between my hands and hold her gaze.

"It is your blood that runs through me, Serena. It is you that I am sworn to protect. It's you that I choose."

"That's what I am afraid of. Freya has made it crystal clear that if you choose me, my friends will suffer for that choice."

"They won't."

"They will."

I'm so mad that my hands are shaking.

I need to get my emotions in check here, because I'm starting to feel as though no one is on my fucking side. No one trusts me, or my motivations, and their constant reminders of failure, fate, and obligations are grating on me.

The truth of the matter is that I'm unsure if Freya will snap and truly go after Serena's friends. I've put a plan into action that will stop any attack, but she doesn't know that yet. I can do this; I can save us. She just needs to trust me.

But she doesn't, and therein lies the problem. I sigh and cast a rueful look at her, needing to show her we are more.

"Trust in my love for you."

She sucks in a quick breath at my statement. Her watery eyes roam over me. "You can't have one hand on the throne, and one on my heart. Our love won't save us from this."

I smile. That's the first time we've admitted our feelings aloud to each other. She loves me, which means there is fucking hope.

"Then it's settled," I state.

Serena's face pinches in confusion at my announcement.

"We love one another, which is good, because my realm happens to be on the brink of war, and as its future king, I could really use a protector to save me." I hold her gaze.

So many opposing emotions cross her face, like she is waging her own personal war inside herself. "I told you last night, we're done, Tristan. There can't be an *us* anymore."

My chest aches as I search her face. "I know."

"Then let me go," she whispers, the fight now gone.

"No."

"But—You just said—" she begins, but I cut her off.

"I said, *I know*, meaning I know that's the bullshit line you threw out last night while you were pissed off," I reply.

Ticked off, she stands and starts for the door, but I grab her by the arm and wrench her back to me.

"Let me go."

"No!"

"You have to!" she screams. "I won't be the reason they die as well," she cries, and falls to the floor in a sobbing mess.

I drop to the floor and crawl over to her, taking her face in my hands and wiping away the tears. "I love you. So damn much it hurts my heart. I need you," I croak. "Like I need air to breathe. And I'm too fucking screwed up to convince you, or myself, to want anyone or anything different. I'm too selfish to allow you to walk out when—" I take a soothing breath. "I just got you back. You are mine. And I am yours. Trust me to protect you. Us. Your friends. Our realms and families. Trust in me. In us, as equals."

Her eyes search mine. "Aequus—in the name of love?"

"Aequus. In the name of love," I confirm.

"Heard some commotion and thought I'd check it out," Zander knocks on the door as he lets himself in. "Everyone okay in here?"

I stand, taking Serena with me.

She buries her face in my chest, and Zander eyes us.

"Everything is fine," I blow out.

"It doesn't look, or sound, fine," he counters. "I'd hate to have to rearrange your face, because we both know your looks are all you have, with that shitty personality."

"We're fine. We're just coming to an understanding."

"Serena has agreed to the plan, then?" he asks.

"What plan?" she mumbles.

I look at him, figuring she wants a moment to compose herself. "Would you mind?" I shift my gaze to the door.

"I would. Is she . . . ," his eyes fall to Serena. "Crying?"

"What the fuck is it with you and her crying?"

"Champ?" Zander's voice becomes excited.

Serena growls and pulls away from me, flashing my brother an annoyed look. His expression turns almost victorious.

"This doesn't count," Serena tells him.

"Hell yeah, it does. It totally counts." His grin spreads.

She growls out an exaggerated breath and turns her irate gaze to me. "This is your fault. I lost because of you."

"Lost what?" I look between them. "What the hell is going on?"

"How did it happen? Did he tell he loved you? Wants babies? Killed your mom?" Zander ticks off, and Serena rolls her eyes at him, standing and crossing her arms in defiance.

"Did you kill my mother, Tristan?"

"No," I reply, confused. "What the fuck, you two?"

"I win!" Zander raises his arms in victory. "I WIN!"

"Win what?" I snarl.

"We had a bet. Winner takes all." He rubs his hands together in a triumphant but calculating way. I don't like it.

"Bet?" I repeat, still in the dark.

"Zander and I bet that I wouldn't cry. I did. He won." Her explanation is short and clipped. She's pissed she lost.

"What did he win?" I inquire.

"Anything I want. At any time. I decide," he grins.

I study Serena. She's frowning, watching Zander.

"I warned you. Nymphs can't be trusted."

Her eyes meet mine. "A lesson I learned last night."

FOURTEEN
THE LION GUARD

SERENA

I CAN'T BELIEVE I LOST THE bet. And the way I did was so unfair. Once Zander finished gloating, they told me about Tristan's meeting with Gage, and the plan they've put into motion.

While I still have my doubts, and worry for my friend's safety, I agreed to be part of it. Mainly because we're out of options and time.

Gage sent word to Ethan and Lucas in Paris of Freya's nymph snipers, and in turn, they've reached out to Mags, Ireland, and Ryker, so they're all on alert. I know they all can protect themselves, but it doesn't ease my fears. I love them all.

Tristan walks into the living room. Following closely behind him, like a puppy, is Maria, his housekeeper.

She's a pretty, young, Hispanic woman, whom he relies on to run his house, as well as for his mere survival, since he doesn't cook. Or shop. Or clean, which of course she loves.

The first time we met, we didn't exactly hit it off.

I don't trust her. She has secret feelings for Tristan.

Today, her shiny, straight, black hair is pulled into a professional bun, making her seem even more beautiful and petite than the first time we met, which makes me hate her.

Tristan smirks, seeing me eye her with suspicion.

"Serena, you remember Maria?" he asks, amused.

"I do." I stand and hold out my hand, which she sneers at but takes for show. "It's nice to see you again."

"Likewise," she fakes.

"Maria dropped off some groceries for us."

"Great. Thank you."

"All of Tristan's favorites," she smirks at me.

"How," I pause, "thoughtful."

Maria grabs Tristan's hands in hers and smiles up at him brightly. "I have to go, but I'll see you tomorrow. I wish you nothing but happiness. Freya is a lucky nymph."

At the mention of Freya's name and the wedding I cringe. He hugs and thanks her before she takes her leave.

Once she's gone, his eyes meet mine.

"Still jealous, raindrop?"

"Jealous? No. Suspicious and mistrustful? Yes."

He bites down on his bottom lip trying not to smile, and immediately my eyes zoom in on his mouth. Desire floats over me, and the sudden need to taste him consumes my thoughts. His mere presence awakens every nerve.

Tristan takes a step closer.

"What are you doing?" I whisper.

"Approaching you." His tone is low, lulling.

This is a game he likes to play.

One where he stalks me like he's a lion and I'm his prey.

Always wanting to devour me.

He prowls toward me slowly, so I won't spook and run.

"Stop," I plead, barely audible.

"I can't, raindrop. You're giving me sexy eyes again."

"Am not," I counter. But I am. I totally am.

Tristan smiles at me, coming closer. Once there's no space left between us, the back of his hand runs down my cheek.

The cool metal of his rings sets off warm sensations within me. In one movement, he grabs my waist and tugs me to him, forcing my hands to clutch his forearms while his body lines up against mine.

His fingers dig into my sides as he leans forward.

I feel his breath on my lips as he whispers, "Caught you."

I suck in a sharp breath.

From under my lashes, I see his lids are hooded.

Someone needs to walk into the room and stop us from what we're about to do. I'm sure Freya is close by, watching.

At the thought, I jerk back, moving quickly away from him. A frustrated noise rumbles from his chest at my sudden withdrawal. From a few steps away, I watch as every muscle in his neck tenses and strains while he catches his breath.

Ten seconds later, Zander enters the room, and relief washes over me.

"Hey," I greet him.

Zander grants me a small smile before his focus shifts to his brother. He watches him with an overprotective expression and military stance, as if ready to strike out if need be, at anything or anyone that might attack Tristan.

"Branna will be here shortly," he reports in a dull tone.

"Thanks." Tristan replies.

"Gage also wanted me to let you know, and I quote, 'The nymphs shadowing Serena's friends at the Academy have taken their last breath.' As have the ones at Notre Dame," he adds.

"That was fast. How did he find them so quickly?" I ask.

Tristan's eyes darken. "He's well connected."

His words are meant to be final. I exhale a deep, grateful sigh of relief that my friends are safe. "Thank you both."

Without warning, the air in the room shifts, and a pretty woman about our age materializes. My eyes rake over her porcelain skin sprinkled with a layer of light freckles.

She has waist-length hair, which is a vibrant, reddish-orange color. And poufy. I mean, untamed, crazy curls are flowing out of her head everywhere, in disarray.

She blows a strand out of her face before her grassy eyes take us in and she pulls her peach lips in a friendly smile.

"Beannú," the stranger greets in Irish and waves at us.

"Are you Branna?" Tristan's tone is full of distrust.

"Aye," she answers with a bright smile.

"The Maleficium witch?" he confirms.

"Aye," her kind smile widens.

Tristan shifts next to me protectively. "No offense, but you seem a little too cheerful to be studying dark magic and sorcery. You look more like a magical leprechaun."

Within seconds, Branna's expression turns from light and airy to fiery and dark. "For the record, I speak and understand English just fine," she admonishes, with a heavy Irish brogue. "And leprechauns are evil little bastards. I don't appreciate the insult," she huffs. "And here I thought it was only Nassa who had a stick up her skinny little arse."

Zander sidles up to her. "Zander," he winks at her.

"Control yourself," I hiss at him.

"What?" He gives me an innocent look. "Accents are hot."

"What Tristan meant to say was thank you for coming." I apologize on his behalf for his rude behavior. "And sorry, for that." I point to Zander, who's giving her puppy eyes.

"You are the one I am to glamour, then," she smiles.

"I am."

"Strong-willed. Vocal. A fighter you are. I'll do it."

"Wait," I stop her from approaching me. "I need to know how all this is going to work before you just . . . spell me."

The brothers exchange a glance before Tristan locks eyes with me. "The real Freya was taken last night. Gage gave her a taste of her own medicine by drugging her. His team went in while she slept and quietly removed her from the castle. A stand-in that Branna glamoured to look like Freya slipped in and stayed in her place. She'll remain in the castle until you take over, so as not to create suspicion."

"Where is Freya now?" I ask.

"The witches of the Black Circle are keeping an eye on her until after the ceremony tomorrow," Zander replies.

"She's unharmed and comfortable," Tristan adds.

"The glamour is the easy part, Your Highness. I conjure a simple spell, and to the outside world you will look, speak, and act like Freya. Only you and Tristan will be able to see the true you beneath the façade," Branna says.

"Why Tristan too?" I ask.

"Your bond. It means that you and he are the only two beings that can see the real you—all the time. No matter what," she points out. "Even dark magic can't trick a link."

"How long does it last?" Tristan interjects.

"Forty-eight hours," the witch replies.

"Are there side effects?" Zander inquires.

"No. You will feel like you, Serena, only look like Freya. It will wear off as fast as it comes. Aye?" she replies.

"Is that enough time?" Zander asks.

"It should be," Tristan answers. "Once Serena becomes Freya, we go through with the ceremony tomorrow. We allow Oren and the dark army to attack. And end this. Once and for all. The realm and our family will be safe. As will Serena." He turns to me, taking my face between his hands.

"You sure about this?"

"Yes."

"Let's get it over with then."

Zander steps in and hands two photos to the witch.

One of me and one of Freya.

Branna smiles brightly and steps closer to me, taking my hand and leading me into the kitchen. With a few ancient words muttered quietly in chant, a flowerpot, a saucer, soil, and a watering can appear on the counter.

"All right, Serena. Firmly pack the soil into the pot," she guides, and I do as she instructs. "Next, place the image of Freya onto the soil." I do. "Now, pour the water onto the photo until it is completely wet and her image fades."

I pour while she chants next to me. Within seconds, the outline of Freya begins to disappear from the photo and I hold my breath. I keep watering until the soil turns to mud.

"Good girl," she encourages. "Do you see how the saucer is branded with your image?"

"Yes."

"You must pour the mud onto the saucer until the image is completely covered," she coaches.

Once my picture is hidden under the wet dirt, she guides us over to the sink and runs the faucet.

"Now, at the same time you wash away the mud from your photo, you need to picture Freya in your mind, aye?"

"Okay." I place the saucer under the water stream and watch as the dirt mixes with the clean water and swirls as it disappears down the drain.

The entire time, I picture Freya.

"See your current appearance draining away harmlessly into the earth. The image in Serena's mind is the image that she shall find," Branna chants next to me, on repeat.

"What in the realm is going on here?" Queen Ophelia's angered voice filters in, causing me to jump and drop the saucer into the sink. It shatters against the steel.

We turn our attention to the irate queen and the warrior standing by her side. Rionach stares at me, a question in his eyes.

Zander inclines his head, and the rest of us mirror the respectful gesture to the queen and her husband.

Ophelia's eyes find mine and widen, which has me nervous. Immediately, Tristan steps in front of me.

"What are you two doing here?" he asks.

"Looking for you, Tristan," her tone is stern.

"Me?" he questions.

"I feared you had forgotten that you have a wedding to attend tomorrow, as I have not seen you since you ran out of your engagement gala the night before last. An unattractive pattern you seem to have picked up as of late, this . . . disappearing from realm celebrations held in your honor, leaving behind your betrothed."

"Apologies, mother, I was just—"

She holds up her hand to stop him. "Don't bother. I know what you were just," she says, giving him a pointed look.

A heaviness falls and lingers among the group.

"Where is Serena?" Rionach asks in a rich voice.

I move around Tristan and my lips part to speak, but Zander's wide-eyed stare stops me, suggesting I shouldn't.

Tristan clears his throat. "Serena sends her regrets. She was summoned back to the Academy due to the sudden and unexpected deaths of the chancellor and his secretary."

Queen Ophelia flattens her hands on her stomach and pales. "A most unfortunate occurrence for the protectors."

"Yes, well—" he trails off.

"And who is this, son?" Rionach points to Branna.

Zander slides over to the witch and takes her hand.

"This is Branna, a friend. She will be joining me tomorrow for the wedding in Serena's absence."

Queen Ophelia steps over to Branna, who offers her a toothy smile. "Your Majesty, it is an honor," she says.

The queen eyes her. "What realm do you hail from?"

"Ireland. I prefer the human realm over the supernatural ones," she replies.

The queen's unimpressed eyes shift to Zander. "Please tell me that a second courtship will not be asked of me."

"No, Your Majesty. Branna and I are just friends. My heart belongs to a very special gargoyle." His statement is meant to allude to me, but I know he means Magali.

Ophelia steps in front of Tristan and me. "Freya, we missed you at your fitting this morning."

Her brows rise, perplexed by my silence.

Zander and Tristan both cough.

I guess the spell worked and I now look like Freya.

Awesome.

And super fucking weird.

"Princess?" Ophelia attempts, and I flinch at the title.

Seeing my reaction, the queen's eyes narrow. I curtsy and stumble to recover. "Apologies, Your Majesty."

"Are you all right, Freya? You don't seem quite yourself."

Rionach steps to the queen's side and smiles down at me with a quick wink. "I'm sure she's fine. Just a bit nervous about tomorrow's events. Isn't that right . . . Freya?"

I nod, grateful for the rescue.

The queen's gaze stays on me for a moment before shifting to Tristan. "Walk me out, son."

"Of course," he waves his hand for her to go first.

Rionach follows closely behind them. They step onto the front porch, leaving the door open slightly, and with my heightened hearing, I listen in on their final exchange.

"You will be present tomorrow, won't you?" she asks.

"Yes, Mother. I'll be present at my own wedding," Tristan replies, in an almost teasing manner.

"Rionach, dear, may I have a moment with my son?"

"Of course." He disappears, leaving them in privacy.

Ophelia faces Tristan, her expression downhearted yet maternal as she places her palm on his cheek. She leans in so that she can speak in a soft tone. "Hear me now as your mother, and not the queen. You must take care, my brave son, or you will bleed for a girl who will never be yours."

WE STEP FORWARD, UNDER THE CANOPY of a thousand branches, and take in the sight in front of us. I breathe in, telling myself that this is not a trick of my eyes, but reality. An army of warriors stand before us, spanning as far as the eye can see.

Their swords are drawn as they stand at attention, waiting to follow their commander into battle. To fight for their realm and bleed for their king should the need arise.

Behind us, a stirring in the air rises, making itself known. Something blacker than the darkness that appears when war is on the horizon. The veil of gloom holds firm, alerting me that the dark army is close by, ready. Waiting.

"May I introduce the Lion Guard," Tristan says.

"Your army is insane," I quiet my tone. "Why are they called the Lion Guard?"

Zander points to Tristan. "They protect the lion."

"The lion is the Paris clan of gargoyles' symbol," he explains, with his gaze on his army. "My blood may be mixed, and I may not carry the lion on my back, like Gage, but Rionach wanted me to have a connection to the lion. In my heart, at my core, in my blood, I am a gargoyle."

His words stir a hunger within me. He turns his head and looks at me, but doesn't react. He only stares back at me with the same look of desire I have for him, our eyes locked.

Tristan's scent hovers heavily in the air. A warm breeze wraps me in his scent. I want him. I long for him to touch me so much that it aches. My skin tingles everywhere as his eyes roam over my body before landing back on my gaze.

"For fuck's sake, would the two of you stop? I'm standing right here," Zander whines, pulling us out of the moment.

A shaky breath escapes me as Tristan and I both turn our attention back to the mass of men and women below us.

"What does Rionach think they're doing out here?"

Zander chuckles. "Practicing safety drills and formalities in preparation for your big day tomorrow."

I feel Zander's turn on eyes on me. "B-T-W, I'm not going to lie, champ, it's creepy that you look just like Freya now."

I narrow my eyes. "B-T-W, it's just for show. I'm still me."

"So, if I grab your boob, is it your boob or Freya's?"

I sigh. "Mine. Still. Me."

He smiles wickedly. "Just checking."

"Branna get back to Ireland?" Tristan asks Zander.

"Yeah. She'll be back tomorrow, just in case the spell goes wacky and Serena shimmers back into, well, Serena."

"Let's hope that doesn't happen," I shiver.

"You two do realize that tomorrow is a real wedding?" Zander points out. "Flowers, guests, champagne, vows, etc. If you're still you, won't you two technically be married?"

My pulse jumps nervously at the idea of being married.

I hadn't even thought of it as a possibility before.

"Just pointing out the obvious," Zander winks.

"Leave us," Tristan demands.

With a knowing smile, Zander shakes his head, amused, and runs off into the sea of lion guards awaiting his command.

Panic crawls up my throat at the thought of what will happen tomorrow, and suddenly breathing is hard. I close my eyes and try to draw in air, but it's not working. Zander is right. If I say the vows, even glamoured as Freya, technically I—me, Serena—am the one marrying Tristan. Fear suddenly grips me.

"Breathe," Tristan whispers in my ear.

"I can't," I barely manage to say.

"Serena," he says, but his voice feels far away.

All of a sudden, I'm overcome with the need to escape.

The desire to run away—from him, the glamour, the realm, everything—wins out and without thought, I turn.

Unsure of where I'm going, I stumble through the forest and ignore the sound of Tristan's voice calling for me.

Instead of stopping and waiting for him to catch up, I keep moving forward. After a while, I tire and clumsily trip over a large branch, falling face first into a section of the forest floor that is covered with heavy dark brown mud.

Worn out and overcome with apprehension, I drop back into the muddy earth and wait, knowing he's approaching.

I feel him before I even look up, his presence hovering in the air. My lashes lift, and he watches me lay in the wet dirt with no expression on his face.

"Your response to the idea of marrying me was . . ." Tristan pauses, searching. "Unexpected."

I lift my mud-covered arm and drop it over my face, hiding from him. No doubt the mud is now smeared all over me.

"I'm scared of frogs," I mumble.

"I know that."

"It's why I don't like fairytales."

"Not surprising."

"I can be insecure at times."

"Not a shock."

"I'm very stubborn."

"Not new information."

"I hate pizza."

"Well, clearly, that is a reason not to get married."

"I leave wet towels everywhere."

"I have a housekeeper."

I lift my arm and glare at him for mentioning Maria.

He smirks. "Are you done yet?"

I push up and lean back on my elbows.

"I'm not even me. I'm spelled to look like someone else."

Tristan crouches down and unsticks a mud-covered strand of my hair from my face. "All I see is you, raindrop."

I open my mouth to respond, just as his lips slam against mine. The force causes him to slip in the mud. Without releasing my lips, his arms drop to either side of me, preventing the weight of his body from crushing me.

I fall back onto the ground, spreading my legs so his body can settle between them and cover my body with his.

The moment our lips touch, every fear I was holding on to fractures, replaced by a raw, basic desire to claim him as mine. My mouth is desperate as it glides across his. His full lips are demanding. Heat travels through me, down my spine and between my legs. I shove my mud-covered hands into his hair, pulling him closer to me, and yet, it's not enough. His tongue slips past my lips and an animalistic moan escapes from my throat. He reacts immediately to the sound, his own dirtied fingers digging into my hips, drawing me into his body as our kisses turn from needy to frantic. The damp, wet earth cools my overheated skin.

My legs clamp around his waist, the mud making it hard to keep a firm grip on him. I feel Tristan's hands under my ass, lifting me up into a sitting position, while he continues devouring my mouth. He stands, lifting me with him. My legs tighten around his waist and my arms wrap around his neck as he flattens me against the smooth trunk of a tree.

Through his jeans, I can feel him hard and ready. My body responds by arching into him. At the reaction, he releases a low growl, and the world around us just disappears. Suddenly, I can breathe again. The panic is gone, replaced by the feeling of being home.

His hands move under my skirt, cupping my ass. I lift my knees higher, the heel of my knee-high boot catching on one of his empty belt loops. His lips withdraw from mine, but stay close enough so that his heavy breaths fan my face.

Warm fingers slide under the fabric of my panties and my eyes roll back at his touch. He kneads my ass cheeks, and steps farther between my legs, lining us up perfectly.

Tristan leans into the crook of my neck, biting and licking, and I lose all sense of myself as desire surges and my fingers drop to the top of his pants, unbuttoning them.

I slip past his boxers, my fingers finding the length of him. At my touch, Tristan's groans are loud and deep. My fingers glide over the silky, smooth, warm skin, and he pushes me harder against the tree with each stroke.

His fingers dig into my ass in pleasure.

Seeing his reaction to my touch makes me feel powerful.

"Fuck." His voice is thick and full of need.

As my hand explores him, he takes in staggering breaths. He pushes the lace fabric of my panties to the side. I draw the tip of him to me and his forehead meets mine, his eyes focused on me as his hands slide over the back of my thighs, pulling my knees higher. The leather of my boots rubs his upper arms, and the material of my flowing skirt bunches on my thighs and drapes over my legs.

In one thrust he's inside me, and my head falls back, hitting the smooth bark on the tree. My mouth falls open to make a sound, but nothing comes out. Without moving his body, Tristan lifts a hand and tucks a piece of my muddy hair behind my ear. His head dips lower. His mouth is so close to mine it taunts me. His hand grazes the inside of my thigh and I shiver under his touch, filled by him. My hands skate down, landing on his ass, the muscles flexed under his skin.

I gasp into his mouth as he claims mine again. My fingernails dig into his skin and my muscles tighten around him, pulling him farther and farther in. Everything in me is bursting with need for him to move. And then he does.

Without pulling out, he dives deeper inside me, hitting my core. I arch against him and my body clamps down on him, greedily accepting the depth to which he buries himself inside of me with each thrust. I let him take me, against the tree, out in the open, over and over again, for anyone and everyone to see that he's claiming me.

It's sweaty. It's aggressive. It's almost brutal in the way our hands grab and our bodies fight to get closer and take more of one another. It's perfect. It's beautiful. It's us.

He moves at a calculated pace, building friction and pleasure. With each thrust, he dives harder and deeper. With each thrust we claim one another, feeding our bond.

And when my body flutters and spasms around him, gifting me release, I scream his name and it echoes across his realm.

The sound causes him to find his own release. Even as the last spasm runs through him, he remains inside me. For a few moments, we both just stand here, breathing heavily and covered in sex, sweat, and dirt. I feel boneless.

My hands run over his lips and face, smudging his skin with black, and I notice the amount of drying mud on me.

"I'm so dirty," I pant out.

A cocky grin appears on his swollen lips.

"Yeah, raindrop, you certainly are dirty."

FIFTEEN
QUIET MOMENTS

TRISTAN

DARKNESS HAS DESCENDED AND I'M ON edge. Without waking Serena, I sit up, throw my bare legs over the side of the bed, and stare out the glass doors onto the lake. Tonight, the moon seems larger and brighter than it ever has before. It's almost as if I can reach out and touch it. Even its reflection off the water seems grander and more intense.

Serena sighs softly in her sleep. I look over my shoulder and take her in, admiring how the silvery-white glow streaming in through the doors lights up her pretty face.

Slowly, I move my fingers, tracing along the edge of her cheeks and jawline, soaking up the feel of her skin against my fingertips. Two of my fingers glide over her neck, and I stop to caress the pulse beating calmly on the side of her throat. Nothing will ever compare to the feel of her life steadily pulsating under my touch. Nothing.

Today there was a tangible shift between the two of us. It went beyond sex. It went beyond wanting what we shouldn't. There is a simple acceptance now that it's not her or me, it's us. Good or bad. We're finally in this together no matter what the outcome might be. We're a team. Equals.

Her eyes flutter open lazily and she gazes up into my eyes with a sleepy, glazed look in hers. With my thumb I brush under one, noticing for the first time the cognac flecks spreading within the sapphire blue. My chest squeezes.

"Hey," she breathes out, and all I can do is stare at her.

This beautiful, smart, fierce, stubborn, strong protector is mine. Truly mine. In every sense of the word. And what's more, I am hers. She owns me. Every fiber in me is hers.

Picking up a piece of her soft hair, I twirl it between my fingers. "Go back to sleep, raindrop," I breathe out quietly.

"You okay?" she asks with a soft voice.

Her fingers reach out and lightly trace the tattoo of her decorating my upper arm. Her gentle touch shakes my core.

"No," I rasp.

A frown crosses her lips and she pushes up, resting her head on one elbow. She leans forward and plants a gentle kiss on my back. "What's wrong? Are you uneasy about tomorrow?" she asks, her fingers running down the skin on my spine. My muscles spasm under her caress. "If so, don't be. You have a royal gargoyle protecting you. You're safe."

I ignore the tease. "I'm not worried about the attack."

"Then, what?"

"I'm worried about you."

"Me?"

Silently, she sits up and slides closer to me. Her uncovered legs fall on either side of me, caging me in as she presses her chest against my back. Once she's comfortable, she rests her lips on my shoulder and her hands on my biceps. The cotton of her tank top is soft against my exposed skin, and my body soaks in the heat coming off her.

"Talk to me," she whispers across my skin.

My eyes focus on the inky, star-kissed sky, with her wrapped around my body, cocooning me in a safe embrace.

"You freaked out earlier. And while the ancient protector vows won't be said tomorrow, the satyr ones will be. It might be for show, but for me, it means something."

She stills. The even breaths that were tickling my skin are gone as she holds her breath. I wait, knowing she's processing.

"What are you saying?" Her voice is barely audible.

"That someday, I want you. This. Us. Forever."

Serena falls silent again for what feels like an eternity.

I can feel her thoughts waging war in her mind.

And I wait.

Her heartbeat picks up, and I swear it echoes throughout the room. Her silence is palpable in the dark.

Just when I decide to give up on this conversation, her hands tighten on my shoulders. She pushes up on her knees, twisting so she can swing her leg around me. Seated now on my lap, she leans closer and her flowery scent wraps around me. I don't hold or touch her. I let her cling to me as she needs.

My eyes focus on the pulse beating a mile a minute at the base of her neck. Suddenly, I long for the steady beat from only a few minutes ago. Her hands settle on the sides of my neck, her thumbs running over the scruff on my jawline, coaxing me to look at her. And when I do, my breath escapes me.

"When we are ready to take this step, and make forever promises to one another, I want to be surrounded by friends and family. With both the woodland priestess and Sora, the leader of the Spiritual Assembly of Protectors, blessing us." She shifts closer. "When we mix our bloodlines for the final bond, we will both be gargoyle and nymph. We'll be one and the same. As will our blood. One."

I brush the back of my hand across her cheek.

"I would rather have hope with you than certainty with anyone else. You deserve everything. All of it, raindrop."

"As do you . . . one day."

"All right. Tomorrow will only be about ending this."

Serena looks down at my lips, taking in a deep breath.

She leans in, leaving no space between us, and tenderly places her lips on mine. I don't devour her mouth like all our past kisses. This time, our lips remain unmoving in a sweet, meaningful touch. A promise for her. A lie for me.

The dawn brings war.

Blood will be shed.

Lives lost.

And the truth is, I can't promise our one day will ever come.

SIXTEEN
ACTS OF WAR

TRISTAN

FAR TO THE EAST OF THE woodland realm's borders, there is a stirring in the air. A writhing and shuddering force waits to strike at any moment. I sense it. The Lion Guard senses it. Hell, even the realm is shaking today, trembling with fear.

An impending war hisses with rage and stands in the shadows. I gaze across the library at Serena. My mother and Freya's ladies are fussing over her. They're all talking over one another in quick statements, bustling about. They believe her to be, and see her as, the water nymph princess.

Her calm eyes lift and lock onto mine. I can't help but notice the red highlights in her auburn hair as she's bathed in sunshine. For a moment, I just stand here and admire her.

Feeling my mother's stare on me, I shift my gaze to her. The queen is watching me with a crestfallen expression. I incline my head toward her and with a small, sad smile, she nods back to me before her gaze shifts to Serena. Or Freya.

"The humans believe it is bad luck to see the bride before the wedding," Rionach states, sidling up to me.

"A myth, like their fairy tales," I reply, watching Serena.

"It's a strange thing," he says, smiling at my mother.

"What's that?"

"How a being can hate another so passionately, yet in the next moment, love them so fiercely." He tilts his head, staring at the side of my face. His words are meant to ruffle me.

I don't return his glare, for fear he'll see my unease.

"You look at your bride with love, son," he throws out.

Fuck. My gaze shifts, locking onto his.

He offers a polite smile. "And no longer with distaste."

"Perhaps my feelings have changed."

"Perhaps." He lifts a shoulder. "Or perhaps, my dear boy, you're getting what your heart really wants. No?"

I don't answer. He knows. Shit.

Rionach grants me one of his paternal looks.

"I need to go check on your brother and the Lion Guard."

"Why is that?" I feign ignorance.

Rionach turns and places a hand on my shoulder, squeezing affectionately. "I've been around for a long time, son. And while you boys are men, you two have been scheming with one another since you were small children." His hand taps my cheek with admiration. "I love that you two are closer than blood, but I'm not stupid. Did you and your brother think I wouldn't notice my army preparing for battle, or sense a Maleficium witch in the realm?" He gives me a pointed look. "I did not become commander of the queen's army by lacking attention to detail."

He knows. Everything. I open my mouth to defend our actions, but he shakes his head once, warning me not to.

"Oren has been planning to take over this realm for years. He saw your love for Serena as an opening. I'm guessing he's made a deal with the dark army and they threaten our borders today. Your brother is a good general. The army will be ready to fight and protect. Believe in him," he says.

"Does my mother know?"

"If she does, it's not at my word."

"I'm sor—" I try to apologize, but he stops it.

"Trust in our world is hard to come by. Over the years, I've tried to be the best father to you that I could, while protecting the realm, your mother, brother, and you. I love you as if you were my own, Tristan. Your actions here show me that your faith in me is not as strong as I had assumed. Something for us to work on in the future, son."

I dip my chin in understanding.

He isn't mad, because Rionach never gets upset.

He's disappointed. With a brief kiss to my temple, he drops his mouth near my ear and whispers, "I don't know what you three did with Freya, but after today, make sure she is returned to her realm, unharmed. You owe her that."

"I will."

He nods and leaves the room to find Zander.

I exhale and catch Serena's questioning look. I shake my head, letting her know that everything is fine. It will be.

THE SUN IS WARM AND SHINING brightly, coating the ceremony in its glowing rays. Vernal purple and cream flowers, draped from the blooming canopy above the guests, sway in the breeze.

The colors are mirrored in the rose petals dotting the grassy floor. Vernal purple evokes sadness within the nymph community. When Freya chose it, we all questioned it. Now it just seems fitting, on this solemn day, for it to be so prominently displayed around us.

I pull at the collar on my white dress shirt, pretending to be the nervous groom, as my eyes roam around the realm, seeking out danger. My mother and Rionach are seated in the front row. Oren sits at Rionach's side and Lily at my mother's. Zander and Branna are seated behind them.

In our world, the father of the bride doesn't walk her down the aisle. She presents herself of her own free will.

Trepidation chokes me as I look over the hundreds of unsuspecting guests, some of whom may get caught in the cross fire of battle. Once again, I am forced to make a choice.

Fight.

Or run.

I close my eyes, trying to mask the pain at my choice.

I'll fight.

Because of my honor and respect for who I am and what I am destined to become. It's time to let go of who I was and step into a new reality, a new life, because some stories don't have happily ever afters. At the thought, Gage crosses my mind, and I realize all those months ago that is what he was trying to tell me.

"Tristan," Gage's voice deepens before I teleport. "It's not allowed. She isn't yours. Don't start a war over her."

I motion my chin toward Nassa and slide my gaze toward Gage. "Enjoy living in your happily ever after."

Gage scoffs. "I'm not the happily-ever-after guy."

Nassa's expression falls the slightest bit at his words.

In this moment, it truly sinks in.

I really am Gage's son.

In more ways than just a shared bloodline.

My hands shake at my sides. I open my eyes and all I see is Serena standing in front of me. And I take a breath.

She isn't wearing the dress Freya chose, but instead a long cream gown that hugs every curve of her perfect body. Some type of lacey material, with large flowers in the design, hangs over the entire dress and cascades into the grass. The thin straps holding the fabric to her body are designed to look like branches. I keep my eyes fixed on her.

Serena smiles and everything around me fades away.

All I see is her. My heart pounds in my chest as she steps to my side. The sound of it beating erratically echoes in my ears. I may stroke out right here, in front of everyone. Our hands touch and I notice hers are warm, not clammy, but confident, as strong fingers wrap around mine.

The nymph priestess begins reciting a message from the deities, followed by greetings and ancient Greek words.

We are asked if we were here of our own free mind and we both remain silent, saying nonverbally that we are.

Everything is going smoothly and quickly. I am halfway through my vows when the air shifts.

"Until death do we pa—" I don't finish.

A veil of darkness moves in, hiding the sun, draping the forest in black. Guests begin to panic, get up, and are ushered out quickly by members of the guard we staged in certain areas, hoping for the least amount of innocent casualties as possible. Zander barks orders as more of the guard storms into the area, ready for battle.

The sounds of violent stomping, chanting and loud battle cries has us motionless. The Diablo Fairies. They slide out of the shadows in the forest, between the trees, as they perform their rhythmic body slaps and choreographed march into the mostly empty ceremony area.

When they are in place, they stop and stand at attention.

I search the tribe for Kupuva, their leader, but she isn't to be found. I glance at Serena; she's noticed this as well.

"She isn't here," Oren stands and narrows his eyes.

"Who?" I ask, pretending not to know.

"Let's not play games. The dark army is under my command. Kupuva would have been here, but, sadly, Serena isn't. Therefore, she was needed elsewhere," he snarls.

My heart sinks, knowing he means the Academy. That is where they think Serena is. I hear her growl behind me but don't risk looking at her. We need to focus on the realm first; we can worry about the Academy later.

Oren claps maniacally, delighted at the scene in front of him. "Wonderful timing," he praises the army. "Tristan, I believe you were about to say, 'until death do we part,' which might come sooner than you think," he threatens.

My mother and Rionach step in front of Serena and me.

"What is the meaning of this, Oren?" she demands.

"My apologies, Your Majesty, but plans have changed," he replies. "My daughter will no longer be marrying your son. I realize it's late notice. But I simply cannot allow my only child to wed your mixed-blood mutt of a son."

The queen takes an angry step toward Oren, but Rionach steps up and grabs her arms, holding her back.

"Freya," Oren holds his hand out to Serena. "Come."

Serena looks at me for a moment before dipping her chin and going to him. Oren pushes her behind him, thinking she's his daughter. Serena's fierce gaze locks onto me.

"There, now everyone is in place," he says, excited.

My mother narrows her eyes at him. "Are you planning to take over my realm, Oren?"

"Isn't it obvious, Your Majesty?"

Rionach releases his hold and my mother lifts her chin.

"If you want my realm, you will have to go through me."

"My dear Ophelia," his voice becomes deadly. "I plan to."

The sound of metal knives sliding against each other comes quickly, as Serena drags her daggers out of her bouquet, tossing the flowers to the ground and wrapping her arms around Oren, placing the weapons across his throat. I smirk, seeing the gargoyle warrior use her speed.

"FREYA!" Lily screams. "What are you doing?"

Oren's wide-eyed stare falls on me. "Where is my daughter?" he seethes.

"What are you talking about, Oren?" Lily screeches.

"Tell the army to retreat, or your life ends," I state.

"WHERE. IS. MY. DAUGHTER?" he yells.

"You have ten seconds before you bleed out," I reply.

A chill races up my spine at the way his expression turns pleased. As if he planned this all along and we're just playing along. Oren no longer looks scared. He lifts his chin and smiles wickedly, a response that has me on edge.

"My son gave you an order, Oren," Rionach barks.

"Ophelia," Lily pleads. "Stop this."

"Five seconds," I bite out.

Oren falls silent and I nod my head.

Serena's daggers slice across his neck, deep. Crimson liquid seeps out quickly, as Lily shrieks next to her husband.

Within seconds, his lifeless body falls to the ground.

Lily turns to Serena, who is still glamoured to appear to everyone as Freya, and looks at her with fear. Her eyes roam and search her daughter's gaze before they fall on her heaving chest and then drop to the blood dripping off her downturned daggers. Confusion appears to flow through her.

"What have you done, Ophelia?" she whispers.

"Lily," my mother says calmly, and steps toward her.

"No," Freya's mother snaps, before bending down and grabbing Oren's sword, pointing it at the queen.

Rionach slowly steps forward. "Lily. Calm down."

Lily looks between the two. "How could you?" she demands, the hand holding the sword shaking in fear and anger. "I was your most trusted friend. Your lady. Your confidant. We had a plan. I safeguarded your secrets. All of them." Her eyes slide to me, before locking back on my mother. "For years, I protected you. Your son. Your realm. And this," she waves to Oren's body, "this is how you repay me? My loyalty? Where is my daughter?"

My mother's expression turns regal. "I did not kill Oren. He did this to himself by threatening my realm. Look around you. He's brought darkness to my borders. An act of war, Lily. He was so hungry for power and control that he made a deal with the devil. That was not my doing."

"It wasn't supposed to be like this," Lily whimpers.

"I know. I'm sorry. I will help you and Freya. I swear."

Slowly, the empress lowers the sword, and we all relax our stances. At the last minute, she changes her mind, turning the steel blade on herself. "You can't help me; you've become weak," she whispers, and before anyone can stop her, she runs the weapon through her own heart.

"LILY!" my mother cries out, and stepping toward her, but Rionach once again steps in and holds her back.

A few moments later the empress's body collapses next to her husband's as she chokes out her last breath.

The queen covers her mouth in shock and sadness.

Under my lashes I see Zander, motioning with his chin to the dark army. They still need to be dealt with. With no one to command them, they can't attack first. Hating what I am about to do, I give him a slight nod and he instructs our army to attack.

Almost on cue, large droplets of water fall from the sky. The rain hits the forest floor at the same time the armies collide in the middle of the open space. The sounds of blade against blade echo around me.

I yank off the black tailored coat I had on and pull my sword from its sheath behind my back. When my fingers clasp the handle, my arm dips with the weight of the metal. I widen my stance and heave up the blade, gripping it tightly, ready to fight. Serena's determined gaze meets mine before she turns and begins to fend off the dark army.

Zander's face glows with delight, rejoicing with every strike his weapon makes against the enemy. He was born to fight, to defend and protect.

The rain begins to fall fast and hard, muffling the yelling and death that starts to surround us. I lick the rain falling on my lips, feeling the fire in my gut to fight and protect. A demon comes at me, barely giving me a moment to respond, and I swing my sword, ending his existence quickly. Another follows on the heels of the first, and meets my sword on the backswing. This cycle repeats over and over again. I lose track of how long they advance or how many of them I run my blade through.

After what feels like hours, I swivel around to check on Serena and see her on the other side of the field, matching me demon for demon. She moves and glides through the battle like a skilled warrior, her daggers in her hands as she inserts them in each being that attacks.

With each of her strikes, pride comes over me.

Another demon comes at me. "Come on, prince. Afraid to fight me?" I grit my teeth and barrel forward, slamming it into the ground. Its sword goes flying into the mud now building on the ground. The demon dives for the sword, but I step on the weapon and kick it away before running my own blade into the back of its neck, ending the creature.

Serena catches my eye; I watch her let out a cry as a demon jumps on her and pins her to the ground, straddling her. She rotates her arm and stabs the demon upward, felling it. Instantly, she rolls out from underneath it and stands, facing me.

Even with speckles of mud and black tar-like blood covering her, she still looks gorgeous.

Calm begins to surround me as I look around and take in what's left of the battle. Whatever demons remain, they are now retreating, back into the forest.

The fact that Kupuva and the other half of the army aren't present tells me they didn't expect us to fight like this. Oren probably thought we'd just hand over the realm.

I take in the carnage. Splattered on vernal purple and cream flowers is the demons' black, tar-like blood, mixed with the crimson blood of the nymphs. I look around and see that, for every five or so demon bodies lying dead, a nymph was lost.

Sadness turns into fury. The roar inside me fills every place that I feel pain at the loss of my kin.

A loud female scream comes from behind me, and every hair on the back of my neck stands up. As if everything is in slow motion, I turn just in time to see Rionach step protectively in front of my mother, at the same time as one of the demon's raised axes slices through the air and connects with Rionach's neck, lopping his head off.

"No!" I draw out in a scream and run toward them.

Zander and I approach at the same time, his sword going through the front of the demon, and my sword going through the back of its body, crossing inside its heart.

The demon falls as my mother's shocked gaze lifts and locks onto mine. With a desperate wail, she throws herself on Rionach's lifeless body.

Zander I both lock tearful gazes, not yet knowing this act of war just changed the future of our realm and our lives.

Forever.

SEVENTEEN
GOODBYES

SERENA

A MORBID SADNESS HAS BLED INTO and settled across the once vibrant realm. It feels the same as when a deep freeze seeps into the humans' world. Coldness and gloom crawls into every living thing. Every flower petal, each blade of grass, all the leaves, everything in the land has turned dull and lifeless. It feels as if when Rionach was killed, the realm's spirit disappeared along with his existence.

The castle is no longer warm and filled with life and light. It's cold, damp, and dreary. It's mourning. Along with all the beings in it. It's a shell of what it once was.

After the battle, Zander and Tristan carried Rionach's body back to the castle. The queen followed regally, but all signs of life had disappeared from her. She's numb.

The moment we stepped into the castle, Ophelia began her husband's funeral arrangements, as well as arrangements for the guards who were lost during the battle.

Standing in the castle entryway, I watch as the staff move about quietly and solemnly, so as not to disturb the ghosts and emptiness filling the halls. Freya's mother was right about one thing: it wasn't supposed to be like this.

Witnessing this terrifies me. The possibility crosses my mind that this is what it would be like if it were Tristan who was taken from me, after I'd loved him so hard. My eyes fill with tears, as I question whether I'm worthy of his love after all this.

A throat being cleared pulls my attention.

"Apologies for the interruption, Your Highness," the page says, Freya's glamour now gone. "The queen requires your presence in her chambers."

I dip my chin and follow him to Ophelia's doors. He opens them, letting me into the darkness, and closes them behind me. I inhale. Black fabric now drapes over the mirrors and oil paintings, covering them out of respect for the queen's bereavement.

Ophelia stands by the window. A sliver of light shines on her black satin dress, giving the appearance she's spotlighted on a dark stage. She looks too young and beautiful to be a widow. Sadness clogs my throat.

"Your Majesty," I croak out. "You asked to see me?"

Ophelia doesn't look at me; instead she studies the realm from the window. When she speaks, it's low and clear.

"I see the glamour has worn off."

I fall silent and still at her words. She knew?

She turns to me and offers me a pitiful look, then turns back to the window. "You flinched, in my son's cabin when I called you princess. I knew at that moment."

"Oh."

"Oh," Ophelia repeats, void of emotion. "Take comfort. That is not why you are here, Serena. Though, it should be," she adds, harshly. "You and my two sons have shown a great deal of courage this week."

"Thank you, Your Majesty."

She sighs. "You've also shown a great deal of stupidity."

I flinch.

Ophelia swallows a few times, having difficulty speaking. Her hands flatten on her stomach as she inhales twice, composing herself, before straightening her spine.

"War. Death." She squeezes her eyes closed before opening them. "These are the burdens, Serena, that come with the royal titles we carry. Men and women give their lives so that we may rule." She turns and faces me with a pale, drawn look, and tears in her eyes. "Love has no place when you become queen. It blinds you. It changes how you reign. And most of all, it makes you weak. A lesson I'm afraid Tristan has learned the hard way. As have we all."

"Weak?" I whisper. "I'm afraid I don't understand."

"You see, Serena," she takes a step toward me. "Oren would never have overthrown me. Our realm is too strong. The emperor lacked the army that my husband built and commanded. Oren was power-hungry and his ego got in his way on more than one occasion. Over the years, Oren was nothing more an annoying nuisance. A pest who, after his daughter's wedding, was slated to die by wine poisoning."

I ponder her words and my brows draw together.

"Freya was Oren's only heir and female. The rules of the water realm state that she is required to have a king by her side to reign. It's archaic, but realms' decrees are just that—decrees—which we must follow and respect."

Unable to speak, I stand motionless.

Ophelia takes another step toward me.

"Tristan's marriage to Freya would have allowed her to become queen of the water realm and rule with her mother's guidance. Lily happened to be a very good friend of mine over the years, as I'm sure you are aware of now. There would have been peace. The realms equal. She and I had been planning this before any of you were even born."

Ophelia takes the final step in my direction, leaving no space between us. With a sad smile, she takes my chin in one hand, tilting my head to the side, and with the other, she brushes my hair over my shoulder, exposing Tristan's mark. When she sees the insignia, she inhales. "It is true."

"Yes, it is." I speak the words quietly.

"Lily and I thought it was a perfectly laid out plan, really." She steps back and releases my face. "One that Tristan never wanted any part of. As children, Freya would chase him around the castle and forest. Lily and I delighted in seeing this. Until one day, Rionach pointed out—" she stops again, taking a breath at the memory. "He pointed out that Tristan was in actuality running away from Freya, not trying to make her catch him. As he got older, Tristan's pull to something unknown outside of the realm grew. We thought perhaps it was his protector blood calling to him. After his brief stint at the Academy, and with Gage, we knew it wasn't. Still, he yearned for something. After you joined our son the first time in our realm, my husband saw it. He said Tristan was in love with you. Perhaps I didn't want to see it, knowing our plan was in motion to dispose of Oren. But then, that night you walked into the party, and your bond severed, I saw it. Plain as day on his face. And yours. Your love for one another. It was blinding."

I exhale slowly and watch a tear escape her eye.

"So, you see, love has everything to do with this. The two of you have rewritten your fates. And that is commendable. The mother in me, Serena, wants to hold you and tell you to love him until your last breath, as I do."

"And the queen in you?" I ask, already knowing.

Her hands lift and wipe the tear away, and with one deep inhale, her face becomes expressionless. "As queen, I cannot allow the future heir to the throne to have weaknesses." My eyes meet hers. "If you truly love him, you will let him go."

A LIGHT MIST FALLS HAUNTINGLY FROM the gray sky into the lush realm. The trees lift and stretch their branches, embracing the droplets, grateful to be quenching their thirst. I inhale the smell of fresh rain. It's been too long.

Tristan steps onto the balcony and takes the few steps to stand next to me. Leaning his elbows on the railing, he stares at the cloudy canopy that has settled over his realm.

"The rain will always fall." He opens his hands and waits for a few droplets of water to collect and pool in the middle of his palms before he shows me. "We can either collect the raindrops and hold on to them," he opens his palms and lets the water fall to the earth below us. "Or we can release them, and let them be free to do what they are meant to."

The undertones in his words give his statement a deeper meaning. His cognac eyes linger on me. I want to tell him I love him. To hold on to me and not let me go. Before I met Tristan, all I wanted was to be free of who I am. Now, all I want is him. And yet, the irony of all this is that if I hold on to him, it's he who won't be free to become whom he must.

My knees go weak. A hard lump grows in my throat, making swallowing impossible as my deepest fears slam into me, clawing at my gut—I'm leaving, him, forever.

"I'm leaving," I say, my voice falling into a whisper.

His expression is distant. "I know. Your things are already packed and your suitcase is by the door downstairs."

"I need to get back to the Academy." My voice is coming out fragmented and soft. "My clan was pissed I put myself in harm's way with the dark army. Once again, they're disappointed with my lack of commitment and consideration to my title and position with the protectors."

Tristan exhales and stares at nothing and everything.

"I wish—" I start and his eyes hold mine.

"You wish what?"

My breath catches and I have to wait a moment before I can respond. The sheer desolation in his gaze is too much.

I part my lips to tell him, but then change my mind.

"How is Zander?" I ask, refocusing the conversation.

He stares at me for a long time, searching and waiting before he sighs and answers. "Sad. Lost. Angry. We all are."

Tristan is silent as he studies me. The coldness between us is heavy. My nerves rattle around, clenching my chest.

Everything is uncomfortable and awkward between us now. I hate the sudden distance between us. I feel like we're broken and I can't put us back together. I fidget with my protector bracelet, rubbing my fingertips over the stones.

He focuses on my squirming. "Look at me," he demands.

"I am looking at you."

"No, raindrop, not like that."

"I'm staring right at you."

"No. You're staring through me."

He stands straight and cups my face. "I don't want you to just see me. I want you to look at me the way you did yesterday, and the day before that. Like you're trying to climb inside of me, craving the safety and security of being one with me. I need you to need me. Where did you go?"

"I'm right here."

"No. You're miles away."

"I just—"

"You just what, raindrop?" He steps closer, his lips a sliver from mine. "Tell me."

"I can't," I barely manage.

It hurts saying the words out loud; it hurts more than I realized it would. Without thinking about what I'm doing, I move forward and brush my lips against his. Our kiss is soft and sweet, just a tease. Tristan's hands tighten on my face as the kiss becomes heated and urgent. It's pleading.

He's asking me to stay.

To be his.

The realization causes a ripple of fear to run though me, recalling Ophelia's words. She's right. I make him weak.

I jerk away from him and hug my stomach as I take in his confused expression. A sad smile crosses my lips.

"I'm sorry. I can't," I whisper, and start toward the door.

Tristan grabs my elbow and spins me around, his face in mine, his breath fanning me. Without a word, he places his palm against the base of my throat, reading my conflicted emotions. He eyes search mine for answers.

I just stand here, letting him do it, knowing he needs to.

"You're so fucking stubborn," he spits out.

"Tristan."

His darkened gaze drops to my bracelet. "My father just died. And you're running away from me." He steps back and pins me with a cold glare. "Someday, you will trust in me."

I stand there staring at him for a brief moment before bowing my head and, with a sigh, forcing myself to move toward the door. Taking one step at a time. With every inch of space that I put between us, I feel my heart crumble.

Right before I walk inside, his hoarse voice hits me.

"I told you once before, I don't like to repeat myself. Let this be the last exception. I'm going to let you go. Let you walk away right now. Not because I want to, but because I have to. But you and I—we aren't over. We've just begun."

My heart tears into a million pieces.

"Goodbye, Tristan," I say quietly.

"See you around, raindrop."

EIGHTEEN
DARKEN THE HEART

TRISTAN

MY HEART IS SHADOWY, WHICH IS nothing new, but today, it's the pain of loss that has darkened it. Loss of the ones I love.

Rionach.

Serena.

Even my mother and brother are shells of the beings they were before Rionach was killed. Death is nothing new in my world, but that doesn't mean it hurts any less, or that it doesn't further darken one's heart. Mine is now black.

Merciless rain pelts the realm, the gloomy day matching my gloomy mood. It hasn't stopped fucking raining since Rionach died and Serena left. The spongy wet ground sinks beneath my heavy boots with each step I take.

With purposeful strides, I make my way to the Celtic cross marking his grave. A few last steps, and I find myself in front of the large, gray stone. Crouching down, I wipe away the blades of freshly cut grass that are sticking to it.

With a heavy heart, I run my fingers over the engraved words Rionach had chosen: *In love, he found peace.*

I close my eyes as the sting of fresh tears threatens. I'd let him down—so many fucking times. Yet, he continued to love me like I was his own son. He believed in me. Loved me. Taught and fought for me. Unconditionally.

And here I am, about to disappoint him all over again.

Even in death.

With a hard, ugly sniff I wipe away an escaped tear.

"I'm sorry. I know—" my voice cracks. "I know you'll be disappointed in me, again. It's my pattern with you lately."

I stare at the stone marker for a long time, internally speaking to him. Wishing things were different. Thanking him for loving me and my mother. Asking that in death, he watch over all of us, as he did in life. Apologizing for my shortcomings and failures, both past and future.

"If I could do it over again, I would have . . . I would have been a better son. A better warrior. A better being. Now, it's too late. And we are cursed to roam the realm without you."

"For what's it worth, I don't think he was as disappointed in you as you think he was," comes a smooth voice behind me. "On the contrary, I think he was, and is, proud of you. Of who and what you have become, Tristan."

My jaw tightens at the gargoyle's intrusion, as I stare at Rionach's final resting place. "Your opinion is worth nothing to me. Don't pretend to know anything about him."

"I might not know about you, or Rionach, or your relationship with him, but I certainly know about death, loss, pain, and a dark heart. I know the shadows that follow you when you feel it was your fault. I know the suffering of living without someone you love, and the constant internal battle to be better after their death than you were during their life."

I keep my eyes trained on the gravestone. The irony of this

moment weighs heavily on my heart. The only father I've known and loved is in the ground, while the one I've never known looks over my shoulder, offering me comfort.

Standing, I turn and face Gage. Since losing the love of his life, his mate, Camilla, he has done nothing but mourn and suffer at his own hand in her name.

"Is that why you're always dressed in black?" I ask with an even tone. "Because you're still mourning her?"

He stares at me for the longest time before answering.

"Yes."

I hold his gaze. "Are you ever going to stop?"

"No."

A weird feeling settles in my chest at his answer. It's warm, caring, and worry—for him. And I fucking hate it.

"Camilla has been gone for a long time, Gage."

His eyes slide to Rionach's grave. "I know exactly how long she's been gone, Tristan. Do you want to know why? Because every single night that I live in this shithole of an existence without her, I pray. I pray that if I do good, if I try to be a better being, try to love and heal, that I will be allowed to reunite with her again when I'm gone from this fucking hell I live in. Eight thousand seven hundred sixty-two days. You want it in hours? Two hundred ten thousand, two hundred ninety-five hours. That is exactly how long she has been gone," his tone is detached.

We stand in silence. Because what do you say that? Nothing. There is nothing that will undarken his heart. Or mine. I look over my shoulder at the writing on the stone.

"In love, he found peace," I mutter under my breath.

"In our world, they are one and the same," he responds.

"I'm afraid to close my eyes at night, afraid I'll never have peace again. My world is in a constant state of battle," I admit quietly, more to myself than to him.

Gage nods sagely. "I understand simply existing."

A few beats of knowing silence pass between us before I change the direction of conversation to why he's really here.

"Did you bring it?" I ask.

"Yes."

I hold out my hand.

"Are you sure?"

"Yes."

Gage hands over the package to me.

"Thanks."

"They aren't going to like this."

"They don't get a say." The rain becomes heavier and the wind angrier. "Not anymore, anyway."

"I can't protect you if this goes badly," he adds.

I take in a deep breath. "It won't."

He exhales heavily. "It will. Be well, Tristan."

"You too."

With a final nod, Gage teleports, leaving the space he was standing in empty. I might be a grown man now, but there is something comforting in the fact that Gage is in the world if, and when, I need him. I laugh at the thought.

His bloodline is a part of me. One that I have fought every waking minute of every day to keep buried under my nymph blood. Both filled with honor and duty, but only one was considered tainted. Only one followed me, haunted me.

Only one festered in the darkest parts of my core.

Ever since Serena St. Michael blasted her way through the walls I built around my darkened heart, that bloodline has climbed its way to the surface, demanding attention.

Demanding acceptance.

Demanding I embrace it.

Demanding in love, I find peace.

NINETEEN
COMFORT THE GIRL

SERENA

S OMETHING DAMP AND SLIGHTLY MOLDY-SMELLING IS thrown at my face with force. I moan and without opening my eyes, my fingers pluck whatever it is off and toss it to the floor.

The sound of hands clapping angrily forces me to attempt to slowly open my lids. They flutter for a few seconds before a gray, coffee-flecked stare narrows in my direction, aimed by the petite gargoyle staring at me.

I growl at her and pull the blankets over my head, sending me back into the darkness I've been in for weeks.

My annoyingly persistent, nonverbal best friend and roommate tugs the blankets off me, and then walks around the room, opening the curtains and letting the insanely bright sunshine into my bedroom, causing me to squint.

She snaps her fingers at me, her version of growling.

"I'm up. I'm up!" I yell when she continues to snap.

Her slender arms fold over her chest as she waits for me to get my ass out of bed. Throwing my legs over the side, I look down at the towel pooled by my feet and then to her.

"You left your wet towel on the bathroom floor—again!" she scolds me, signing each word with her hands.

"So, you decided to throw it onto my face?"

"Yes."

"Wow, Mags, super childish," I counter.

She rolls her eyes at the ridiculous statement, because we both know I'm the childish one. Magali glares at me.

I frown. "You could have at least let me grab a cup of coffee and fully wake up before you sign-yell at me."

She huffs and continues to yell at me in sign language.

I ignore her ramblings. "What time is it anyway?"

Magali pins me with a glare, but when her eyes lock on to mine and she sees how bloodshot they are from crying, her hands stop moving through the air angrily and she gives me a sympathetic look. Her pity just annoys me more.

"Noon," she replies.

"Great." I pick up the towel and walk to the bathroom.

Magali stands in the doorway watching me as I throw the towel into the washing machine with a dramatic flair.

I shoot her a sarcastic smirk as I shut the door, then sign swear words at her through the back of the door.

She knocks twice, letting me know she knows I'm cursing at her, before I hear her bare feet pad down the hall.

With a heavy sigh, I walk over to the sink, turn on the faucet, and splash cold water on my face. My gaze lifts and I look at myself in the mirror as the water drips in streams off my face, reminding me of rivulets of rain on glass panes. *Come on Serena, you're stronger than this.*

Rain.

Tristan.

I inhale and lie to myself. I tell myself I did the right thing. It was my only option. Tristan is where he belongs, in his realm. And I am where I belong, at the Academy.

I splash another round of water on my face, grab a fresh towel, and gently pat my skin dry. As I do, I stare back at myself in the mirror the entire time. The cognac flecks that have appeared between the deep blue of my irises have spread. It's jarring. Hopefully, it will wear off with time.

After I brush my hair and teeth, I throw the towel on the floor. The instant it hits the tiles, Magali knocks twice on the door again, startling me.

I mumble under my breath at her ridiculous ability to know what I am doing, and snatch the towel off the floor, contemplating placing it back on the sink before I decide to throw it in the washing machine.

Adding a few more items, I turn the machine on and just stand in front of it. I watch the fabric twirl and spin inside the soapy water. Numb. That's what I am. Unfeeling.

Since returning to the Academy, my friends look at me like I'm a wounded puppy. Even Ethan and Lucas stayed with me that first month, holding me every night, one on each side, taking turns letting me cry on their shoulders.

After a while, they had to return to Notre Dame, their protector assignment. Then Ryker and Ireland stepped in.

They mainly treated me like a child. They fought over what and when I should eat, sleep, and get fresh air. The entire time Magali just watched from the sidelines, nursing her own heart. Zander hasn't visited her since Rionach died. Although she's handling it a million times better than I am.

I inhale and ignore the brokenness inside me. With every ounce of strength I have, I open the door and walk into the kitchen in our suite. Magali hands me a cup of coffee and I offer her a small smile before taking a sip and moaning in pleasure. She places her mug down so she can sign to me.

It's her favorite cup. My dad gave it to her for Christmas because Magali always gets annoyed when people assume because she's unvoiced that she can't hear them. It says *I can still hear you, dumbass.* I smile at the memory and mug.

"You can't sleep in tomorrow, Ser."

"Why not?"

"A new chancellor has been appointed to the school and all protectors are required to attend a meeting tomorrow in the main office."

I frown. I knew my family was searching for another gargoyle to take over Chancellor Davidson's position, but I wasn't aware they'd found someone. It's been two months since my Uncle Keegan stepped in temporarily, acting as the head of the Royal Protector Academy. To be honest, I'll be glad when his rough, grumpy ass returns to London.

"You'd think my mom or dad would have warned me."

"Especially Abby, since she calls eight times a day."

"She's gotten better, it's only four now."

"Only because Callan keeps hiding her phone."

"True. He keeps putting in the same spot though, so . . ."

We both fall into a laughing fit at the thought of my parents and their insane, childish behavior with each other.

It feels good to laugh. To be home. To be normal again.

"Do you miss Zander?" I ask quietly.

She shrugs. "His dad died, Ser. He needs time to come to terms with the loss and find his place in the realm. I'll be here when he's ready."

I admire her strength. "He's lucky to have you."

She winks. "I know."

"I'd hug you, if you didn't hate hugs."

"I do," she nods.

"And public displays of affection."

"Yup."

We fall silent again, lost in our thoughts.

"Want me to lick you instead?" I ask.

"No," she laughs.

"How am I supposed to show you my love for you?"

"You could pick up your wet towels."

"Wet towels symbolize love to you?" I ask in disbelief.

"No. Wet towels not on the floor expresses love to me."

"Fine. I'll work on it."

"And that's why I love you back."

The door to our suite swings open, and Ryker and Ireland stroll in, champagne and chocolate in hand.

"We're here to comfort the girl," Ryker announces.

"Which one?" Mags and I say at the same time.

He stops and looks around, his dark brows falling over his eyes. "Shit! I'm officially the only one left standing."

"What do you mean, Ry?" Ireland asks.

"I'm the only guy left." He heads into the kitchen, mumbling to himself about needing more male friends.

Ireland drops onto a stool and flicks her strawberry blonde ponytail over her slender shoulder. Her gray, emerald-flecked gaze shifts to me, while Ryker puts the champagne in the fridge and the chocolates on the counter.

"So," she says.

"So?" I repeat.

"Who is the new chancellor?"

"Oh." My eyes shift to Magali. "I don't know."

"What do you mean you don't know?" Ryker questions, walking around the island and sitting on the other stool.

Mags makes and hands each of them a cup of coffee, then opens the box of chocolates and bites into three before deciding she's found one she likes. The other halves are returned to their positions within the box. No one responds to this. It's her way; we're used to it. Ryker will most likely eat the other halves. It's this weird habit they have together.

"I just found out there is a new one this morning."

"What?" Ireland shrieks. "How is that possible? Your family runs the Academy, Serena," she points out.

I bite my lip. "Well, they're not exactly . . . pleased with me. You know, after what I did." I don't meet her eyes.

Ryker pins me with a look. "What you did?" he parrots. "You mean, leaving your assignment and running off to the woodland realm? Or are they pissed that you hung with a Maleficium witch who glamoured you?" he ticks off.

None of my friends were amused by my actions.

"Oh, I know," Ireland says, excited to join in. "They're mad that you tried to steal a groom from a bride who went all psycho and killed Henry." She adds, as if this is a game.

"No, wait," Ryker interjects. "Their anger must stem from the fact that you schemed and placed yourself in the middle of a dangerous battle, with the dark army that is trying to end your existence, all while killing an emperor."

I sigh at the two of them. "I was there. You don't need to point out the week's events to me. I remember, vividly."

"Shit!" Ireland exhales. "You did all that in a week?"

"Imagine what she can do in a month," Magali adds.

"Hey," I say defensively. "Zander helped me."

Magali's face turns sad, and instantly I feel horrible.

"Sorry, Mags. I didn't—"

She waves me off.

"Anyway, my clan is upset—at all of it. The only member of my family who is speaking to me is my mother. And that is through secret text messages and voice mails, reminding me to brush my teeth and eat broccoli."

Ryker shivers. "Broccoli. Yuck."

"They haven't entirely cut you off. I mean, your sexy and stoically hot uncle has been acting as the Academy's temporary chancellor," Ireland mentions brightly.

"I'm sitting right here," her boyfriend retorts.

"I see you." She smiles flirtatiously. "But I also see him. A lot."

I roll my eyes. "Uncle Keegan isn't the warmest. And watch how long you gaze upon him—my aunt Kenna will spoon out your eyes for looking at him with anything other than hatred or disinterest."

"Why is she bitchy?" Ryker inquires.

"Maybe she needs a puppy," Ireland suggests.

"She'd probably kill it. For being cute. And lovable," I respond. "Anyway. None of them are speaking to me."

"If you had to guess, who would you think they'd appoint?" Ryker inquires, sipping his coffee.

"I don't know. They've always talked about replacing Henry with someone from the Irish or Scottish clans if he ever retired. My guess is it will be someone like that."

"Old and female would be good. Then maybe my girlfriend won't be ogling her," Ryker blows out.

"Or maybe I will," Ireland teases back.

My gaze roams over Magali, who for the first time in three years hasn't flinched or looked crestfallen at the mention that Ryker and Ireland are together. A tightness seeps into my chest. She must really like Zander if she no longer cares.

"I didn't say old, or female. I said Irish or Scottish."

Ryker plucks the half-eaten chocolates out of the box, popping them into his mouth. He chews and swallows.

"Take comfort ladies, we'll find out tomorrow."

TWENTY

BACK TO YOU

TRISTAN

THE SUN IS BARELY ABOVE THE horizon when I push open both french doors leading out onto the balcony and step outside. Brilliant bursts of orange and yellow flood the whole skyline as the sun rises from the horizon. The weaving shadows draping the wooded land disappear, replaced by beams of warm light streaming through the forest.

I inhale the early warmth of the morning air as my eyes roam over the picturesque landscape. A light breeze sighs through the land, awakening the foliage and vegetation. The emerald blades covering the ground bend and shift.

I don't understand how someone can see the beauty here and not crave it day after day.

For a moment, at least, the world is quiet.

The clock inside ticks and then chimes.

I step back inside as the doors to my office open and Maria walks in with a cup of coffee in hand. She presents it to me and places a plate of fruit on the paper-covered desk.

"Thanks," I grunt at her, grateful for the caffeine.

She frowns. "You looked like you need it."

She's right. I rolled out of bed this morning and got into the shower, hoping it would aid in waking me up. It didn't.

Maria looks around, disgusted. "This place is so dusty. You've been holed up in here too long. Want me to clean it?"

I look around and shake my head. "No. Leave it."

She pins me with a stern look. "Other than to sleep and shower, you haven't left this room. You have twenty-four more hours. Then I'm coming in here and taking care of the mess. It's what you pay me for. And for the record, it smells like death in here," she adds, and I place the coffee down.

"Fine." I go to pick up the drink, but her words stop me.

Maria gives me a sad look. "Are you sure you want to keep isolating yourself like this, Tristan? Is this," she waves around my office, "where you want to hide away?"

I ignore her and harden my expression.

"Rionach's death wasn't your fault. Queen Ophelia and your brother would hate that you're doing this to yourself."

With a sharp exhale, I look to the doors. She's right.

"When they arrive, direct them in here," I clip out.

She sighs and dips her head before leaving me alone. I sink into the leather chair, staring at the closed doors.

Frustrated, I scrub my hands down my face, wishing Zander were here with me.

I know why he isn't, but still.

The sound of the clock ticking fills the room again.

And I wait with the ghosts that linger in the shadows for the shitstorm that is about to go down as I grab the file and open it. A photo of Serena stares back at me.

"Everything comes back to you," I whisper to her.

Noise from outside my door draws my attention. I close the file and throw it onto my desk with the rest of the paperwork I've been studying for the past week.

I remain seated as Maria opens the doors and lets everyone I've summoned enter. They're speaking in hushed, curious tones, no doubt wondering why I've called them here so early. As they enter, each looks at me with surprise.

All but one.

Who is late.

Twenty minutes later, the doors open again.

"Miss St. Michael, it's nice of you to join us this morning," I welcome from behind Henry's desk.

At the sound of my voice, she freezes and pales. Her sapphire gaze lifts and locks onto mine as her lips part.

"Um," she manages, and I smile at the familiar conversation we're having.

"My favorite word of yours," I reply, as I did before when she had the same reaction to my being a professor here. "As you are aware, I don't like tardiness. Take a seat."

Confused, Serena looks around before staring at her friends, who are smiling at her. They've been here for a while, and I've already given my speech to all the protectors on assignment here. They all know why I am here.

"What's going on?" she whispers, stumbling over to Magali and sliding into an empty seat next to her friend.

Magali lifts her hands to sign. "Tristan is the new chancellor of the Royal Protector Academy, apparently."

Serena's gaze darts around the office, in complete shock.

I keep my expression blank as she processes.

She presses her lips into a flat line. "Wait, what?"

"If you had arrived on time, you would have heard my speech and been fully briefed," I snap out. "The rest of you may leave. Miss St. Michael, stay seated," I demand.

In shock, Serena watches the other gargoyles who have been assigned to the Academy as their protection duty stand and leave. They respectfully incline their heads or shake my hand as they head to their morning posts and watches.

When the last protector has left, I close the door and lock it, swinging my gaze to her narrowed one. She's silent.

"Chancellor?" her voice questions, and my tongue gets stuck to the roof of my mouth. "What the hell, Tristan?"

My expression remains blank as her eyes hold mine. All of a sudden, she bolts out of the chair and begins pacing in front of the desk, nervously fidgeting with her bracelet.

"You can't be in charge of the protector academy if you are planning to be king of the woodland realm someday."

"Then it's a good thing I'm not planning to be king of the woodland realm someday."

She abruptly stops and faces me, without a word.

After a second, I take a step in her direction.

She takes a step back, putting space between us.

Unable to help myself, I stalk toward her, closing each stretch of space she's grasping for. Eventually, she bumps into the desk, and curls both hands around the ledge, leaning onto it. I slam my hands on the top, trapping her in my arms, and lean in, my lips almost brushing hers.

"Your silence isn't helping here, raindrop."

"I don't understand," she breathes across my mouth.

"I've renounced the throne," I speak clearly.

Her stare bores into mine, as if she's trying to find the untruth in my statement. Unfortunately for her, she won't.

"I don't believe you," she whispers.

"I didn't ask you to believe me."

"Why? Why would you give up your birthright?"

"For you, because it all comes back to you."

Serena sits back farther onto the desk, as if she can no longer stand and needs support.

"I never asked—I mean, I never wanted you to."

"I know."

"What about your realm? Your duties?"

"Zander is going to step into them."

"And your mother?"

"Is pretty pissed off, but she'll get over it."

"Zander. King?" She blows out.

"Given his pure satyr bloodline, my brother will be a better king to the realm than I could or would have ever been. He understands the realm's needs. And honestly, at his core, Zander is a far better being than I will ever be."

"No," she replies sharply. "He is not."

"He is. For the simple reason that he doesn't live with the darkness of the gargoyle blood running through his veins."

"Your mixed bloodline doesn't make you inferior."

"Don't you see? I no longer belong in that world."

"Because of what you perceive to be tainted lineage?"

My eyes hold hers. "Because of my love for you."

I push into her space so our chests are touching, and she closes her eyes and takes in a deep, shaky breath.

"My clan won't allow it."

"They already have," I mutter across her lips.

Her eyes snap open and the cognac flecks woven into the sapphire color blaze with recognition of me being hers.

"How?"

"Gage. He went to your uncles and father on my behalf. Explained the need for me to explore my gargoyle lineage and let them know that I was renouncing the nymph throne. After a few days of questions and seeking out my true intent, it was agreed that I would be allowed to take my rightful place within the Paris clan, so long as I proved myself as chancellor of the Academy. And as your royal protector."

"My uncles and father agreed to that?"

"No. Your mother and aunts did. Forcing their hands."

She pinches her face. "Even McKenna?"

A smile tugs at my lips. If she only knew. "Kenna fought hardest."

"For us?" She inhales the breath I've exhaled.

"For us."

"You've forsaken everything, for me?" she confirms.

"In your love, I find peace."

Serena's lips touch mine and with a groan, my hands dig into her hips, lifting her so she's fully sitting on the desk.

Assaulting her mouth, I step between her legs so our bodies align. Her lips are wicked, promising me all things dangerous. Suddenly, I feel like I'm drowning and I cling to her body harder, to prevent myself from completely falling under. My hands slide up her sides, causing her body to arch against me as she squeezes her thighs around me. I push into her and she gasps at the sensation. Fear and barriers are no longer attached to the way we kiss—only temptation.

My body buzzes with awareness and my blood surges with the need to claim her, and to have her claim me. To complete our bond.

I slow our kiss and with everything in me, pull away. She groans in protest, and I swear the sound is more erotic than it should be. I fight the instinct to throw her on the desk, rip her clothes off, and get lost in the warmth of her body. Instead, I step back, putting some space between us.

"Where are you planning to stay while here?" she asks.

"At the chancellor's house—"

"Or, you could come home with me," she cuts me off.

"Home?"

"To your home. Where I am. Our suite. We need a third room-mate anyway, to help with the pizza and beer, bills and stuff . . . ," she rambles and trails off, waiting for my answer.

I smile at her tease.

"I have a condition," she breathes out.

I raise my brows. "What's that, raindrop?"

"Maria has to go."

"Jealous?" I ask, already knowing she is.

"Yes. You're mine. The End."

"Done," I reply without hesitation.

Serena stares at me for a moment. "Tell me this is real," she pleads. "I'm afraid that this . . . unknown shadow is going to descend on us and take you from me. Leaving me alone."

My fingers stroke her cheek as I stare at her intensely, allowing my thumb to run across her bottom lip. "Trust me," I whisper, "nothing is going to happen to me, or you."

TWENTY-ONE

FATED

SERENA

THE FARTHER THE SUN SINKS IN the sky, the eerier and darker the nightfall is. My gaze roams over the trees. I'm suddenly chilled, feeling like thousands of eyes are hidden in the forest, watching me. I'm on edge; my plan has to work.

The silence of the campus steadies my breathing and my mind, making me believe that my eyes are just being cruel and attempting to make me see something that isn't there.

I remind myself there is nothing to fear. Not with Tristan by my side, which he is now. He's finally mine.

Inhaling, I relive each moment and word spoken today. I'm still in shock he gave up his position within the woodland realm and his rights to the throne.

Even stranger, Queen Ophelia agreed to allow him to renounce his birthright. I'll have to figure out a way to change his mind, to fix it. He can't walk away from what he is fated to rule. Tomorrow, I'll take him back to the woodland realm, so that everything goes back to the way it should.

Warm, strong arms wrap around my waist. I close my eyes and lean my head back on Tristan's shoulder, basking in the protectiveness and sense of happiness I feel with him near. I just want to hold onto this feeling forever.

His lips are at my ear. "You okay?"

I nod, afraid if I speak he'll see right through the lie.

"Magali is still on watch for another hour," he whispers, and my heart leaps with excitement and anticipation.

This—this is what I've been waiting for all afternoon. Secret moments in one another's arms. The chance to hear him tell me he loves me as he slides into me, and secures the bond between us as it was fated to be by the deities all along.

He turns me in his arms so we're face to face.

"You've been quiet all afternoon," he points out.

"I'm just happy. That we're finally together again."

The intensity in his stare is unnerving. I feel like he reads me too well. The way he's watching me forces me to control every single facial expression and breath I take, hoping to fool him into believing this is real. I'm real.

He takes my chin between his fingers, lifting my face.

"What is it?" I ask.

He's staring at me, trying to gauge something. After a few moments, he shakes his head and smiles at me, easing my fears. "Nothing, it's just, your eyes are more sapphire in the evening's light. Earlier, they felt . . . warmer, I guess."

I close my eyes, knowing he's staring, trying to get a sense of where I am and why I am acting differently. Gods.

Reopening my lids, I smile, as the air shifts next to us and Zander appears out of thin air. Tristan is slow to release my gaze, but finally does, shifting his focus to his brother.

"I see you've still got your hands on my girl," Zander accuses, and I stiffen, unsure of his meaning, or how to act.

"I think we established that Serena is mine," Tristan replies, with an easiness about him. One I haven't ever seen.

Zander snorts. "So you've chosen then, champ?"

An odd silence falls between the three of us.

"Serena?" Zander prompts in an even voice.

"What?"

Tristan and Zander both look at me with odd expressions.

"I mean," I catch myself. "Yes. I choose Tristan." I release a hollow laugh, hoping to seem calm and controlled. Feeling uncomfortable under their scrutiny, I shift on my feet and look up from under my lashes at Zander. "What are you doing here?"

Zander's gaze slides to Tristan. "I'm here to see Magali." His voice is gentle, almost hesitant. Concerned.

I smile. "How lovely. Did she invite you?"

"Ah," Zander begins to answer. "No. Then again, she never does. Hey, is something going on here between us?"

I bristle. "What do you mean?"

"Listen, champ, I know I haven't been around lately, but with my father's death, and you know, having the throne thrust at me un-expectedly," he narrows his eyes in annoyance at Tristan, "I've been preoccupied. If Mags is upset with me, that's between us. I get it, but you don't have to be mad at me too. I'm under a lot of pressure here."

My brows pull together. "Why would I be mad at you?"

Zander exhales. "Well, she's your best friend. Isn't there some sort of girl code? If one is mad at a boy, the other is?"

"I'm not aware of such a code," I reply.

Tristan steps in front of me and takes my face between his hands. "Zander will work things out with Magali and since she won't be back for a bit, let's go inside and relax until she does return. Then we can . . . chat a bit."

I pout. "No."

He rears back as if I slapped him. "What?"

"I mean, I just want some alone time with you," I seduce.

Tristan's expression and tone turn hard. "Alone time can wait. You seem a little tired and off tonight, Serena."

I stare at him. He's waiting for me to say something, but I have no clue what he wants me to say, which causes his mouth to frown, and me to swallow in panic. I suck at this.

"BEER!" a male voice yells from within the suite.

Zander rubs his hands together. "Ryker's here."

Ryker steps onto the balcony and does some sort of hand-shake-greeting thing with both brothers.

"It's good to see you both. It was getting a little girly up in here for a while. No offense, Ser," he winces.

"None taken," I reply.

"Chancellor, are we cool to have some beers together?" Ryker asks Tristan. "I figured now that you and Serena are together, that makes us more like friends than employee and boss."

"I like the sound of that, man," Tristan smiles.

We enter the suite and the guys run over to the pizza boxes and beer. Zander leans in and whispers something to Tristan that I can't make out, and I stand here, lost and annoyed that I'm running out of time.

"Ser, can you grab us some napkins?" Ryker asks, and I roll my eyes, begrudgingly stepping into the kitchen.

Once there, I look around for a few moments before Zander sidles up next to me. He leans over me and opens a drawer to my left, pulling out napkins, and I smile at him.

"You okay?" His tone is off and his face is serious.

"Fine." I quickly reply, and move to step around him.

Zander's hand snaps out and he grabs my elbow, stopping me. He leans into my ear and speaks low.

"Remember that time you let me touch your boob?"

My gaze lifts to him in question.

"Why don't we sneak into the bathroom and you allow me to feel you up. I'm dying to hear those sounds again."

A blush creeps up my cheeks at the way he's speaking to me, and

I fluster. "Zander, whatever happened between us before can't happen again. I'm with Tristan now."

Zander tightens his grip on my arm. "Just tell me one thing, champ," he pops his *p*. "How devilishly sexy do you really find me?"

I exhale, racking my brain for the right answer.

"I've always thought you were very sexy, Zander."

"Is that so?" he questions in an odd tone.

"Yes," I assure him, so he'll leave me alone.

Before I can blink, the napkins are on the floor and Zander spins me, pulling my back to his chest and pressing a knife across my throat, causing me to scream out in both surprise and fear as I meet Tristan's and Ryker's gazes.

"What the hell?" Ryker stands and steps toward us, but Tristan places his hand on Ryker's chest, stopping him.

Tristan looks at Zander with nothing but respect and suddenly, I'm confused. Shouldn't he be stopping this?

"You were right," Zander growls. "She's glamoured."

"What are you talking about?" I grate out.

Zander leans close to my ear. "Serena would slap the shit out of me at the mere mention of touching her boobs. And never once did she agree I'm sexy. Even though I really and truly am. And she chose wrong."

I exhale, having been caught.

Tristan steps into my space. "Freya?"

"How did you know?" I ask Tristan.

"Serena has flecks of cognac taking over the sapphire in her eyes from our link. Mated gargoyles share eye color, and though we haven't completed our bond, the stronger our link, the more her color becomes one with mine."

"This isn't Serena?" Ryker asks, in seeming disbelief.

"No, it's Freya, glamoured by dark magic to look like Serena," Zander explains.

"The psycho water nymph princess?" Ryker poses.

"I'm not a psycho," I snap.

"You killed two gargoyles. And you're pretending to be Serena. I'm pretty sure that qualifies you under the category of mentally unstable."

Ryker takes a menacing step toward me, but Tristan places his arm out, stopping him from coming closer.

"Where the fuck is Serena?" Tristan yells.

I smile and fall silent. The knife on my throat is pressed harder and the sting of the metal against my skin causes my eyes to water. A frightened chill seeps through my skin.

Tristan leans into my face. "Either you tell us where Serena is, or I will have Zander kill you."

"You can't. You gave up your authority over the realm, and nymphs, when you denounced the throne," I reply, my tone full of spite. "If you give the kill order, you will sign your fate. And never find her."

"WHERE IS SHE?" he bellows, coming apart.

"Gone."

Tristan's icy eyes are fixed on me, narrowing and assessing me. He's trying hard not to kill me on the spot.

Zander tightens his hold on me. "How the hell did you escape from the Black Circle?"

"With help. The same help I had in making Serena disappear." I smirk wickedly at Tristan.

"I certainly don't need permission to kill you," Zander states coldly. The knife glides across my skin in the barest of touches, opening the skin with a sting, and I cry out.

"Probably not the best time to say this, but it's kind of nice being part of this guy shit," Ryker states.

"Yeah?" Zander asks, sounding pleased.

"Normally, I'm stuck feeding the girls champagne and chocolates. Murdering a nymph is kind of a nice change."

"Where is she, Freya?" Tristan's cold glare locks on me.

The emptiness in his eyes tells me that he won't let up until I tell him. So, I won't. He'll have to kill me first.

"Let's start with something easy. Who is helping you?"

This is the part I'm going to enjoy. Where Tristan finds out that for years, he's been deceived by those he holds dear.

"Maria," I choke out around Zander's hold.

"What?" Tristan asks, incredulous.

"Maria helped me escape the sorceresses. Maria helped me devise this plan. Maria helped drug Serena and hand her off to the dark army," I admit. Each time I say her name, he flinches and looks devastated at the betrayal.

"Keep talking, nymph," Ryker demands.

The high I'm getting from seeing Tristan hurt, angry, scared, and confused is making me giddy, so I decide to continue to show him how stupid he really is. "It was innocent at first. When you hired Maria to take care of you, I befriended her. I was worried that you would fall in love with her. When it became evident you had no romantic interest in her, we became friendly. She would share your likes and dislikes with me. And I listened. I learned what pleased you, knowing that someday I would be your wife."

"Holy shit!" Ryker blows out.

I ignore him. "By the time you brought Serena into the realm, Maria already felt protective of me. She shared what happened during her first visit. And her second." I wait for him to put the puzzle pieces together.

"That's how you knew about the bathroom? Maria?"

"Yes," I answer, and Zander tightens his hold.

"Keep going," Tristan demands.

"Maria never left that day that Branna came into your home. She stayed in the shadows, listening on my behalf like she always did. Watching you. Studying your patterns."

"The fuck?" he responds.

"When Maria heard you had me drugged and sent to the Black Circle, she listened and learned. Then she came to me, rescued me, and told me all about your little plan."

I swallow, because the blade on my throat is painful.

"What did you do?" Tristan asks with evident disgust.

"We drugged the coffee Maria brought you this morning. Having studied your patterns, she knew that if she spoke in circles, you wouldn't sip it. But that Serena would."

"That is why Maria suggested a morning assembly?"

I nod. "When you left Serena in your office, Maria entered, encouraging the princess to drink the coffee, since she appeared so tired from the early morning meeting. She did. Within seconds, she collapsed and I slipped in, replacing her under the glamour," I barely manage to say.

Tristan's face turns murderous. "You drugged her?"

"I did."

"What did you do with her?"

"Wouldn't you like to know," I whisper.

"What happened to you? How did you turn into this?"

"Nothing happened to me!" I shout, as much as I can. "I have always loved you this deeply. My father wanted your realm. I simply wanted you. Want you. Even after you had my parents killed, and chose her, I still want you—only you."

Tristan studies me. "You're delusional."

"I did this for you!" I shout, trying to get him to see.

"For me," he repeats, eerily calm.

"The glamour wears off, Freya," Zander interjects. "In the light of the morning, Tristan would have discovered you weren't Serena. What were you planning then?"

"By then, it would have been too late."

Tristan's eyes narrow. "Meaning?"

"I just needed you to sleep with me. To tell me once that you loved me, and then the mark would have switched to me, instead of Serena. Don't you see? You think you love her. You've walked away from your family and realm for her. But it's okay, I understand. You're under the influence of the prophecy. But if I bear your mark, you will love me in the same manner that you love her. We can go back, Tristan. With my father gone, I can rule the water realm and you the woodland in peace. Together. You will love me as you do her. I promise.

This was all for you. To show you how much I love you. Even after you've destroyed my realm and took away my family, I still love you. In time, with Serena gone, and me marked, you will love me as well."

Tristan's face softens as he nods his understanding.

Zander releases me and I take a step toward Tristan, relieved he's agreed to all of this. "With me there is peace and light. With her there is only war and darkness."

Without a word, Tristan turns, giving me his back. After a moment, Ryker leans in to make sure he's okay and the sound of metal being unsheathed fills the room as Tristan pulls out Ryker's dagger, spins, and drives it into my heart.

Tristan leans into my face. "Wherever your soul lands after this, may you go knowing that Serena is the one I am fated to be with. In her love, I find peace."

My wide-eyed gaze locks on him, as I gurgle blood and fight for breath. With every bit of strength I have left, I smile, as the glamour disappears, revealing my true self.

With my last breath I deliver my final blow to him in a barely understandable whisper, "Serena was always fated to die at Asmodeus's hand. And now, she has met her fate."

TWENTY-TWO
STONE COLD

SERENA

AFTER SEVERAL ATTEMPTS, I OPEN MY eyes, gasping, desperate for air. My body is drenched in sweat, and I try to get my mind to clear, catch up, and assemble the pieces of the puzzle that has led me here. Wherever that may be.

My gaze darts around wildly, taking in my surroundings. I don't recall how I got here. The last thing I remember is the feel of Tristan's lips against mine before my mind went fuzzy and my body shut down, slipping into darkness. The unfamiliar bed I'm lying in crushes any hope that this nightmare isn't real.

The pitch darkness of the room makes it difficult to see, and my gargoyle vision feels like it's on the fritz.

Strangely, I can't feel any of my gift's essences, or even my bond with Tristan.

Panic grips me. More so at the thought of my link to Tristan being gone than anything else. I inhale. My body feels heavy, as if I've been drugged. When I swallow, I notice dryness in my throat and the taste of coffee on my tongue.

Coffee.

Maria.

My body becomes stone cold at the thought.

The office. She handed me the coffee and I drank it. I promise myself I'll snap her neck for this the next time I see her. By the grace, does Tristan even know I'm gone? He must by now, although I have no idea how long it has been.

Low voices filter through the wall. They must be coming from another room attached to this one. A female and male voice. The language being spoken is unfamiliar to me, but I'm relieved that my heightened hearing is still intact.

An ache rolls over me as I try to force myself to sit up. My head feels as though it weighs a thousand pounds. The heaviness of it almost makes me want to pretend that nothing is happening, go back to sleep, and wait for Tristan or my clan to come save me. My heart and head, though, ignore my suffering body. Whatever fate has in store for me, this darkened room is not it. I need to fight for survival because whatever Maria is up to, it can't be good.

I need to escape before anyone comes in here. My lashes flicker a few more times, trying to clear my drug-blurred vision. Slowly, my sharp protector sight returns, allowing me to see I'm in an empty, four-walled room with only a mattress on the floor. I try to push myself up, but my arms won't comply. The pressure around my limbs is so heavy that I almost give up. Almost.

As my anxiety mounts, adrenaline spikes through my blood and with a final effort, I sit up, my breathing labored. What the hell did that crazy nightmare of a bitch give me?

I look around in a desperate search for a way out. There is no door. Only smooth walls. Damn it. I sigh and close my eyes, envisioning being out of this room. Almost instantly, I feel the warm air shift around me and suddenly, I'm sitting in a hallway, no longer in the room on the mattress.

Confused, I look around. Did I just teleport? Holy shit! How did I do that? Blowing out a quick breath, I envision my suite at the Academy. After a few failed attempts, I give up. If I want to find a way out of this place I need to focus more on escaping and not on why the hell I just teleported.

With every ounce of strength in me, I roll and push off the ground, getting myself up into a standing position. My palms press flat on the wall as my vision swims and I become light-headed. I close my eyes and take in a few deep breaths.

As I stumble through the darkness of the shadowy passage, the smell of sulfur assaults my nose. I attempt to hold onto the wall for support, but the dim bass vibrations, mixed with a loud buzzing sound coming from an overhead light, is making me even more dizzy than before.

I manage two steps before I fold over and empty the contents of my stomach in a heave on the thin, worn-out carpet beneath my feet. My head pounds and all I want to do is collapse again and shut my eyes.

Definitely drugged.

My arms and legs are heavy, and my mind is sluggish as I continue to force myself to move forward. Everything surrounding me is bathed in a deep burgundy hue. The color, mixed with the thumping sound, is playing tricks on my eyes as I search for a way out of the unfamiliar place.

A sharp pain in my face causes my hand to lift to my mouth. When I pull it away, blood coats my fingertips—I stare at the crimson color and wonder how I got a cut lip.

I can't remember.

Anything.

My knees are about to give out again, but I fight through it and keep standing. I try to take another deep breath, convincing myself that I can find a way out of wherever I am, but without signs or doors or windows my hope is becoming less and less of a reality.

Pain grabs my lungs and squeezes them. A cracked gasp pushes its way out of my broken ribs. I know they'll heal soon, but *fuck* it's painful in the now. When did I break ribs?

A steel wall at the end of the hallway catches my eye. Fighting through the agony, I manage to stagger forward, faltering with each pathetic step.

When I have only two steps left, I lunge for it and place my hands and forehead on the steel. Breathing heavily. Shit.

As I sway, I notice the cool iron under my fingers is a door. With a great deal of effort, I try to push it open.

It doesn't move. Not even an inch.

I growl in frustration, close my eyes, and focus on taking even breaths. The air around me shifts again, and suddenly I'm on the other side of the door, in a dark alley.

Cold, fresh air hits me as I stumble into the concrete alleyway, away from where I escaped. My body folds over and I throw up again in the street from all the effort I exerted. Once I'm done, I lean on a brick wall across from the door. The noise, along with the hustle and bustle of a city, echoes in my ears. I study the steel exit and notice there are no signs on it. Where the hell am I?

Adrenaline only rallies my system as I realize it doesn't matter. I'm free. I need to keep moving. "Third time's a charm," I whisper into the cold evening air, and close my eyes, envisioning a forest. Within seconds, I disappear and reappear in a park. I release a humorless laugh at the fact that not only did I teleport on command, but that I can now.

Quickening my pace as best I can, I trip as I make my way through the darkness. I hold on to tree branches as I go. They offer their protection like strong arms ready to lift me. My instinct to survive drives every wobbly step I take.

Tristan crosses my mind. He's going to feel so betrayed and deceived when he discovers what Maria did.

No matter how much my heart refuses to give up on the love that binds me to him, a sinking feeling settles in my gut that I won't see him again—ever. I chastise myself for thinking this way and keep going for a few more minutes.

Needing to rest, I collapse under the safety of a tall oak tree. Pins and needles pierce my entire body, worsening with every breath

I take. The bottomless abyss of pain devouring me from the inside makes continuing unbearable.

After a brief time out, the desperate desire to get back to Tristan makes me ignore the pain and focus on moving forward. Before I force myself to stand, I notice the scrapes and bruises on my legs.

"I wonder why I am not healing as quickly as before," I mutter under my breath to myself.

"The drugs they injected in you are why you can't heal," a velvety smooth voice answers.

My world tilts again as I look around for the voice's owner. An incredibly sexy, African American vision of beauty steps out from the shadows of the trees.

His chocolate eyes look me over with sympathy.

"With the amount in your system, you should be dead."

"Dead. Are you an angel?" I slur, fighting to stay awake.

The twenty-something guy releases a warm chuckle and his eyes twinkle as he watches me. "No. Definitely not."

The heaviness in my head is taking over as it falls back against the tree's bark and I laugh for no reason. "Do you know Lady Sequoia?" I ask, reminded of her smooth trunk.

"Not personally," the stranger replies and winks.

"Did you just . . . wink at me?" I babble, feeling drunk.

"I did. It's my thing."

Now that I've stopped running, I can't move.

Hottie steps forward and crouches in front of me before he looks around, assessing our surroundings.

"You're very brave, princess," he whispers, brushing a strand of hair off my face, "to have escaped as you did."

"I am," I agree, dazed. "B-T-W, I hate that title."

His lips pull into a small smile. "No doubt."

"I need to sleep." My eyes flutter open and closed.

His mouth is suddenly at my ear. "I'm sorry we have to do this, Serena," he apologizes, sounding sad.

My half-lidded eyes are blurring in and out of focus as I attempt to maintain my grasp on reality.

"How do you know my name?" I drone.

Another man steps out of the shadows with a syringe in his hand. He crouches next to the dark stranger and gently takes my wrist, pushing my sleeve up before turning my arm over. I don't struggle, because I physically can't.

With his teeth the second stranger pulls the cap off the syringe. With an apologetic look, he forces the needle into my arm. It breaks through the skin, burrowing into my vein. I want to fight, tell him to stop, but I don't.

Heat rushes into my veins.

I cry out and my vision continues to swim.

Everything dims and unconsciousness takes over my body, pulling me into the deepest depths of the darkness.

TWENTY-THREE

DEVASTATION

ZANDER

TRISTAN IS ANGRY. THAT MIGHT NOT be the right word. Then again, what is the right word for how you feel when the reason for your existence is gone? Vanished without a trace.

My brother's tension, anger, and fear assaults the air around us. I take Magali's hand as we sit in the hallway of her suite, outside the bedroom Tristan is in the process of destroying with his bare hands. And even though I know she isn't, she looks fragile—lost without her best friend.

In silence, we watch my brother as he falls apart, his world crashing down around him. There's no sense in trying to stop him from destroying everything around him.

He needs this outlet, to breathe. To exist without her.

These past two days have been dark.

The light in him is gone, replaced by emptiness and rage. Behind his eyes is nothing—except fear.

Fear is the one that scares me the most.

Emptiness and rage can be channeled, but his fear—it leaves him vulnerable and weak. Devastated.

It's been forty-eight hours since Freya died with Asmodeus's name on her lips. Tristan and I, along with Serena's friends, have torn apart the entire world searching for her over the last two days. With no leads. No rest. No food. All we've done is search for Serena.

And Maria, who is also nowhere to be found.

And here we are.

Empty-handed.

And running out of time.

Overpowered by the need to console my brother, I look up and am disappointed to find him struggling to breathe. Her absence is like a noose around his neck, choking him.

Tristan's eyes flash to mine as he throws the last piece of intact furniture—a lamp—against the wall with a roar.

It shatters into a million pieces on the floor and I imagine the shards of glass match the state of his heart.

Ireland and Ryker walk into the hallway and nod to me.

Understanding, I stand and hand Magali over to Ryker for safe-keeping. He pulls her into an embrace as Ireland rubs her back in comfort.

Knowing she's in good hands, I take a step into Serena's bedroom and close the door behind me, taking in the mess—both the room and Tristan.

I let out a low whistle, looking around. "Too bad Maria is missing," I joke, stepping on the broken wood that was once a bed. "This place is a disaster."

He ignores me.

I stare at my brother.

Incapable of taking my eyes off him.

A dark, dangerous energy grips his heart.

He's lost.

And right now, I feel as though he'll be lost forever.

Tristan's muscles flex as he clenches his fists at his side, haunted in this room by Serena. Her scent. Her essence.

"I can't do this anymore," his voice cracks, as he chokes out the words. "I feel like I'm dying without her."

"I know."

"No. You don't," he clips out.

A fresh pain slices through him and he covers his heart.

I tense and cringe, watching him suffer.

"What do you want me to do here, Tristan?"

"Bring her back. Just . . . fucking bring her back."

Devastated by the anguish in his voice, I flinch. I would give anything to give my brother what he's asking of me.

Anything.

Tristan sinks to the floor, exhausted.

With his elbows leaning on his knees, he drops his face into his hands and pulls his hair. Crouching in front of him, I make my brother promises I know I can't possibly keep.

"We'll find her," I use a reassuring tone. "But you can't go on like you have been. We need to come up with a strategy and focus our efforts. We've been running around blind, man. Maybe . . . maybe it's time—"

Tristan's tear-stained face lifts and his bloodshot eyes pin mine. "No." The word is final and deadly.

My lips flatten in a grim line. "I don't know how else to save you from drowning in the darkness like this."

"Save me?" he snorts. "I already feel like my life is over. That everything I ever was is now twisted and out of place." His icy, lifeless eyes meet mine. "There is no saving me."

"I know you're losing your shit here, Tristan, but it's not helping. Destroying her room won't bring her back."

"WHAT ELSE DO YOU WANT ME TO DO?" he shouts. "I can't feel her, our bond, anymore."

My palms become slick with sweat at his meaning. If he can't feel her, it's possible Serena doesn't exist anymore.

"Stop." The word catches in my throat because I've never seen him like this.

He's always been the strong, stoic one.

Nothing ever bothers him.

He isn't afraid of anything.

Except losing her.

He's terrified of existing without Serena.

"I want her home," he whispers.

My expression turns sad.

"I know you do. We'll find her and bring her home."

"I can't breathe anymore without her."

"Hang on, just a little longer, man. You can do it."

Tristan sighs and nods his head.

"You need rest. Maybe a shower and food."

"You're right. I'm so drained I can't even teleport anymore," he says, rubbing his hands over his drawn face.

"If I were you, I'd also clean up this shit. When Serena does get back, she's going to be pissed off that you destroyed her room. And in your current pathetic state, I'm pretty sure she'll kick your ass." I attempt to make him smile.

Something flashes in his eyes at my words—resolve.

Knowing he heard me, I pat his shoulder.

Tristan's hand snaps out and he yanks me into a tight hug. I hold him tightly as he clings to me like I'm a lifeline.

We don't talk. No words are needed between us.

A short time later, he takes in a deep breath and lets go.

"Thank you," he whispers.

"You're my brother. I love you, Tristan." I reach up and, trying to act natural and easy, sweep my hair out of my eyes.

His empty eyes fixate on me with fiery intensity, narrowing in annoyance. "Set up the meeting."

I nod.

I know how hard it was for him to come to this decision and ask this of me. Proof he'll do anything for Serena.

I step out of the tense room into the quiet hallway and close the door gently behind me. I lean back against it, slide down and hang my head between my knees. Worried.

Actually, that is a lie.

I'm fucking terrified.

I have no idea how to help Tristan.

I've never experienced this type of love or devastation.

But I know someone who has.

TWENTY-FOUR
TORCHES AND DRAGONS

TRISTAN

FATE IS A FUNNY THING. IT waits for us. Hidden deep within the shadows, wrapped in darkness, planning its strike. And when it does, most of us fight it before we accept it.

I'd say it's human nature, but I'm not human.

For Serena and I, fate has led us back to the beginning.

The gargoyle heir destined to reign, needing to be safeguarded from those who hunt her. And the reluctant protector who must educate her in the ways of her reality.

It is a vicious cycle.

Only this time, I'm not reluctant.

And we are no longer fighting separate wars.

We're one—aequus.

I wasn't supposed to want her, because it wasn't supposed to be about me. It was supposed to be about blood, oaths, and protection. Loyalties and obligations that we are, and were, both tethered to.

Now, I'm enlightened.

I realize those loyalties and obligations we're bound to have always been about each other. Our fate.

Acting on our attraction triggered a shitstorm of darkness to fall over both our futures. These past few days have been pure fucking hell. During the day, I force myself to stop imagining what is happening to her. Wondering whether she's suffering. But nights are completely different.

At night, in the darkness, I can't guard my thoughts.

And with the darkness comes the madness and anger.

For the first time in my life, I will destroy everything and everyone in my way to fight for, and hold on to, my fate.

Her.

I'll protect her, even if it takes me to my grave.

Because I love her.

Which is the only reason I'm staring at the dragons and torches in front of me. The wrought-iron gates creak open and we drive into the underground garage. Zander parks next to handful of expensive-looking vehicles.

I take in a deep breath and exhale it slowly.

Magali and Zander get out of the car, but I sit for a moment, talking myself off the ledge. Reminding myself how much Serena needs me to do this, in order to save her.

A harsh knock on the glass window next to my face forces me to snap my gaze to my brother.

He offers an encouraging nod and motions for me to get out of the vehicle as he opens the passenger door.

I step out and we walk to the elevator.

Once in, Magali presses the button for the first floor.

With a quiet ding, the door to the elevator slides open, and we step into a short entry.

The walls are a light gray and the floors a dark hardwood. I know this because my gaze is focused on the tips of my boots until we arrive at the black lacquered door.

The three of us stand in front of it. Wordlessly.

Stretching my neck from side to side, I sigh.

Magali tugs at my elbow, signing it will be all right.

Zander and I exchange a final look.

I raise my fist and pound three times as instructed.

And we wait.

In silence.

For what's to come next.

A moment later the door swings open.

I inhale sharply at the sapphire eyes narrowed at me.

"It's about fucking time you showed up," she says.

Nox

THE ROYAL PROTECTOR ACADEMY
MY FINALE

NOVEMBER 2017

Love has revived an ancient war.
Jealousy has risen and torn lives apart.
And one prophecy demands the ultimate sacrifice.

WHAT IF REWRITING YOUR DESTINY MEANS that you must sacrifice the one you love? Serena St. Michael has forsaken her future—for him. Tristan Gallagher has renounced the throne—for her. The Vergina Sun prophecy has been fulfilled, but at what cost? Their love has renewed an ancient war. With Serena gone, will Tristan save her in time? Or will the dark army of Diablo Fairies descend upon the Royal Protector Academy, destroying the London clan's legacy and ending the existence of the gargoyle race forever? Nox is the finale in the Royal Protector Academy series.

EXCERPT FROM STOLAS

(THE DARK SOUL SERIES, BOOK ONE)
MAY 2017

"THERE IS NO REASON THIS HAS to be difficult, Miss Annandale."

Startled by the voice, my eyes blink rapidly and I pull my stare away from the dark figure hiding behind a snow-covered tree. Its constant presence is the reason my mind has turned.

"Miss Annandale?" the inquisitive voice firmly repeats.

I exhale and slowly shift my attention to the warm, vibrant gentleman who is assessing me with a curious expression. "I'm sorry, what did you say?" I manage.

The expensive leather groans under his weight as he sits back in his executive chair, quietly scrutinizing my disposition. Dr. Cornelius Foster has been studying me since I walked through the door, fingers tented under his chin. It's unnerving. Even so, I don't show my discomfort.

I've learned that exposing alarm is cause for medication.

And the meds only serve to darken my mind further.

I focus on the prestigious degrees and awards the good doctor proudly showcases on the rich burgundy wall behind his mahogany desk. They're impressive. *He's* impressive. None of it matters, though. He can't help me. No one can.

"Let's talk about the voices. Are you still hearing them?"

The voices are constant. Never ending. But that isn't what he wants to hear. The hundreds of thousands of dollars he's spent on those framed degrees won't allow the voices to still be there.

If years of conventional medical treatments and medication haven't helped, one hour in a Swiss *healing spa* certainly isn't going to. I fake a smile. "They're much quieter now."

Dr. Foster dips his chin. "And the demons? Do you still see them?"

I can't help but notice how bright his crisp button-down shirt looks against his dark chocolate skin. The white almost appears to glow. I pretend he's an angel sent from Heaven to protect me from evil.

"Hope?" he prompts, stating my name.

"I haven't seen one since landing in Switzerland," I lie.

Dr. Foster's brows furrow and he runs a large hand over his full beard. The gesture causes me to stare at the few strands of grey mixed in with the black. For a man in his early forties, Cornelius Foster certainly is easy on the eyes. His features remind me of that actor, Idris Elba. Unlike the other doctors before him, he's sharp and seems to be able to read me.

Lost in thought, I don't realize he's now leaning on his desk in front of me, his muscular arms crossed.

"Hope," he commands my attention again. "You're safe here. Our patient-doctor relationship only works if you are candid during our sessions. I can't help if you don't truthfully tell me what is going on inside your head. While you are here, I expect open and honest communication. There is no judgment. I'm here to aid in your healing."

An awkward silence lingers between us.

It's been two years since my twenty-first birthday; two years my mind has been haunted by visions of suffering, pain, and torture. The images are burned into my memory.

I squeeze my eyes closed and attempt to push them away, along with the bile.

A small knock at the door breaks through our quiet standoff.

"Come in," Dr. Foster answers, without taking his gaze off me.

I twist my focus to the girl who slides into his office. With her presence, a cold chill spreads through my limbs. The stranger's brown eyes are vacant. Just like mine.

She's young, around my age, and looks to be of Native American heritage.

Her straight brown hair falls to her waist and is parted down the middle. I watch as she flips one side over a slender shoulder. The gesture is odd. There is no feeling behind it. It's almost as if someone programmed her to blink and move every few seconds as a way for her to appear human.

"Hope, this is Lore," Dr. Foster says by way of introduction. "She'll be your roommate during your stay here at Shadowbrook."

I frown. "Roommate? I thought my parents requested a private suite?"

The psychiatrist smirks. "Human nature thrives on community. I believe it's healthy to be social. Having a suitemate will be beneficial to your healing. You'll see."

I don't answer him as I once again meet Lore's unresponsive expression.

"We're done for the day." Dr. Foster walks around and sits behind his desk. "Lore will show you around the campus and help to get you settled in. I'll see you tomorrow afternoon for our private session."

Relieved at the dismissal, I stand and face my new roommate. She's silent as she opens the door and waits for me to walk through. Maybe Lore doesn't speak. I can certainly understand the desire to remain quiet and keep people at arm's length.

Walking through the door, I watch as inky shadows swirl around her aura.

Demon.

START AT THE BEGINNING
EXCERPT OF REVELATION

(THE REVELATION SERIES, BOOK ONE)

I'M RUNNING, AND NOT VERY WELL, might I add. My lungs burn and my shallow breathing erratically bounces off the slick stone walls. I keep moving forward, forcing myself farther and farther into the dark underground passage. It's cold, damp, and smells like musk.

"What the hell is following me?" I ask myself, as confusion sets in. The only thing I'm certain of is that I'm bone-chillingly terrified, down to the core of my very soul. I'm frightened that whatever is chasing me will catch me, because when it does, there's no doubt it will kill me. Its hatred and anger rolls off it in waves, crashing through me like a sharp gust of wind, suffocating me. I'm positive it's pure evil.

Just as I reach the end of the tunnel, I hit a solid wall, ceasing my progress and ending my futile efforts at escape. "Shit," I whisper out loud, while I strike my palms against the water-slicked stones. Feeling defeated, I place my forehead to the damp wall and release a soft whimper.

I need to figure out my options, quickly. I sense its presence closing in, dropping the tunnel's temperature from cool and damp to downright frigid, the glacial air settling around the passageway. My breath comes out in a cloud in front of me. My heart rate increases as I stifle the gag reflex being challenged by the rancid smell of sulfur and sour milk.

"Eeeve," it hisses, mocking me. Sensing my deepest fears, it begins to play with me by using those emotions against me. "Oh God," I exhale, as I close my eyes and rub my temples, trying to ease the dread rising in my throat.

Panicked, I start talking to myself. "Think, Eve." I turn around, allowing my eyes to scan over the dark enclosed area. All I can see in front of me is black. Blowing out a harsh breath, I begin to pray for a miracle as I wait for it to manifest.

"*Nope, nothing,*" *I say dejectedly to no one.*

I twist back to the wall. In a frantic state, I push and pound on the large, dark gray stones, trying anything. I'm desperate, and there's an off-chance that located somewhere is a hidden opening that could grant me freedom.

Then I hear it. The thing I fear most. I spin and freeze, fixed in my spot at the hissing sound of slithering snakes. Oh shit, now I'm really afraid. My heartbeat echoes in my ears as a severe chill runs down the length of my spine. My lips force air out sharply in a frenzied state, causing strands of fallen hair to jump away from my face with each irregular breath.

Without warning, the tunnel goes silent. The only sound ricocheting off the wet stones is my strained breath being forced into the dark abyss. I remind myself to inhale before I suffer from a full-blown panic attack. With great slowness, I rotate to face my attacker.

No one is there.

As I swallow hard, my eyes shift down to the floor and take in the dark tendrils of smoke that crawl around my ankles, rooting me to the ground. What the hell? My eyes dart around wildly, searching for the point of origin of the wisp, but there isn't one.

With my back pressed flat against the cold concrete wall and the dampness seeping into my shirt, I've resigned myself to the fact that this is how I'm going to die. I close my eyes in acceptance and attempt to steady my breathing, listening to the droplets of water hitting the ground.

Drip.

Drip.

Drip.

I try to convince myself it will be okay as the dark cloud works its way up my body, wrapping forcefully around my neck and cutting off the oxygen supply sustaining me.

Black spots form behind my closed eyelids as I become light-headed and dizzy. The lack of oxygen begins to take hold of my body, and I start to lose consciousness. Crap.

"*Dimittet eam, Nero,*" *I hear a strong male voice order, in a calm yet deadly tone.*

I can't see my savior. Everything is shrouded in darkness. Maybe he isn't even here, and I'm hallucinating in my final moments of life.

The black mist loosens its choke hold on my neck while hissing angrily. "Deus tuus, ibi est filia eius."

A putrid gust of air blankets my face with each seething mock. Changing its mind, the evil smoke cackles, wrapping around my throat again and gripping firmly, causing me to wheeze. What the fuck?

"Dixit mittam tibi pergat ad profundum inferni, sive," my liberator says heatedly in Latin.

Nero releases me, then turns to my rescuer, morphing into the outline of a man. At the discharge of its hold, my body slides down the slick wall, landing harshly on the glacial, water-soaked stone floor. I begin coughing and gasping for air as I place my head between my legs, willing air into my lungs.

"Et subdit quod me putesssss?" Nero hisses.

"Yes, you repulsive excuse of an existence, I do think I can send you back to the depths of Hell," my protector replies calmly, yet cockily.

"Et veniunt ad me ut, gurgulio," Nero states, in a final slithery tone. At that command, my savior pulls out a long, black, granite sword that reflects the water cascading down the passage walls.

"Delectabiliter," the dark knight replies coldly, before he attacks.

Even wrapped in blackness, I can sense he's a trained warrior. His body moves with ease and agility as he engages Nero. I hear each whoosh the sword makes as it slices effortlessly through the air, making contact with each thrust.

I can't make out any of the warrior's facial features, but I know he's large and moves fast and efficiently. I close my eyes for a brief second, only to throw them open in alarm at the high-pitched shriek coming from the thing called Nero, as it bursts into blue flames and vanishes.

That's when I officially lose control over my emotions and begin to shake uncontrollably, with tears flowing down my pale cheeks. The blackness engulfs me, choking me. I shut my eyes, wishing that everything would just stop, and that I was anywhere else.

All of a sudden, I feel warmth and calm flow through my veins, as my guardian kneels down next to me and pulls me into his safe embrace with gentleness. He strokes my hair, trying to pacify me as I cling to him for life.

The masculine scent of smoky wood and leather fills my nose, as his deep voice whispers in my ear.

"Hush. It's all right. You're safe. No harm will come to you. I've got you."
His tone is slow and soft, as if speaking to a wounded animal, lulling me into
a state of calmness.

With great tenderness, his large, warm hands cup my cheeks and lift my
face to meet his, wiping the tears away with his thumbs—a pointless effort, since
the flow increases with the kind gesture.

My gaze lifts and connects with a pair of glowing indigo eyes. They're staring
at me with such intensity and affection that his look creates an ache deep within
my chest, as my body draws itself to his of its own accord, like it knows him.

The voice belonging to those eyes speaks with a firm vow. "I will protect
you . . . always."

Gasping for air, I abruptly sit up in bed and swallow down a
scream. My fists clutch my blanket in a severe death grip, as pieces
of my light brown hair fall from my ponytail and stick to the sweat
on my face and neck.

I drop my head into my waiting hands and realize my cheeks are
wet, most likely from the tears that escaped my hazel eyes during my
nightmare.

The dampness causes my long, dark lashes to stick to one another while I rub them. The lids open, then close again, and I order
myself to take even breaths to calm my erratic heartbeat. As I slowly
open them for the final time, my heart rate picks up once more, at
the realization of what's coming next.

I turn to my left and steel myself.

"What. The. Hell. Eve!" Aria, my roommate and self-appointed
best friend, screeches, and I wince from the high-pitched octave. *Crap.*
I woke her up, again.

She's sitting on her bed, looking like a pissed-off fairy. Her normally cute pink, pixie-cut hair is suffering a major case of bed head,
sticking up in all directions.

"Are you okay?" Aria asks, with an irritated yet concern-laced
voice, and her petite hands on her curvy hips. She's staring at me,
waiting for an explanation as I open and close my mouth like a gaping

fish, trying to form intelligent words.

"Sorry, I um, bad dream," I mutter inarticulately.

"No shit," she says, with sarcasm dripping from her lips. "Same one?" The question is thrown out along with some serious stink eye radiating from her round chocolate orbs.

Arianna "Aria" Donovan dislikes being woken up in the middle of the night. I know this because we've been college roommates for all of one month now. Which means I've woken her up more times than I care to count.

We met over the summer during freshman orientation, and according to Aria, it was "friendship at first sight." As new students, we were placed into groups of ten and forced to play this ridiculous get-to-know-you game where each person had a photo of a particular cartoon character taped to their back. The goal was to ask the group questions in an attempt to gain enough information to guess who your character was, so you could partner up with your match for the rest of orientation.

Aria was *Bert* and I was *Ernie*. We've been inseparable ever since, even requesting to room together this semester. Well, in truth, Aria demanded we room together, and since I'm pretty easygoing, I didn't put up a fight, figuring it would be nice to know someone.

At the moment, I'm thinking she's second-guessing her choice in roommates.

She sighs and prowls to the minifridge, grabbing a bottle of water and shoving it in my hand before turning on the crystal-embellished lamp on the pink thrift-store-revived table between our beds.

Our dorm room is a decent size. We got lucky in the housing lottery and managed to snag a suite. Unfortunately, that means we share it with two other roommates.

The space consists of two shared bedrooms, a common lounge area, and an attached bathroom. Overall, it's your typical college dorm room, amped up with Aria's thrift store finds reincarnated into amazing pieces of art, because she is an eternal optimist and believes everything can be redeemed.

Her décor style matches her schizophrenic personality to perfection—Barbie meets Marilyn Manson. She's the only person I know who can pull off pink combat boots, black nail polish, and dark black smoky eyeliner with a pink sundress, and have it look adorably sexy.

I like her one-of-a-kind style. It offsets my average, girl-next-door fashion sense, which usually consists of skinny jeans, knee-high boots, and a cotton long-sleeved shirt. I suppose it's what originally drew me to her—opposites attract. I also presume that's what makes our friendship fun.

The cousins, our other two suitemates, are a different story. Speaking of which, I need to take cover as the door to our room crashes open in dramatic fashion and both Abby and McKenna enter the room like a Victoria's Secret pajama commercial.

Abby, the younger of the two cousins by only a few months, smiles with her delicate arms folded, allowing her long red hair to cascade over her refined shoulders.

"You okay, Eve?" she asks with concern.

Even at three in the morning, Abigail "Abby" Connor is ethereal looking. She's wearing her black flannel pajama bottoms and a cute green T-shirt that says, *Kiss Me, I'm Irish.* The green brings out the flecks of shimmer in her crystal-blue eyes.

I force a casual shrug. "Yeah. Just another bad dream. Sorry to wake you guys up again."

She responds with a warm smile.

On the other hand, McKenna just grunts. I've deduced it's simply because she hates talking to people.

Now that I think about it, McKenna "Kenna" McIntyre just dislikes people in general. She's always ranting about the "human race" being inferior. Inferior to whom, she's never clarified. Most of the time, her off-handed comments go in one ear and out the other, because they're so frequent.

I exhale and take a sip of water, the cool liquid hydrating my dry throat.

McKenna narrows her sapphire eyes, outlined with lush black

lashes, at me. "Seriously, Eve. I'm tired of waking up to your fucking screaming every night," she comments in a harsh tone.

I grimace. "Was I screaming? Sorry, I had no idea," I offer. Of course I was screaming. I was being choked to death, for God's sake. The shrieking might also be why my throat feels like sandpaper, making it painful to swallow or talk.

Turning like a graceful but angry swan, McKenna heads toward the doorway, stopping just before making her dramatic exit. "You look like shit, by the way," she snarls, and flicks her long, platinum-blonde hair over her shoulder to enhance her point. With that, she storms out, fuzzy slippers and all.

Most of the student body on campus is terrified of McKenna. It would be wishful thinking to assume they're put off by her "sass" and "straight shooting" attitude.

I think she just gets off on intimidating people. She also has no filter, a vocabulary rivaling any truck driver, and can make even the strongest person fold into her- or himself with her malevolent stare.

Needless to say, the jury is still out on our friendship. It's only been four weeks. Abby, on the other hand, is extremely likable, and is becoming a good friend.

"Sorry," I mutter, for the fourth time this week.

The nightmares began on my eighteenth birthday. Each time, I wake up in a cold sweat, gasping for air, crying and screaming from being terrified and tortured in the outlandish dream. It's been rough, to say the least.

Lying back on my pillow, I put my arm over my eyes, willing my body to calm itself down, as the adrenaline still pumps wildly through my veins. I try using the breathing techniques I've learned through years of studying yoga. It's not working.

Abby fidgets with unease. "Kenna doesn't mean to be bitchy. She's just tired," she excuses the poor behavior, a maternal habit of hers.

With poise, she sits on my bed, removing my arm from my hidden face. "Do you want to talk about it?" She offers a small smile. "It might help make it less scary and real if you say it out loud." Abby pauses before continuing. "You'd be surprised at my level of under-standing when it comes to fear-provoking things," she says at almost an inaudible level.

"No. Thanks, Abby. I'm good. Just a bad dream," I say as persua-sively as I can, for both our sakes, because if she knew what lurked in the darkness of the dreams, she'd have me committed.

Abby studies my face for a moment, searching for a hint of deceit. When she's convinced I'm all right, she stands to go back to her own room. "Okay, but if you change your mind, come and get me. I'm happy to listen, Eve. Night, girls," she utters in a sweet voice before leaving.

McKenna and Abby are both tall and built like dancers. While Abby exudes grace and regality, McKenna radiates fierce warrior princess. When they're together, it's intimidating.

Aria just stands there, staring at me, taking this all in while wearing her favorite pink T-shirt and matching boy shorts. All five feet of her looks both adorable and annoyed.

"Fine," she huffs, and relinquishes the idea that I want to elabo-rate on my nightmare-induced state. She crawls back into bed, pulls up her ruffled pink blanket, and turns off the light.

We sit in silence, the moonlight shining through the window, bathing the room in a blue glow and twisting the shadows on the walls. I turn my eyes upwards to the ceiling, focusing on it with immense concentration, wishing the terrifying dreams would stop so I could have a normal night's sleep.

After a few moments, Aria rolls over to face me as the night's silver light bounces off her features, masked in sympathetic concern. She goes to speak, but I cut her off.

"Please don't, Aria. I just don't have it in me tonight," I whisper, pleading for her to back off.

"Okay, but at some point we need to figure this out, Eve. I'm worried about you." She sighs, turns over, and goes to sleep.

I'm left to contemplate my dreams and their meaning while, once again, staring into the abyss of darkness.

TWO

ENCOUNTERS

CTOBER IN MASSACHUSETTS BRINGS COOL FALL temperatures. Little by little, this charming New England campus, crammed with brick buildings and puritan heritage, is filling with warm autumn colors. I close the required reading for my Rhetorical Criticism class and take in a deep, cleansing breath, allowing the crisp air to fill my lungs while I sit on my favorite bench under an old oak tree in the campus quad.

I have an unusual connection to the tree. Perhaps it's the sheer size that comforts me, deceiving me with the sensation of being secure and sheltered. I've been on edge lately, as if a dangerous storm is coming—an illogical sentiment, since Kingsley College has been voted the safest college campus in the Northeast for the past ten years.

It's for that reason alone my overprotective aunt allowed me to attend in the first place, using some of the trust fund my parents left me after their deaths. Well, that and five forced years of studying Krav Maga. My beautiful and crazy aunt required I take it in high school and continue in college, because a girl can never be too safe or prepared. Her words.

Buried within a small town, the college epitomizes educational greatness and is steeped in rich academic tradition. At least that's what it says in the brochure. With a small community of just under six thousand students and flawlessly manicured estate-like grounds, Kingsley overflows with scholarly charm.

The entire campus sprawls out on three hundred acres, meaning you could walk from the west side to the east in under twenty minutes, or if feeling lazy, you can take the shuttle bus in five, which I'm sure I'll appreciate in the snow-filled months.

I'm currently on the west side of campus in the main courtyard. It has well-kept landscaping for miles, adorned with brick walkways, blooming fall flowers, and oak-tree-lined streets proudly boasting their warm orange, gold, and brown fall leaves.

My bench faces the centerpiece of the campus. Belmont Hall is an impressive brick building, showcasing four thick white pillars. Ten massive steps lead up to the large white double doors. It sits at the head of the quad like the queen of all university buildings. It's also the picturesque structure used on all the brochures to lure you into academic life here, promising exemplary education leading to a productive and fulfilling post-educational life.

I could sit here for hours and people-watch. Wrapped up in my reverie, I barely notice a small area near the trees harboring a soft blue glow. As my eyes focus on the illuminated area, my skin heats and warmth begins to flow through my veins. I'm having the oddest case of déjà vu.

I narrow my eyes, trying to get a better look at the radiance that has captured my interest, but whatever it was dissolves into thin air. As if nothing happened, I feel myself being released from the seize it had on me, leaving me empty and alone as coldness emanates through me, replacing the warmth.

"Great. Now I'm seeing glowing blue spots," I mutter under my breath. "I'm also talking to myself. Yep, Eve, it's official. You're starting to friggin' lose it." I seriously need a good night's sleep, or Aria's going to have me admitted to the psych ward.

My thought process is interrupted and my attention shifts to a group of giddy girls, whispering and giggling. Internally rolling my eyes, curiosity gets the best of me and I turn to see what the uproar is about.

Leaning on a classic black Wiesmann Roadster, in the parking lot near Lexington Hall, is a tall, lean, good-looking guy. He's smiling at his fangirl harem.

Smoldering hot guy is the type of male that females instantly drop their panties for. No doubt he makes every girl feel as if they're the only one on the planet. Damn if he didn't have the chiseled cheeks and blond scruff along his perfect jawline to solidify the cliché.

He runs a large hand through his golden hair, which falls to the midway point on his neck in a sexy cut, a stark contrast to his all-black outfit consisting of tailored dress pants, a V-neck T-shirt, a watch, and designer shoes that probably cost more than my tuition.

This guy's obvious love for black reeks of trouble. God, I need to stop gawking and drooling.

Lighting a cigarette, he turns, catching my eye with his. He gives me a slight nod as if he knows me. Then he shifts his sea-green eyes to the area I was just staring at in the courtyard, narrowing them while blowing out the nicotine-infested smoke from his mouth. He methodically rubs his lips with his thumb in contemplation.

Confused, I look back and forth between the quad area and him, but can't make out a connection or reason for his peculiar behavior. He refocuses his gaze back to me, bestowing a sexy but emotionally void smile.

Wariness runs over me. There's something aloof and conniving about him. He gives the impression of being standoffish, but it's too controlled, forced even. As if he knows what I'm thinking, the boy sneers at me and turns back to the scatterbrained girls vying for his attention. He says something that appears to be brilliant, because I swear they all swoon and blush simultaneously.

"Hey. Who's the hot guy?" Aria inquires, plopping down next to me, chomping on her pink bubble gum.

Is everything this girl touches pink?

"I don't know. He just appeared, looking all cunning and surrounded by his fan club," I say, feigning disinterest but keeping my eyes glued to him, watching his every move with an abnormal curiosity.

"Well, he's YUMMY. I wouldn't mind licking him up and down like a lollipop," she states with enthusiasm, wiggling her eyebrows.

I glance matter-of-factly at her. "Don't you think the other ten guys you're currently sleeping with would be upset if they saw you licking him in broad daylight, in the quad no less?"

"I'm not sleeping with ten guys," Aria fakes offense. "It's only three." She pretends to sulk.

I offer a smug smirk. "My apologies. I didn't mean to over exaggerate your promiscuity."

"Listen, I can't help it if the male species is drawn to my raw magnetic pull," Aria says. "I think it's the pink hair combined with my fishnets and combat boots."

"I imagine it's the short skirts, C-cups and open-door policy, but, hey, that's just me," I jest, and stick my tongue out in an adult fashion.

She pushes my shoulder with little effort behind it. "Jealous, Eves? If someone would let go of her virtue, someone might be less tightly wound," she adds in a dry tone. "Maybe your night terrors are caused by sexual frustration?"

She blows a pink bubble with her gum and pops it.

I exhale, tired. "Maybe." The girl has a valid point.

"In my professional opinion, a good orgasm is just what you need to help end the nightmares." Aria uses her fake psychiatrist tone to make me smile.

I stand and grab her, yanking her off the bench. "Come on, Freud. We're going to be late."

She bats her eyes prettily at me. "What? We're learning about psychosexual development in Psychology 101."

I bark out a short laugh. "That explains today's unfortunate probing into my nonexistent sex life."

We begin to walk over to the Art Center, and Aria grabs my hand, halting my movement as she looks over her shoulder. I follow her line of sight to a set of smoldering sea-green eyes.

"At least admit hotness has a really cool car," she purrs, and smacks my ass, causing me to yelp in surprise.

"Aria! Come on," I order. My tone is laced with annoyance as I glance once more toward the parking lot.

She's right. The car is smoking hot.

AS A COMMUNICATIONS MAJOR, ARCHITECTURE IS not a class I'm overjoyed to be sitting in this semester. However, it does fulfill my art prerequisite and it's the only afternoon class that fit into my schedule. So here I am, begrudgingly awaiting my instruction on "the fundamental devotion to the examination of the built environment," according to the first line in my textbook.

Professor Davidson is not known for easy grading or motivating lectures. As a matter of fact, he's notorious for his rather lengthy and tedious explanations, specifically his sermons focused on Gothic architecture during the medieval period. I hear they're as appealing as pulling out your own fingernails.

I'm planted in my normal seat in the back of the lecture hall, hiding in the throng of the hundred students suffering along with me, and internally cursing myself for not putting this credit off until the semester before graduation.

My eyes follow Professor Davidson as he walks into class, holding his beat-up old brown leather satchel and playing with his salt and pepper hair. His thick glasses and tweed suit add to the ensemble, topped off with a bow tie no less. I sigh. It's been a long month, meaning it's going to be an even longer semester.

Aria left me at the door to head to her design class. She's hoping to work for a large advertising agency, like her dad, when she graduates as a graphic designer, much to the dismay of her mom. As a doctor, she would prefer Aria join the practice. I envy Aria for her perfect family.

My mom and dad both died when I was a baby, leaving me to grow up alone with my mother's only sister, Elizabeth. Aunt Elizabeth loves to dress in long, billowy skirts, and is a bit scatterbrained, but she's warm, affectionate, and has loved me every day like I was her own daughter. She's also a very talented jewelry designer and owns a shop on Martha's Vineyard.

She never married nor had kids of her own, which surprises me, because she's quite beautiful; blessed with the same light brown, long hair as Mom and me. Her warm hazel eyes just draw people to her. I actually look so much like her that people tend to think she's my older sister instead of my forty-year-old guardian.

Smiling at thoughts of my aunt, I don't notice class has started and I should be taking notes. *Crap.* I turn on my iPad while Professor Davidson drones on and on about architecture's effect on art in the thirteenth century.

Midway through the lecture, I stifle a yawn, stretching my neck to the left, then the right, while my wandering eyes lock on a set of full, kissable lips. I lift my gaze to see whom said lips belong to. The very attractive owner is seated one chair over from me, looking every bit as bored and annoyed as I am.

Everything about him attracts me, especially his indigo eyes outlined in dark lashes that fan softly over his cheeks. He has dark brown hair, short in the back and sides, but longer and styled on top in sexy, messy pieces. I fleetingly contemplate what it would be like to run my fingers through his hair as I chew on the inside of my cheek, a nervous habit of mine.

His five o'clock shadow highlights a chiseled jawline that, at the moment, is clenched so tightly it's triggering a slight tic in his striking cheek muscle. *Odd.*

My eyes travel down the right side of his body, roaming over his forearm. A striking Celtic cross tattoo is displayed on the inside.

He has on a plain white T-shirt, worn blue jeans, and kick-ass black motorcycle boots. There are two thick, black leather bands adorning each of his wrists, adding to his masculine style.

Hotness crosses his arms, showing off his toned biceps and blocking the taut chest I've been staring at, hidden under his cotton shirt.

I lean closer, drawn to him like a magnet.

Suddenly, he narrows his eyes at me, with an intensity that could be construed as anger. At the force of his stare, my heart lurches and breathing becomes difficult. The warm sensation from earlier begins to run through my veins, causing me to shift uncomfortably in my seat.

Without me noticing, he's leaned over the empty seat between us. "See something you like?" his deep, masculine voice asks in a malicious whisper.

Those plump lips are now set in a hard line. Our eyes lock and hold one another's for what feels like an eternity, before I drop mine.

My cheeks flush with embarrassment as realization sets in. I was just caught openly checking him out. *Crap.*

Ignoring his question, I snap my attention back to the front of the lecture hall just as Professor Davidson ends my humiliation by dismissing us for the day.

Haphazardly, I throw things in my messenger bag and hurry to escape, only to find the six-foot-plus Adonis already blocking me in by leaning against the door frame in a casual stance.

I breathe out sharply, partly in surprise and partly in nervousness. Shit, he's even hotter standing up.

He's also abnormally fast. I look back and forth between our seats and the doorway, wondering how the hell he got down here so quickly. *Eve, attempt to focus,* I internally scold myself.

I move toward the exit. Not trusting my voice, I release the breath I've been holding and give him an *excuse me* look.

He motions his hand, encouraging me to walk through.

"After you," he says, his smooth voice warming my cheeks again.

I walk through the door, rolling my eyes at his dramatics and my lack of vocal control. Once outside, the fresh air hits me, clearing my head and offering relief from the embarrassing exchange.

"No need to thank me. It's truly my pleasure." I hear his condescending voice come from behind me.

I spin around in front of him, causing him to stop abruptly to avoid walking into me. Not expecting my sudden movement, his hands grasp my upper arms to steady himself and prevent me from stumbling backwards.

Heat pools on my skin where he touches it. Against my will, I close my eyes at his close proximity.

His scent fills my senses—a heady, masculine combination of smoky wood and leather. I inhale and sway, slightly light-headed from the whiff, which ignites warmth in my veins.

The good-looking guy leans in closer and his lips softly brush my ear. His minty breath comes out in a cocky whisper, "Falling for me already?"

This snaps me out of my daze. I look up and give him my best *what the hell* look. He watches me for a second as confusion crosses his face, then he releases my arms abrasively, as if I burned him.

We study one another, each waiting for the other to say something or make a move. Both of us are in a defiant stance with our arms crossed.

I speak first, clearly a mistake.

"What the hell is your problem?" I bark, narrowing my eyes.

"The siren speaks," he says, feigning awe. "I was beginning to question your familiarity with the English language."

One side of his mouth tilts into a smirk. It's obvious he's pleased with himself and his lame answer.

"Charming," I reply, annoyed. "I happen to be well versed in the English language."

He places a long finger to his closed mouth in contemplation. "That's astonishing, considering that earlier, I caught you openly gawking at me." Indigo eyes scan my face as he leans in and lowers his voice to a sensual tone. "Pink lips parted, beautiful hazel eyes locked onto my chest, drooling as if I were a piece of chocolate." He pauses for effect. "Yet not a single word flowed through that pretty, pouty mouth of yours," blue eyes retorts, staring at my lips, waiting patiently for my response.

I swallow. Between his scent and his nearness, my body is over-heating. "Shows how much you know. I prefer salty over sweet," I throw back at him, proud that my voice sounds strong.

It would be in my best interest to gather my dignity and just walk away. This infuriating guy is getting under my skin, distracting me with insults that appear to be compliments.

He snorts and gives me an insolent smile. "Yeah, I can tell sweet isn't your thing, sweetheart."

My jaw tightens. "I have a name, and it's not Sweetheart," I snap.

He crosses his arms, amused at my outburst, and gives me a crooked smile. "What would that name be?"

"Eve Collins," I offer in an even tone.

"Eve," he says in a husky voice.

The way my name rolls off his tongue does crazy things to my body. I secretly curse his good looks for causing my stomach muscles to clench and the butterflies to take flight.

"Eve," he repeats, as some form of understanding sinks in. "Without doubt, a suitable name for you."

The cute guy stands taller and puffs his chest out in some sort of proud posture.

"Meaning?" I question tersely.

"Wasn't Eve the mother of mankind? Of course, she was also seen as weak, allowing evil to succeed in tempting her to the forbidden." He challenges me with his eyes.

I pull my brows together, confused by his bizarre statement. "Are you implying I'm weak?" I question, with a slight octave change.

He just stands there, calm and unfazed by my growing temper. For some reason, his lack of reaction makes me even more irate.

"I can assure you that's not the case," I say. "As a matter of fact, I could punch you right now and you'd be seeing stars for weeks, followed by a plastic surgeon to reset your nose, pretty boy."

Clearly unaffected by me, he laughs deeply, placing his hands up in mock surrender while backing away from me. "There's no need for threats of physical harm, Eve."

His gaze locks onto mine, assessing me, probably waiting to see if I'll actually punch him. I angle my head to the side in annoyance and continue to watch him watching me.

As soon as he finds what he's searching for in my eyes, he nods, seeming to have had some sort of internal dialogue with himself. His face turns impassive.

"Your lack of knowledge with regard to your name means nothing," he says, casually shrugging me off.

I feel a migraine coming on. This conversation is nonsensical and it needs to end. "I don't think this is working." I motion between us while giving him an irritated glower.

A mischievous grin forms on his face. "Do we need couples therapy already?"

My frustration is now off the charts, so I exhale loudly, hoping he'll get the hint. "That's not what I meant."

He leans into my personal space and narrows his eyes, attempting to intimidate and fluster me more than he already has, and for the love of God, it's working.

"Would you please stop? I can't think with you in my face," I grumble.

At this, he leans away. "I make you nervous?" It's a question with a hint of curiosity.

"Ah, no. Far from it," I answer, still a bit shaken.

"Your unconvincing tone says different," he retorts.

I'm just about to offer my witty comeback when his eyes snap up, quickly scanning the area behind me before redirecting his focus back to me. He frowns.

Before I can glance at what caught his attention, blue eyes speaks, ending my inquisitiveness.

"As delightful as this conversation has been with you, I have somewhere I need to be. Try not to walk into anyone or anything," he mocks, as he begins to walk away.

"Whatever," I mutter, and add under my breath, "ass."

He stops and turns back toward me, stalking me slowly, like a predator. "Tsk. Name-calling is very unbecoming of you, Eve." My name comes out like a dig. "Perhaps you should consider your choice of words within the English language with more care when conversing with others."

I just stand there, glaring at him, racking my brain for a smart-ass response. Unfortunately, he has me all tongue-tied and at a loss for witty repartee.

Hotness, of course, wastes no time conquering the silence. "I'll be anticipating your retort, siren.

ABOUT THE AUTHOR

RANDI COOLEY WILSON IS A BESTSELLING author of paranormal, urban fantasy, and contemporary romance books. Randi was born and raised in Massachusetts, where she attended Bridgewater State University and graduated with a degree in Communication Studies. After graduation, she moved to California, where she lived happily bathed in sunshine and warm weather for fifteen years.

Randi makes stuff up, devours romance books, drinks lots of wine and coffee, and has a slight addiction to bracelets. She currently resides in Massachusetts with her daughter and husband.

Visit randicooleywilson.com for more information about Randi or her books and projects.

Or via social media outlets:
Twitter: *@R_CooleyWilson*
Facebook: *www.facebook.com/authorrandicooleywilson*
Goodreads: *www.goodreads.com/RCooleyWilson*
Randi's Rebels: *www.facebook.com/groups/randisrebels*

ACKNOWLEDGEMENTS

THERE ARE SO MANY PEOPLE TO thank who are a part of this amazing journey I'm on. A simple thank you to them for encouraging and supporting me just doesn't seem like a strong enough show of gratitude on my part.

To my husband and daughter, thank you for loving me and sharing your time with the characters I write and being understanding of my deadlines. And for bringing me coffee.

Hang Le, By Hang Le. I love you like I love dancing squirrels. Thank you for always visually capturing my stories and being my design soul mate.

Sarah Hershman, my agent, and the team at Hershman Rights Management, thank you for your ongoing support.

Rick and Amy Miles, and the entire Red Coat PR team, thank you for allowing me to be part of the author family.

Liz Ferry, thank you for coming into my life and polishing these stories so they shine. You're amazing.

Christine Borgford, at Type A Formatting, thank you for making the interiors of my books look badass.

A HUGE thank you to Randi's Rebels. Y'all are the best reader group a girl could ask for. You keep me sane when I need it, provide me with endless book recommendations, and fill my days with man candy and laughs. Rebels Rock!

Special shout-outs to Joanne Cowan, who named Aoife; Cassie Colosimo, who named Branna; and Alisha Tetreault, who named Laven. Adrienne Clark, Emma-Jayne Mills, Sarah Burke Evans, Gemma Louis Bailey, Kelli Rasmussen, and Helen Adamson, thank you all so much for the dresses for the vision board!

Thanks to my family and friends, I love you all.

To the readers, thank you for reading my stories. Thank you for continuing to take chances on me and the stories I write. Thank you for trusting me with your imagination.

I'm honored to be part of your literary world.